The Edge of Safety

Mara Lennox

Copyright © 2024 by Mara Lennox

All rights reserved.

No portion of this book may be reproduced in any form without written permission from the publisher or author, except as permitted by U.S. copyright law.

Contents

1. Prologue — 1
2. Chapter 1 — 3
3. Chapter 2 — 12
4. Chapter 3 — 18
5. Chapter 4 — 25
6. Chapter 5 — 31
7. Chapter 6 — 39
8. Chapter 7 — 49
9. Chapter 8 — 56
10. Chapter 9 — 67
11. Chapter 10 — 75
12. Chapter 11 — 86
13. Chapter 12 — 96
14. Chapter 13 — 104
15. Chapter 14 — 114

16. Chapter 15 — 123
17. Chapter 16 — 131
18. Chapter 17 — 139
19. Chapter 18 — 149
20. Chapter 19 — 160
21. Chapter 20 — 171
22. Chapter 21 — 180
23. Chapter 22 — 189
24. Chapter 23 — 197
25. Chapter 24 — 204
26. Chapter 25 — 211
27. Chapter 26 — 218
28. Chapter 27 — 225
29. Chapter 28 — 232
30. Chapter 29 — 241
31. Chapter 30 — 247
32. Chapter 31 — 257
33. Chapter 32 — 265
34. Chapter 33 — 273
35. Chapter 34 — 283
36. Chapter 35 — 292
37. Chapter 36 — 300
38. Chapter 37 — 308

39.	Chapter 38	314
40.	Chapter 39	321
41.	Chapter 40	329
42.	Chapter 41	337
43.	Epilogue	348

Prologue

Blood pooled around the dead body that lay in the middle of the lounge room floor. The body already cold from the blood loss and the once cream carpet was stained with murder.

Jessica stopped immediately in her tracks as she walked through the front door and assessed the scene that lay before her. Her breath caught in her throat, heart beating erratically and her body began to shake. Jessica's aunt was dead. A kitchen knife stuck out from her motionless body.

On instinct, Jessica's hands flew up and covered her mouth, in fear she may make a noise that would alert the attacker to her presence. Her eyes darted around the room; ears pricked up listening for any indication that the attacker was still in the house. Everything was still.

Without a second thought, Jessica sprinted from the house, with nothing but her school backpack. Tears trickled down her cheeks. She didn't look back. Her anxiety told her if she did, she would see him. That he would catch her.

It was obvious to Jessica what had happened in the house. No-one needed to confirm her nightmare. She knew what she had to do.

Run.

Run away and not look back.

He had found her.

Chapter 1

The rain teemed down on the front windscreen and even with the wiper blades on high speed it made it difficult for Sandra to see clearly. She drove slowly to avoid having an accident, the headlights on the car giving little guidance. Thick sheets of water blurring her vision.

A shadow on the footpath came into view and she slowed the car further, recognising someone was walking in the torrential rain. Who would be crazy enough to be out in this weather? Sandra thought to herself.

As the car slowly approached the figure, Sandra noticed it was a teenaged girl, who couldn't be much older than seventeen, the same age as her son. The girl wore a hooded jacket, pulled up close to her face to keep from getting wet, and a backpack hung on her shoulders. Maternal instinct kicking in, Sandra pulled the car up alongside the water sodden girl, rolling down the car window to speak to her.

"What are you doing out in this weather?" Sandra asked in a caring tone.

The girl froze instantly when the car stopped beside her, like a deer in headlights, her eyes wide with fear. At Sandra's voice, her body eased slightly, and she glanced in both directions as if to check her surroundings.

"Get in the car and I will take you home," Sandra offered, leaning across the passenger seat to open the door closest to the curb.

"I-I'm fine," the girl stammered.

"Not negotiable," Sandra said in a firm, motherly voice and a wave of her hand to usher her in.

The girl glanced around once more before sighing and climbing into the car, closing the door behind her.

"Where can I drop you off to?" Sandra asked, pulling the car gently back onto the road and continuing on her journey.

"Uh..." the girl thought for a moment, unsure with what to answer with.

"Where's home?" Sandra asked, glancing sideways at the girl who avoided her eye by looking out the window and not answering. "Well, I guess you will just have to come home with me then."

"No," the girl started to argue, reaching for the door handle.

"Not up for discussion. You need to get out of those damp clothes," Sandra smiled at the girl, briefly taking her eyes off the road. "Just for tonight, you can stay with me and my family. Tomorrow we can work out where you're going."

The girl took a deep steadying breath, letting go of the handle and tried to think of an excuse to not go home with the generous lady, but she couldn't think fast enough. She could hardly tell her the truth.

"I'm Sandra by the way. What do people call you?"

The girl searched the car for an answer, her eyes falling on a magazine on the back seat. Sandra watched her from the corner of her eye, she knew this girl's type sadly too well.

"Elle," the girl replied simply. Sandra nodded in response.

It wasn't long before they arrived at a two-storey suburban home, with a large tree out the front. In the driveway was a black Jeep and a silver sedan already parked in the garage as Sandra parked her own car alongside it.

Elle watched behind her as the garage door started to close behind the car. Anxiety crept up inside of her, she gripped her backpack tightly to her chest.

"Let's get you out of those wet clothes first. I'm sure Kelly will have something to fit you," Sandra commented, climbing out of the car.

Elle followed Sandra cautiously into the house, looking around and taking in the foreign surroundings.

Kelly, Sandra's fifteen-year-old daughter, sat with her legs folded underneath her in front of the television on a modular lounge. She was writing in a notebook with a textbook opened beside her. Her blonde waves swept over one shoulder.

Elle stood awkwardly behind Sandra, suddenly nervous and unsure of the situation she had found herself in.

"Hi honey," Sandra greeted Kelly, who looked up for the first time and her eyes falling on Elle in question. "This is Elle. She's going to be staying with us tonight. Can you take her up to your room and get her some clothes and show her where the bathroom is to have a shower?"

"Sure," Kelly climbed off the lounge to lead Elle upstairs to her room. Elle was sure she saw a slight eye roll as she did so.

Elle, rocked nervously on her heels. Only when Sandra nodded to assure her, Elle followed Kelly up the stairs.

Kelly tried to engage Elle in conversation. Elle remained silent. Kelly quickly realised it was pointless as Elle wasn't about to open up to the stranger she had just met.

Finding some clothes for Elle, Kelly directed her to the bathroom down the hall and left her alone to have a shower, wandering back downstairs.

Glancing around her, Elle took in the white tiled bathroom and touched her hand to the soft, fluffy towels that hung on the wall. It had been a long time since Elle had known such comfort.

Taking her time, Elle allowed the warmth of the water to wash over her, grateful to be able to wash her hair for the first time in what felt like forever, a luxury she didn't take for granted. The scent of blossoms and coconuts swirled around her in the steam and she allowed herself a moment of peace, a break from her reality.

After her shower, Elle dressed in the clean, dry clothes Kelly had given her. Unsure what to do next she wandered down the hall back to Kelly's room where she had left her backpack. Elle brushed her dark brown hair from her face, examining her reflection in the full-length mirror on the wall. Her hazel eyes stared back at her, taking in the shell of a girl she once knew so well and now felt like a stranger. Unable to help herself, she pulled her top up and examined the scar that branded her stomach. She touched it gently with her fingertips and noticed how the redness had faded over time and was starting to look light pink, almost white in colour.

Closing her eyes, she tried to breathe calmly, not letting the memories or panic take over her.

The bedroom door opened without warning and a teenaged boy filled the doorway, causing Elle to jump at the unexpected intrusion, pulling her top down quickly to cover her stomach and hide her ugly scar.

"Kel..." he barked, before stopping, recognising it wasn't who he expected to find in the room. "I'm sorry," he said more calmly, "I was looking for my sister, Kelly."

Elle stood frozen, eyes wide in horror, heart pounding and her stomach tying in a large knot. She tried to breathe normally but found it too difficult to bypass her anxiety. Kelly's brother was seventeen with dark blonde hair, his frame filling the doorway. It was very intimidating to Elle and all too similar.

Not only had his entrance into the room startled her, but he reminded her of someone she once knew which scared her most of all. It reminded her she shouldn't get too comfortable and let her guard down.

"Are you a friend of Kelly's?" he asked, casually leaning on the door frame, but went on before waiting for an answer, "I'm Owen."

Elle just stared at him in fear. Her palms began to sweat and her legs felt like jelly. Any normal girl would probably be weak at the knees to look at Owen, as he was extremely good looking. Elle couldn't bring herself to see it. Instead, she felt like a caged prey with its predator circling.

Owen waited briefly before realising Elle wasn't going to talk to him. Standing up straight he took in Elle's timid stance. Owen gave a small wave goodbye, before leaving the room with a backward glance at the shaken girl. He headed downstairs in search of his sister, leaving Elle breathing a sigh of relief as she listened to him descending the stairs.

Entering the lounge room, Owen found Kelly sitting on the lounge studying. His parents were in the kitchen discussing something in hushed but serious tones.

"Kel," Owen announced as he entered and flopped down beside Kelly on the lounge, "Where's that money you borrowed from me last week? I'm heading out with Mark soon."

"I left it on your desk if you had cared to look," Kelly retorted, not looking up from her notes.

Owen ignored his sister's tone.

"So, what's up with your friend?" Owen asked, crossing one leg over the other and leaning back.

Kelly looked up at Owen, "She's not my friend. Mum brought her home with her."

Owen rolled his eyes at his sister's response, "Great. How long is this one sticking around for?"

"As long as she needs," Sandra's voice interrupted their conversation and both teenagers looked up to see their parents standing behind them.

"Whatever," Owen grumbled, standing up and starting to walk out of the lounge room past his parents. "I'm heading out with Mark tonight. Just keep her out of my room. I'll know if anything goes missing."

Without another word, Owen took off upstairs to find the money Kelly had left for him in his room.

Elle sat down for dinner with Sandra, Kelly and Brian, Sandra's husband. She was relieved to find Owen was not joining them for dinner. Even though she was starving, Elle tried her best to eat at a normal pace, not wanting to arouse suspicion. She had resolved she would allow herself one night of luxury; a shower, home cooked meal and a warm bed, but first thing in the morning she would need to disappear. It was too much of a risk to stay in one place for too long.

During dinner the family spoke animatedly about their days. Sandra tried her best to encourage Elle to join in on their conversation. Elle felt rude not being involved, though she could not afford to slip up even in the slightest.

After dinner, Sandra showed Elle to the guest room. She hoped Elle would open up more to her once they were alone, but Elle kept to herself. Maybe in the morning, Sandra thought to herself.

It took Elle nearly two hours before she was able to relax enough and fall asleep. The bed was soft and moulded around her body. It was the comfiest sleep Elle had had in a long time. Yet it didn't stop her body from being on high alert.

The front door closed in the middle of the night, shocking her from her sleep. Her heart began to pound rapidly, her eyes sprang open. Sitting up in the bed, she waited quietly, holding her breath. Elle wondered if she had been found. She only let her guard down for one night, surely it couldn't be...

"Owen," Elle heard Sandra's voice whisper outside the guest bedroom door, "Be quiet. Elle is sleeping."

"Yes, Mum," Owen replied not as quietly.

Owen was home. The thought did not settle Elle considering it could have been worse. Elle couldn't help but feel unsettled knowing he was sleeping in another room in the house. For the rest of the night Elle tossed and turned as she slept.

As the sun rose the next morning so did the house. Chatter and bustle of everyone getting ready for their day's activities. Elle woke from the unfamiliar sounds of a family and discovered her clothes washed, dried and folded on the chair in the corner of the bedroom. Eager to move on, she hurriedly dressed in her own clothes and grabbed her back pack.

Sandra smiled at Elle when she saw her standing on the bottom step of the staircase. Elle stood awkwardly, unsure of what to say or do, the front door was within sight, but her upbringing taught her not to be rude without cause.

"Want some breakfast?" Sandra offered kindly from her spot in the kitchen. Kelly and her husband, Brian sat at the kitchen table eating.

Elle thought about what to say, maybe she could stay for breakfast and then leave. Surely it couldn't hurt to have one last proper meal before she headed off again on her own.

Before she could reply, the sound of footsteps descending the stairs behind her alerted Elle to the presence of the final member of the family waking; Owen. Elle's eyes met his. They weren't friendly, but they weren't cruel either, only nonchalant. It didn't stop Elle's anxieties from creeping up once more. Her decision made; Elle started for the front door.

"I-I'm sorry, but I have to go. Thank you for last night," Elle mumbled quickly, the family watching her in bewilderment by her sudden change of demeanour.

"Wait!" Sandra calledafter her, but Elle didn't wait. She was out the door and running off down thesuburban street without a backwards glance.

Chapter 2

The small grocery store was busy for an early weekday, which surprised Elle. She wandered along the aisles casually. Finding something she needed, Elle carefully glanced in both directions to make sure no one was around or watching, then quickly slipped the item into her bag. Casually, she flicked her backpack behind her as though she hadn't touched a thing.

Half an hour later, she walked to the front of the store, bypassing the registers and out the front door.

"Excuse me!" called a voice behind Elle, but she ignored them and continued on her way, quickening her step. "Miss!"

Elle suddenly felt a hand on her elbow that turned her around. She came face to face with an older man in his late forties, with greying hair and a frown creasing his brow.

"You need to come with me," he stated in a matter-of-fact tone.

"Let go of me," Elle complained, trying to pull her arm free of his grasp. It was useless as he tightened his hold and started to direct her back into the store, Elle struggling the entire time.

The man took Elle into an office out the back and forced her to sit on a chair. She held her backpack on her lap, tight against her chest, not willing to let it go. The man questioned Elle, asking to look in her bag. She simply turned her head and looked away, refusing to say a thing. With a frustrated sigh, the man picked up his phone and rang the police.

Not long after, two police officers came into the office and directed Elle to follow them. They led her, handcuffed, out to their car parked out front. Elle was very much aware of all the eyes watching her as she climbed in the back seat. She tried her best to hide her face with her hood.

At the police station, Elle was directed into a small room with only a table and a chair either side of the table. She sat in one, her backpack placed on the table. Out of the backpack one of the officers pulled out five apples, a small box of muesli bars, a large bottle of water and a box of tampons.

"Let me guess," the young male officer asked while the male partner stood in the corner, "You forgot to pay."

"No," Elle replied simply, speaking for the first time, "Forgetting to pay implies I have money to pay, which I don't."

"Alright," the officer sat down in the opposite chair to hers, "Let's start with your name and then we will have to call your parents."

"Amy," Elle lied, it had come so easily to her now dealing with the police.

"Okay Amy," the officer writing it down on the notepad in front of him, "And what's your parents' number so we can call them."

"Don't have any," Elle replied simply, avoiding his glance in her direction.

"Well, who do you live with?"

"No one."

"Listen, you're going to have to give me something or you are going to find yourself locked up for stealing. What's it going to be?" Irritation was evident in his voice. He couldn't understand why she wouldn't give him any straight answers.

"So, lock me up," Elle remarked, shrugging her shoulders and looking away.

It was probably safest for her and would also mean she would be fed and have somewhere dry to stay. Given she wasn't yet eighteen it would mean only juvenile detention, which wasn't anything new to Elle. She had spent a few nights there previously for the same thing. It wasn't her plan that morning to get caught, but if that was the result it wouldn't be a bad one.

The police officer groaned in frustration and ran a hand through his hair. With only a look to his partner they left the room, closing the door behind them. Elle wondered what they were doing. Normally they would take her to lock up by now.

After some discussion between the two officers outside the room, where Elle could not hear them, they decided to call in Social Services to deal with the young teen. It was obvious she wasn't going to make it easy for them, but they could also clearly see they weren't dealing with a usual shoplifting incident.

The two had seen it many times before with teenaged girls, but normally they would steal make-up, music or movies, alcohol and majority of the time, clothes. This girl didn't have any of that. What she had stolen could be called essential items. Something didn't add up and she wasn't going to give away the answer any time soon. What they couldn't figure out is why she would so readily agree to being locked up.

A woman from Social Services arrived an hour later. She introduced herself to the two police officers and they caught her up to speed with what was going on. The woman looked through the one-way window and her brow furrowed in concern when she saw the girl sitting at the table, eating one of the apples she had stolen.

"Leave it with me," she said to the officers and opened the door, going into the room and closing it behind her.

"Amy? Or is it Elle?" Sandra asked walking over to the table and sitting down in the chair opposite Elle.

Elle looked up in surprise, the blood suddenly draining from her face.

"What are you doing here?" Elle murmured quietly.

"I work for Social Services," Sandra answered, "What are you doing here?"

"Isn't it obvious?" Elle replied, looking away.

"So, let's start with the basics then," Sandra smiled, ignoring the tone in Elle's voice, "Why did you steal these things? Any of these items you could have gotten from my home this morning."

Elle held her tongue, refusing to answer Sandra's questioning. She just wanted the interrogation to be over and done. Elle just wanted to be locked-up and safe.

"Elle, you need to talk to me if I'm going to help you," Sandra pleaded in a caring voice.

"I don't need your help," Elle said unkindly, regretting it right away, she slunk down in her chair.

"Looks to me like you do," Sandra stated calmly.

Elle looked away again.

"Elle, if you don't let me help you they will put you in juvenile detention. Is that what you want?"

"I already told them to lock me up and they went and called you," Elle said crossly.

It wasn't Sandra's fault for trying to help Elle, she was just doing her job and was a kind-hearted person, but Elle couldn't afford to get attached to Sandra or get sucked into her kindness. Putting up a wall between them was her best option.

"Right then," Sandra said standing up and walking to the door.

Elle didn't have any idea what happened after Sandra left the room, but more than an hour later the police were letting Elle go, on the one condition that Sandra took responsibility for her. Elle was one hundred percent against the idea, but Sandra wouldn't hear anything about it.

That's how Elle found herself back in Sandra's car that afternoon and heading back to Sandra's house.

"I don't want to do this," Elle sulked, looking out the window.

"Well, guess what," Sandra stated, "You don't have a choice."

Elle sighed in defeat and wondered when she could run off before it got too complicated.

"First thing we need to do is get you enrolled into school," Sandra announced.

Elle balked at the idea of having to go to school, she would be too visible.

"I can't. You can't" Sandra looked sideways at Elle and Elle continued on. "You don't have any documentation and they aren't just going to let me in."

"You let me worry about that," Sandra mentioned calmly, "All you need to worry about is what name you want to be known as. I know Elle and Amy aren't your real names, so this is your last chance to pick something good."

Elle stared away, out her window. Silence extended between them in the car.

"Fine," Sandra spoke, breaking the quiet, "You're my responsibility according to the officials, so I'll name you. Let's see, Kelly was named after my mother and Owen after Brian's father. What about Evelyn, after my grandmother? You can shorten it to Evie if you like."

"Whatever," Evie shrugged. "Won't matter anyway, I won't be here for long."

Chapter 3

Evie dumped her bag in the corner of the guest room of Sandra's house, where she had slept the night before. Flopping down on the bed, she gazed at the off-white ceiling. She let out a sigh of defeat. Evie knew she couldn't stay in the one spot for too long. It was too risky and dangerous, not just for her, but anyone in contact with her.

Sandra made it difficult for Evie to leave the house for the rest of the day, resolving to work from home so she could keep an eye on Evie. Not wanting to be social, Evie spent the day hidden in the bedroom.

By dinner, the entire family was home, making Evie feel uneasy knowing Owen was somewhere in the house. It wasn't his fault she felt this way, but it wasn't something she could easily move past either.

Kelly knocked tenderly on the bedroom door before opening it and inviting Evie down to the dinner table. Evie ignored her and gazed out the window wishing for her freedom. Kelly left without a word.

Sandra arrived in the doorway.

"Kelly tells me you refuse to come down for dinner," Sandra said as she stepped into the room towards Evie.

Evie remained silent.

"I know you haven't eaten a proper meal since last night," Sandra stated, "You need to come down and eat."

Evie sighed with defeat and looked at Sandra for the first time.

"I'll see you downstairs in two minutes," Sandra commanded, before leaving the room.

Evie took a deep breath to calm her nerves of seeing Owen and headed downstairs to eat dinner with the family who had taken her in.

Thankful, she had managed to position herself at the opposite side of the table from Owen. Evie trained her eyes on her plate, not wanting to meet his gaze she could feel was on her.

The family talked animatedly about their days. Evie's run in with the law managed to stay out of Sandra's account of her day and Evie was grateful. Although, Evie didn't know what Sandra had told her family about why Evie had returned to their house and with a new name, yet they all seemed to take it in their stride and didn't mention anything in Evie's presence.

Sandra mentioned to Owen that Evie would be starting school with him on Monday and that she would like Owen to accompany Evie to school and look out for her. Evie's eyes met Owen's for the first time that night. He seemed bored and unwilling at the idea of having to take on his mother's charity case. Evie bit down on the inside of her lip to steady her beating heart, her breath speeding up.

It was Friday night and Evie knew that she would be long gone from their home before Monday morning or the duty of heading to school would fall upon her. Taking a steadying breath, Evie stood up, excusing herself from the table, leaving half of her dinner still on her plate.

Later that night, silence fell over the house. Evie waited quietly until she was certain everyone was asleep. Looking at the digital clock in the guest bedroom, red lights lit up the numbers, it was just after one in the morning. Evie hadn't heard any movement or talking for nearly two hours.

Picking up her backpack and already dressed in her own clothes, Evie crept to the stairs and started to descend. One of the steps creaked and Evie stood stock still, looking behind her in panic. There was no noise. No indication that anyone was awoken from their slumber by her sudden noise.

As Evie passed the kitchen, she grabbed some food that could be stored in her backpack, keeping her fed for a few days at least. She had already stolen some toiletries from the bathroom earlier on that day. Positioning her backpack on her shoulders, Evie headed to the front door.

Pausing briefly, with her hand on the door handle, Evie looked back at the stairs. Sandra and her family had been so kind, taking her in, not knowing who she was or her past. It was her past that was forcing her to leave. She could not risk staying in one place. She could not risk the lives of the family who had shown her so much generosity.

Not allowing herself to become caught in emotion, Evie twisted the handle and left the house, closing the door quietly behind her. With one last glance back at the house behind her, Evie disappeared into the night, walking briskly down the street.

As the sun began to rise in the early hours of the morning, Evie found herself at a train station far from the family's home. She viewed the timetable, not looking for a destination in particular, more just for whichever train would be departing at the earliest time. Evie was disheartened, noticing the next train wouldn't be leaving for two whole hours. Settling down on a nearby bench seat, Evie laid down using her backpack as a pillow and hugging her jacket around her tightly.

Evie was unsure how much time had passed when she woke to the sound of people talking nearby. Startled that she wasn't on guard, Evie sat up right quickly and looked around her, checking for any dangers. Everything seemed normal. Just some people waiting for the train nearby.

Shaking her head to wake herself from her brief sleep and a rub of her eyes, Evie looked at the clock on the wall. The first train would be arriving soon. Collecting her bag, Evie stood up and walked over to the waiting platform.

When the train arrived, Evie boarded and found a seat to herself and settled down for the journey. It wasn't long into the trip that a ticket collector came into the carriage. Evie tried to hide her face with her cap and the hood of her jacket, pretending to be asleep.

"Miss," the older man spoke to her gently, "Could I see your ticket please?"

Evie's shoulders slumped in despair and looked up at the man.

"Oh, I'm sorry. I was sleeping," Evie lied. "My mum paid for my ticket, but forgot to give it to me. My father is meeting me at the next station. He will be able to show you my ticket."

Evie prayed that her lie was believable and he would move on. Yet luck was not on her side that day.

"I'm sorry, Miss, but if you don't have a ticket, I will have to report you to security."

"But I do have a ticket," Evie argued. If she could just make it to the next station, she could run away. She just had to convince the ticket collector that her ticket was waiting for her at the other end. "My dad has the ticket. If you would just wait, I can show it to you then."

The man eyed Evie suspiciously then nodded his head slowly before moving on to the next passenger.

Evie sighed with relief that she had gotten away with it. It wasn't the first time she had used that excuse while travelling on the trains and buses, but she was careful not to use it too often.

Thirty minutes later, the train arrived at the station. Evie saw the ticket collector watching her, so she waved to a random man who was waiting on the platform that could pass as her dad. She collected her bag and exited the carriage from the opposite end to where the collector was, pretending she hadn't seen him watching her.

Stepping off the train, Evie glanced behind her to make sure the collector wasn't following her. She spotted him hanging out of the door at the opposite end of the carriage. Avoiding his eye, Evie bowed her head and high tailed towards the exit of the station.

Not watching where she was going, Evie rushed forward and straight into a wall. The wall was hard, yet not like brick or wood. Her eyes drifted upwards and found herself staring right in the eyes of a station security guard.

Evie's defence mode kicked in and she turned to run, but he grabbed her arm. She turned and kicked him in the knee, which caused him to shout out in pain and loosened his grip enough that she was able to free herself and run.

"Stop right there," a second voice boomed from behind Evie.

Checking over her shoulder, Evie saw the first security guard limping after her and a second security guard running from the other end towards her also. Picking up speed, Evie ran as fast as she could, down a ramp and along the street.

The security guards soon fell back and Evie felt relief that she wouldn't have to run for much longer. She knew it would be over as soon as she turned a few corners; the first was not far ahead of her.

Sirens wailed in the distance and panic coursed through Evie's body once more. A police car came towards her from in front, the security guards still coming up from behind her. Evie knew she wouldn't make the corner anymore. Her feet slowed and she came to a stop. Flustered, Evie looked around for an escape, but knew she was out of luck.

The police car stopped in front of Evie, the security guards caught up quickly. Before she could think of an excuse, she found herself in handcuffs and in the back of the police car. Slumped over, Evie decided it wasn't the worst thing. Maybe this time she would get locked up for evasion of fair. A few nights in a cell didn't bother her.

That afternoon, Evie slept soundly in her cell. It was a sense of relief to know she was safe for the time being. Small and petty crimes never reached the news. Evie had wondered in the past if she could bring herself to committing a worse crime, but the truth was she was concerned it would end up in the news and she couldn't risk that happening.

The door at the end of the corridor opened, waking Evie. She drowsily sat up in her cot, knowing they were coming to speak to her, as she was the only one in the cells at that time.

"Evie," came a soft woman's voice, Evie had come to know as Sandra's.

Suddenly, Evie felt low about her situation and how she had left in the middle of the night, without even a thank you for the hospitality she had received, Evie bowed her head.

The clunk of the cell door opening brought Evie's eyes upward to meet Sandra's. Concern etched across Sandra's face where Evie had expected anger, maybe disappointment.

"I'm sorry," Evie whispered, so quietly it would have been a miracle if Sandra had heard her.

"Come on," Sandraushered her out of the cell, "You're coming home with me, again."

Chapter 4

Sandra pulled the car into the suburban driveway of her home and Evie looked at the house through the passenger window.

"We're home now," Sandra announced.

"This is not my home," Evie mumbled under her breath.

"Well, it is now," Sandra refuted, "For the next three months at least."

Evie sighed in defeat. Sandra was right. After the incident at the grocery store and then the ticket evasion on the train, the police were ready to lock Evie up for three months in juvenile detention. Evie wanted to oblige happily, until Sandra stepped in and took responsibility for her.

With a sunken heart, Evie sat on a chair in the dining room of Sandra's house while the probation officer fitted her with an ankle bracelet. Sandra signed the necessary paperwork and the probation officer explained how the anklet worked.

Evie looked at her outstretched leg, twisting it back and forth, examining the object that would rule her life for the following three months. She was stuck. There was no escape now. Evie had no choice but to try, keep a low profile while she served her time under Sandra's roof.

Trudging upstairs, Evie left Sandra to escort the probation officer out of the house. As Evie reached the top of the stairs, she became aware of Owen leaning on the doorframe to his bedroom down the hall. She stilled at his presence, caught off guard, Evie felt herself shake.

"Nice accessory," Owen teased, looking at Evie's ankle.

Evie's eyes followed his gaze to her tracking device. She realised she was going to have to figure out a way to disguise or hide it for others, especially with Sandra enforcing that Evie would be attending school starting Monday.

Doing her best to ignore the fear coursing through her body, Evie avoided Owen's eyes and ducked quickly into the guest bedroom, her bedroom, closing the door behind her. Leaning against the door for added measure, Evie slumped down to the ground.

On Sunday, Sandra dragged Evie out of the house to go clothes shopping. Evie did her best to hide her ankle monitor with her jeans. The conditions of the anklet allowed Evie to go to and from school or with a special code only Sandra knew, she could have three hours to go out. That meant Sandra had only three hours to find suitable outfits for Evie to wear to school.

Evie had dug out her baseball cap from the bottom of her backpack to help hide her face while out in public. Her hair hung freely, providing more cover to her face.

Wandering the stores, Evie reluctantly tried on various outfits that Sandra passed to her. When Sandra was satisfied they had enough clothes, Evie breathed a sigh of relief that they would be heading back to the semi-safety of Sandra's home. She was wrong.

"We've still got some time left, I'm going to get my hair done," Sandra smiled at Evie, "Would you like to get something done with yours?"

Sandra eyed Evie's brown locks hiding her face.

"Uh, no thanks," Evie declined, she had dyed her hair dark to protect herself and never looked back.

"Well, feel free to wander while I do." Sandra looked down at her watch. "We still have ninety minutes until we have to be home. Meet me back here in an hour."

Evie nodded as Sandra waved goodbye and headed into the salon.

Ninety minutes seemed like an eternity to Evie. She had managed to avoid large shopping centres for so long, she felt highly exposed at that moment. Sandra had left her with ten dollars. Deciding to treat herself, Evie headed towards the food court she had seen earlier.

After ordering an iced-chocolate, Evie found a seat at a quiet table in a hidden corner of the food court. With a clear view of the entire area, she was able to map out various escape routes if the need arose. She sipped her drink slowly, while watching everyone that walked past, making sure to keep her cap pulled down and covering her face.

A girl screaming across the other side of the food court made Evie jump in her seat, her eyes darting around madly to find the danger. That's when she saw it, a bunch of teenagers, around the same age as her fooling around. One of the girls squealed in delight again as one of the boys picked her up and swung her around playfully.

Evie took three deep breaths, trying to calm her speeding heart rate. As she did so, Evie recognised Owen was a part of the crowd, which didn't make calming herself down any easier. He was laughing, so care free as he sat on the edge of one of the tables with his friends. As he talked to one of his friends, his eyes wandered casually around the food court landing on Evie. She quickly got to her feet, heading for the closest exit of the food court to head back to Sandra.

"Evie," Owen called out to her as he jogged after her, "Hey, wait up!"

When he drew closer, Owen took hold of her elbow and stopped her, turning Evie to look at him. Evie gasped in surprise and froze, backing herself against the wall.

"Aren't you meant to be with my mother," Owen interrogated her, "Or are you doing another runner? You do realise how that anklet of yours works, right?"

"Y-your mother is at the h-hairdresser," Evie stuttered.

Owen's brow furrowed as he studied her.

"Please let me go," Evie pleaded him.

Owen looked down at his hand still holding onto Evie's elbow. He released his hold quickly and took a step back, feeling apologetic for his behaviour.

Without another word, Evie ran off, leaving Owen standing there alone, confused. Evie rushed back to the salon and found Sandra paying the hairdresser, her hair freshly styled.

Evie was silent the entire ride back to the Taylor's home. She didn't mention her run in with Owen to Sandra. Once they arrived back at the house, Evie retreated to her room. At least for the next three months. She wandered aimlessly over to the window that overlooked the street, the large tree out front swayed gently in the breeze.

It had been a long time since Evie had stayed in one place for this long and in the comfort of a home too. It felt strange and foreign to her, like visiting a different country for the first time. She had become so accustomed to life on the run and living on the streets, Evie often had to remind herself of her life before it all.

As she stared blankly out the bedroom window, an unknown four-wheel-drive pulled up to the curb outside of the house. Evie pulled back from the window and hid back behind the curtain, watching to see who was in the car. Her heart began to pick up speed. She attempted to swallow the lump that had instantly formed in her throat. All of Evie's anxieties bubbled to the surface.

The front passenger door opened and Owen climbed out of the car, laughing and talking to the inside occupants. He closed the door and waved as it drove away.

As he turned towards the house, he happened to look up at the house, straight to Evie's window. While watching, Evie had unconsciously moved out from behind the curtain and was in full view. As Owen's eyes met Evie's she gasped and dove down to the floor to hide.

Her heart now racing, Evie slowly peeked over the window ledge once more, but Owen was no longer there. She sat back down on the floor, her back against the wall and tried to steady her breathing.

Three months in a house with Owen was going to feel like perpetuity. How on Earth could she avoid him?

Chapter 5

Monday morning, Sandra woke Evie and instructed her to get ready for her first day of school. Evie aimlessly selected some clothes for school while making sure to cover her ankle monitor. Loose jeans and a white tank top, covered with a long-sleeved checked shirt with the buttons undone.

Sandra had given Evie a shoulder bag to use, filled with notebooks and pens. Adding the final touches to Evie's outfit, she pulled out her cap once more and pulled it down on her head, her hair falling down around her shoulders.

Downstairs, there was the buzz of a busy Monday morning and everyone getting ready for their day. Evie slowly descended the stairs, pausing half way to watch the family happily converse with one another as they went about their daily ritual. Her heart broke a little knowing she could never have that. A life she was slowly forgetting.

"Good morning, Evie," Sandra chirped when she saw Evie standing there.

"Hi," Evie responded quietly, completing her descent down the stairs but being careful to stick to the opposite side of the room from Owen.

Their eyes met briefly, but broken almost immediately by both of them.

"Owen will drive you to school and help you get settled in," Sandra announced to Evie, not noticing the exchange. "Kelly attends a different school. She got a scholarship for the school of arts."

Evie's heart rate picked up at the thought of having to spend time with Owen. She pushed the thought aside, unable to determine if it was from fear or excitement. The idea it was the latter unnerved her.

After breakfast, everyone went their separate ways. Brian headed off to work in his car, Sandra took Kelly in her car to drop her off to her school on her way to work, and Owen wandered over to his old Jeep. The other cars pulled away and Owen looked back at Evie who was standing idly on the front door step.

"Are you coming or what?" Owen queried, holding open the driver's door, waiting for Evie to get into the car.

Taking a deep breath, Evie walked around the other side of the Jeep and climbed into the passenger side. She could feel Owen's eyes watching her every move but she refused to look at him. With hands tightly clasped in her lap, Evie looked out her window in silence as Owen drove them to school.

It had been over a year since Evie had stepped foot in a school and as much has she had missed the normalcy of teenaged life, fear gripped at her throat of being amongst it all once more. It was high school where her old life ended and her new life of running away took hold.

"We're here," Owen announced once he had parked the car, bringing Evie out of her daze.

Looking up at the large building, Evie swallowed down the lump in her throat. She had no choice but to go in. Her only option was to keep as low of a profile as possible for the next three months.

Evie followed Owen as he guided the way through the hallways and the mass of teenagers towards the office. He didn't stick around, leaving Evie to sort out her timetable with a lovely older woman named Julie who worked behind the counter.

With her timetable and a map of the school in hand, Evie wandered down the now empty hallways, checking the map as she checked against her timetable, to find the right room for her first class.

Evie opened the room to her new Maths class and padded over to the teacher near the board to introduce herself. Mr Fisher, a balding old man with thick, rimmed glasses, welcomed Evie to the class and directed her to take a seat. The last empty seat was to the back of the classroom. Evie could feel the entire class watching her intently as she passed them, making her way to her seat.

The story Sandra had told the school was Evie was her sister's daughter who lived on the other side of the country. Evie had supposedly come to stay with them while Sandra's sister was overseas for business.

Once in her seat, Evie pulled the tip of her cap down over her face and lowered herself further into her chair, attempting to be invisible. No one attempted to speak to her and she liked it that way.

On her way to her next class, she stayed out of people's way. It was a large enough school, Evie knew she could easily remain unnoticed for the three months; she just needed to keep her head down and remain quiet.

At lunch, Evie collected her lunch and found an empty table in the far corner of the cafeteria. Not wanting to have her back to any dangers, she sat in the corner with a view of the entire room. Evie watched as various groups of loud teenagers entered to eat their lunch. Keeping to herself, she picked at her food and kept her head down.

A chair screeched against the floor as it pulled out and Evie jumped slightly when she noticed someone sat down across from her at her quiet table. Looking up from her tray of half eaten food, Evie's eyes found themselves staring into a pair of chocolate brown eyes.

Zane Carter leant with ease across the table, picking up a chip from Evie's tray and putting it in his mouth. He smiled a dazzling smile at her. Taken aback, Evie found herself unable to talk. Who was this boy and why was he eating her food?

"I'm Zane," Zane introduced himself with a cocky grin, "Haven't seen you around before. Are you new here?"

So much for being invisible, Evie thought to herself, remaining silent. She wondered if she ignored him if he would lose interest and go away.

In any normal circumstance, a girl in Evie's position would be falling all over Zane and flirting with him. His dark brown, wavy hair was styled and short, but long enough that it made you want to run your fingers through it. Evie ignored that thought.

"Not much of a talker, are you?" Zane pondered aloud.

Evie noticed people at the tables around them, watching and waiting, but she didn't know why. It made her feel uneasy and like she was under a spotlight. Not wanting any more attention from Zane or the rest of the gawking teenagers, Evie quickly collected her bag, left her half-eaten food and got up to leave.

"Hey, I just wanted to talk," Zane laughed, as he gently touched her arm.

It was a friendly laugh and his eyes were kind. Evie knew he only meant well, but regardless of his intentions, they weren't desired. Her shield was up and she didn't like the attention it brought from all the onlookers.

"Do not touch me," Evie growled through her teeth, only loud enough that Zane would hear her, glaring back at Zane.

He stilled, surprised by Evie's reaction, Zane retracted his hand.

"I'm sorry, I didn't mean," Zane started.

"I just want to be left alone," Evie stated calmly, again so only Zane could hear.

Without another word, Evie walked away and out of the cafeteria. She rushed quickly, but not too fast to cause a scene and made her way to the girls' bathroom. Inside she locked herself into a cubicle and tried to steady her breathing.

Panic attacks were common for Evie these days. She knew how to handle them, but that didn't make them any easier. Leaning forward on the lidded toilet, Evie rested her head in her hands, between her knees.

As the bell rang to end lunch break, Evie found her way to her next class, Biology. Entering the already half-full room, she noticed Owen sitting in the middle row talking with some other students. Pretending not to have seen him, Evie checked in with the teacher then did her best to be inconspicuous as she made her way to the back row.

"Evie," Owen's voice called out across the room.

Evie looked up through her lashes, keeping her face down and recognised one of the students he was sitting with was Zane. Her face paled at her sudden misfortune of chance and tried to calm her rapidly beating heart with slow and steady breaths. Evie gave a half smile in Owen's direction as she took her seat and went back to ignoring him.

Even from her seat in the back, Evie could hear the muttered talk between the boys, three rows in front of her. She tried to pay no attention to them while she got her books and a pen out for the start of class.

Evie jumped slightly when she felt someone brush behind her before sitting down in the seat next to her. Scared, she thought Owen or even Zane had decided to join her. She was grateful when she realised it was another girl, Harley.

Harley had long blonde hair that extended the length of her back, tied in a thick braid, which made Evie think her hair was longer than it actually seemed. Her green eyes were like gems and skin the colour of milk.

"Hi," Harley greeted Evie chirpily, "I'm Harley. No, I'm not named after the bike."

"Uh, E-Evie," Evie replied, unsure of herself.

It was the first time she had actually spoken her new name out-loud. Normally she never stuck to a name longer than twenty-four hours, but this time she didn't have a choice.

"You're new here," Harley stated simply, "That must be why everyone is talking about you."

Evie baulked at Harley's statement. She didn't want everyone talking about her. She just wanted to be invisible. Noticing her distain about the topic, Harley pointed the tip of her blue biro in Owen's direction.

"You've got their attention," Harley smiled mischievously.

Evie's glance followed Harley's direction and noticed both Owen and Zane looking in her direction as they talked. She quickly turned her attention back to Harley who was flirtatiously waving at the boys with the tips of her fingers.

"I don't want anybody's attention," Evie muttered, "Least of all, theirs."

Harley shrugged at Evie's comment and turned to face her.

"Two of the hottest boys in school are paying you attention and you don't want it? Girl, there is something wrong with you," Harley chimed.

"You don't know the half of it," Evie mused quietly.

"Well, I would be more than happy to have it, so that makes me your new best friend. Feel free to palm all unwanted attention my way."

Evie eyed Harley, trying to figure out how she could deter Harley from being her friend, but it was obvious Harley wasn't the type to take no for an answer.

Not wanting to drawany more attention to herself than necessary, Evie decided to focus on thelesson the teacher was starting and pray that Harley would eventually loseinterest.

Chapter 6

Harley followed Evie like a lost puppy to her locker. Evie swapped some books over and then headed onto her final class for the day, hoping her lack of speaking would put Harley off, but it only made Harley feel like Evie was shy or scared to step out of her comfort zone in a new school. Harley pushed on to become Evie's friend. Evie wished she could just disappear into the crowd.

Unfortunately, for Evie, it turned out that she shared her final class of the day with Harley and another familiar face, Owen. Evie groaned inwardly and rolled her eyes as she took her chosen seat at the back of the room. Harley sat down beside her once more.

Modern History had never really appealed to Evie, but given the choice between it and Physics, it was a no brainer decision for Evie. At least she knew she had the headspace to sit through history. It wouldn't matter how well she did in class, she would be gone in three months, but her old ways of being a good student rose from within her. Evie missed school.

At the end of the lesson, Evie began to collect her things, when she noticed a shadow fall over her desk. Her breath caught in her chest briefly from fear as she looked up and found herself looking into Owen's blue eyes. They were beautiful eyes, she gave him that, kinder than the blue eyes she knew, but that didn't make her fear disappear all the same.

"I've just got to get some stuff from my locker," Owen announced, "Meet me at the car in ten."

Without another word, he stalked off out of the classroom.

"Hold up," Harley exclaimed excitedly, "Owen Taylor is driving you home?"

Evie shrugged, not wanting to get into details with Harley. It would only lead to more questions and more unwanted attention from Harley and whoever else. The less she said the better.

Thankfully for Evie, Harley's locker was in the opposite direction to Evie's, which meant they parted ways after class. Evie quickly grabbed the necessary books she needed that night to complete her homework assignments and then headed towards the parking lot to meet Owen at his car.

Evie watched cars drive past the school with unease, as she leaned against the passenger side of Owen's Jeep. Owen hadn't arrived yet, even though she was on time. With every passing car, Evie looked for the driver, hoping her fear would settle when she didn't recognise the driver. It didn't help. She felt exposed and vulnerable waiting out in the open of a parking lot. She pulled her cap down lower to cover her face more.

Boisterous male laughter caught Evie's attention and she looked up to see Owen and Zane approaching. Evie froze in fear. Owen was one thing to deal with but adding Zane to the mix was just too much.

Zane smiled warmly at Evie as they approached. Owen's expression gave nothing away like usual.

"Evie, Zane. Zane, Evie," Owen introduced the two nonchalantly.

"We met at lunch," Zane winked at Evie and she glared at him in response.

"Can we go?" Evie asked Owen, ignoring Zane further.

"Zane's coming with us," Owen explained, walking off to the driver's side and climbing in, starting the engine right away.

Zane opened the front passenger door and held it, bowing slightly, "Ladies first."

"I'll get in the back," Evie muttered, before opening the back door and climbing in, shutting the door behind her before Zane could insist further.

Owen eased the car out of the lot and onto the street. Zane twisted in the front seat and turned to face Evie in the back seat, directly behind him.

"So, Evie," Zane spoke to her, "How come you didn't tell me you knew my man, Owen here?"

Evie stopped looking out her window and gazed at Zane with disinterest, saying nothing in reply.

"Not much of a talker, are you?" Zane went on.

Owen's eyes met Evie's in the rear-view mirror. Breaking the connection, Evie looked back out her window at the passing scenery.

Zane continued attempting to engage Evie in conversation for the remainder of the trip home. At first Evie thought Owen was just driving Zane home, but much to her dismay, Zane was going to Owen's house with them to apparently study with Owen, which most likely meant hang out.

Once home, Evie was quick to exit the car and get inside the house. Sandra had just arrived home herself with Kelly. Sandra began to ask Evie how her day was, but Evie rudely ignored her, wanting to create distance between her and the boys who were following behind her, and dashed up the stairs to her room and closed the door.

Evie could hear muffled conversation coming from downstairs through the door. She paced back and forth along the far side of the room, near the window. There was a feeling of entrapment and she couldn't run away, anxiety of being found, her past catching up with her. Absentmindedly, Evie's hand went under her top and touched her scar. She took deep, calming breaths. She couldn't afford to get found out and it was unlikely she would be. There was nothing to link her to the Taylor family.

A soft knock on the bedroom door interrupted her thoughts. Evie stopped in her tracks by the window. Turning around, Evie watched as the door slowly opened and Sandra poked her head through the gap.

"Can I come in?" Sandra asked gently, to which Evie just nodded.

Sandra stepped inside the room, closing the door quietly behind her. Evie watched as Sandra moved across the room, sat on the end of the bed and faced Evie who hadn't moved from her spot by the window.

"How was school?" Sandra asked in a tender and caring mother-type tone.

Evie smiled briefly, remembering her own mother, but quickly dashed the thought away as quickly as it had emerged, looking back out the window to hide her emotional slip.

"Did something happen at school that I should know about?" Sandra went on, not drawing attention to Evie's brief smile, which made Evie grateful.

Evie stayed silent, staring out the window at nothing in particular, just unable to bring herself to look back at Sandra.

"Evie, you need to talk to me so I can help you," Sandra encouraged.

Evie turned to Sandra, not in anger but in frustration.

"You can't help me," Evie exclaimed.

"Explain it to me then," Sandra spoke gently still, not wavered by Evie's tone or volume.

"I can't," Evie shouted at her, "The best thing you could do for me, you and your family is to let me go. You've trapped me like a prisoner in your house!"

"If I hadn't have brought you home, they would have locked you up in jail," Sandra stood up and spoke with force.

"So, send me there," Evie spat back, "Everyone will be safer if I was there, including me."

As soon as the words left her mouth, Evie wished she could take them back. She had said too much. Evie turned away from Sandra, facing the window once more, hoping Sandra would not notice.

"Why are you not safe here?" Sandra asked with her voice soft once more. She was standing now, her concern for Evie evident.

Evie remained silent.

It was the bedroom door opening that made Evie jump as she turned around, expecting to see Sandra leaving, but she hadn't moved. Owen filled the doorway. His eyes swept from his mother to Evie and back to his mother again.

"Everything okay? We heard shouting?" Owen's question directed to Sandra.

"We're fine, thank you Owen," Sandra replied calmly to her son, her eyes drifted to him, signalling for him to leave.

Owen took one last look at Evie, trying to figure out what was going on, before he left the room, closing the door behind him.

Sandra waited patiently for Evie to speak once Owen had closed the door. She sat back down on the end of Evie's bed, which Evie had made neatly that morning before going to school. Sandra had been surprised with how neat Evie had been. Most homeless teenagers didn't care about being organised. She could tell there was something different about Evie though.

Meanwhile, Evie's heart was racing. After shouting at Sandra and then Owen coming into the room, Evie's anxiety was high and her emotions were in turmoil. She felt smothered, finding it hard to breathe. It was obvious Sandra wasn't going to leave Evie and give her the space she needed in that moment.

"I need to get out of here," Evie stated plainly before marching out of the room, Sandra calling after her.

Evie rushed down the stairs, Sandra tried to keep up, but Evie was on a mission.

Owen and Zane were in the dining room with their schoolbooks laid out on the table, both of them looking up, startled, as Evie hurried past them and out the front door. Sandra called out to Evie, but she ignored her and continued.

Evie made her way down the street, running, not caring about the consequences of her actions. She was well out of the boundaries of the house now; her anklet would activate the police. Maybe it would be a good thing, maybe then she could go to jail and be safe. The Taylors would be safe.

After running a short distance, Evie reached a park with a children's playground and swing-set; it was deserted. She wandered over to the empty swings and sat down on one, swaying gently on the chain link.

Evie needed time to think, straighten out her thoughts. She felt horrible for shouting at Sandra the way she had. Evie sunk her head in her hands, covering her face; she knew she would need to apologise. She wanted to apologise.

Nobody knew about Evie's past. At only seventeen, Evie had been through more in the past year of her life than most people had been through in an entire life. She had seen things and experienced loss like no one ever should. All

Evie wanted now was to survive and keep others safe. She couldn't risk getting close to anyone.

Everything would have been so much easier if she was still able to be out on her own once more or even in jail. Why did Sandra have to come to her rescue? Evie wanted to be angry with Sandra, but couldn't. She was only doing what a mother would do, it made Evie's heartache for her own.

Evie dragged the toes of her sneakers through the dirt underneath the swing as she swayed like a pendulum, back and forth. Two small grooves started to form, identical and straight, ridges slowly growing on either side. Evie watched her feet in daze, transfixed on the simplicity of the pattern. Her breathing slowed and heartrate eased into a normal rhythm.

Feet padding gently, crunching quietly against the ground, as someone approached caused Evie's eyes to dart upward in the same direction of the oncoming intruder. She had expected Sandra, maybe even the police, but certainly not the familiar face coming towards her. Evie's heart began to beat quicker from the habitual anxiety once more.

Unsure what else to do, Evie's fingers wrapped tighter around the chain link and her knuckles whitened slightly under the strain. Owen eased himself down into the seat of the other swing, facing the same direction. Evie stared at him in bewilderment, wondering what he was doing there. He was the last person Evie had thought would come for her.

"Listen," Owen talked finally, not looking at Evie, but out into the park, "I don't know what your issue is and quite honestly, I don't care. You're just another teenager my mother brought home and tried to sort out. The thing is though; she does care about you and right now is at home frantic and worried about you. So why don't you get your shit together and come home with me?"

"I told her to just let me leave," Evie muttered, slightly loosening her grip on the chain.

Owen turned to face Evie.

"You're pretty keen to get out of here, aren't you?" Owen asked.

"I don't like to stick around in one place for too long," Evie replied simply, looking back down to her tracks in the ground.

For some strange reason, Evie felt a little more at ease with Owen in that moment. When he said he didn't care about her, Evie felt a twinge of sadness. It was what her life had become. No one cared for her anymore. Yet, there was Sandra, trying her hardest to do the best by Evie and all Evie could do was push away. Guilt riddled her mind at that moment, along with the sadness.

"Most teenagers in your position would love to be in a home, fed, looked after, given a good education and all that comes with it," Owen was confused at Evie's readiness to run away.

"Most teenagers haven't lived my life," Evie murmured as she peered up at Owen through her eyelashes.

Owen held her gaze for a moment before looking back out across the park and standing up.

"Come on," Owen commanded, "We only have another ten minutes to get you home before that jewellery of yours alerts the police."

"Let them take me," Evie argued, not making a move to stand up.

"If your plan is to get away from here, trust me that isn't the way," Owen explained, looking back down at Evie, "My mother is very good at getting what she wants when she puts her mind to it. It could mean you just wearing that jewellery of yours and being with us longer. There's no way she will let you just go to jail."

Evie let out a deep sigh and stood up slowly. Owen was right. Knowing Sandra just in that short time, Evie knew she had a knack of being able to pull strings to get what she wanted. Evie had no choice but to return to the house with Owen and try to survive three months with the Taylor family.

Chapter 7

As soon as Owen and Evie walked into the house, Sandra wrapped her arms around Evie. Over Sandra's shoulder, Evie saw Owen watch the embrace before walking out of the room, back to Zane in the dining room. She was unable to read his expression.

When Sandra released Evie from her hold, she held her still at arms-length.

"You gave me such a fright," Sandra said truthfully.

"I'm sorry," Evie apologised, "I didn't mean to. I didn't think. I just felt trapped and needed to get away. I couldn't breathe. Anyway, I shouldn't have shouted at you and I'm so sorry."

Sandra gave a slight smile, as though she felt she had cracked Evie.

"I shouldn't have pressed you so far, I'm sorry too," Sandra spoke softly. "Next time I will try to be more considerate of your need for space."

Evie forced a weak smile to show her appreciation of Sandra's acceptance. Still, it didn't feel right that she was trapped, forcibly having to stay with the Taylor's.

After the family dinner, Evie excused herself to go to her room, on the pretence of wanting to do her homework. It wasn't a complete lie, but she also just wanted to be alone.

While she sat on her bed, flicking through her notes from that day, there was a knock on the door. Evie sighed, not from annoyance, but more in preparation for what detailed conversation Sandra may now want to have with her.

"Come in," Evie called.

The door opened slowly, as if cautiously and unsure. Evie's brow furrowed slightly in thought and then her eyes widened with the door as she saw who stood before her. The last person she expected. Owen.

"Sorry to interrupt," Owen spoke, breaking the silence that expanded the room.

Evie took a deep breath to gain strength. She felt she needed all she could muster in Owen's presence, especially in the small room with no one else around.

Owen stepped forward, his hand outstretched with a couple of notebooks in its clutches.

"I thought you might like these," Owen explained, his hand waiting in the air, "They're my notes from all my classes for this semester. I know we don't share all the classes, but we do all the same subjects."

Evie extended her hand out and retrieved the notebooks from Owen. She glanced down at them and then back up at Owen.

"Thank you," she said in a small voice.

Owen looked away and cleared his throat.

"Just give them to me tomorrow morning," he said quickly before leaving out the door, closing it behind him.

Evie tossed and turned that night, unable to sleep. When she did sleep, her head filled with nightmares, reruns of her argument with Sandra. Even though she had apologised and Sandra had accepted graciously, Evie was still plagued with guilt from how she had spoken to her.

Visions of her past played like movie before her eyes. There was no escaping.

A shrill cry of fear rang throughout the house as Evie woke from her nightmare. She sat upright in bed, panting and trying hard to breathe normally. The bedroom door flung open and the light suddenly lit up the room. Sandra ran to Evie's side as Brian checked the room for any obvious threat that may have caused Evie to scream.

"Evie," Sandra cooed, "It's okay. I'm here. You're safe."

At the sight of Sandra being there beside her on the bed and Brian standing in the middle of the room, a look of concern etched on both their faces, Evie began to cry tears of relief that they were okay. It was just a dream.

Evie flung her arms around Sandra's neck and held her tightly in an embrace that even surprised Sandra. Yet Sandra held Evie just as she would have her own daughter if she were upset.

After what seemed like forever but was more like five minutes, Evie pulled back from the embrace feeling slightly embarrassed by her behaviour. Evie wiped the tears from her face with the back of her hand. Brian stood by the bed, still watching on. Evie looked around and noticed her screams had woken the entire household and Owen stood in the doorway with his younger sister, Kelly, standing just inside the room.

Anxiety and fear suddenly gripped Evie once more. Seeing Owen standing there, watching her in that moment, scared her. All her insecurities rose up to the surface and she couldn't contain them any longer.

"Get out of here!" Evie screamed at Owen, fresh tears streaming down her cheeks. "Leave me alone!"

Evie backed herself protectively up against the headboard of her bed, pulling her knees up to her chest and sobbing into her legs, rocking back and forth. The Taylors all looked in Owen's direction in shock, Owen confused by Evie's outburst like the rest of his family.

Sandra moved closer to Evie and wrapped a comforting arm around her shoulder.

"Owen," Sandra spoke softly, "Maybe it would be best if you and your sister return to your rooms, please."

"Sure," Owen muttered, taking one last glance at Evie's position and walked off down the hall back to his room, Kelly following to her own room.

Brian looked at Sandra who gave him a nod and he walked out of the room, closing the door behind him.

"It's okay," Sandra assured Evie, rubbing her shoulder gently, "It's just you and me now."

Sandra waited patiently, listening to Evie slowly steady her breathing pattern. Only when she felt Evie had managed to calm down Sandra spoke again.

"Want to tell me what happened?" Sandra asked soothingly.

Evie shook her head slowly, but finally looked up at Sandra, her eyes puffy from crying.

"Did Owen say something to you this afternoon that upset you?" Sandra probed lightly.

Evie knew Sandra wouldn't leave it alone and she did owe Sandra some sort of an explanation for her behaviour, especially after waking the entire household.

"It- it was just a bad dream," Evie mumbled softly, "It felt so real."

"Tell me about it," Sandra offered, "Maybe I can help you figure out what it means. My mother always said our dreams held hidden messages for us."

"No," Evie shook her head and looked down at her finger intertwining with one another, her arms still wrapped tightly around her knees that were pulled up to her chest. "No one can help me."

"If you let me, I would like to try," Sandra pushed further.

"Many people have tried to help me before, but every one of them failed. It would be no different with you. In three months, I will get this thing off my ankle and I can leave again."

"Is that all you want? To be running away? You have so much potential." Sandra's voice etched with sincere concern for the teenaged girl.

Evie gazed at Sandra cautiously, an eyebrow raised in wonderment, trying to understand what Sandra meant.

"I spoke to your school this afternoon to see how your first day went," Sandra went on to explain, "Apparently you had a Maths test today. You scored one hundred percent."

"So?" Evie shrugged, nonchalant.

The result didn't surprise Evie, it had been an easy test. Nothing she hadn't already known. She had always enjoyed numbers, how they were always constant. The answer was there, you just had to figure it out and Evie enjoyed doing that.

"So?" Sandra taken aback by how cavalier Evie was being about scoring so well, "The rest of your class had been given four weeks to study for that test. You had no prior knowledge that it was happening and you scored the best in your class. Only two other students in the entire year level scored the same and I bet they studied their butts off the entire week to prepare."

This didn't surprise Evie. At her last school, she was top of her year for Maths. Her teachers always praised her and asked for her help in tutoring those who were struggling with the topic. Evie had happily obliged and that led to her world falling apart.

Evie didn't respond to Sandra.

"I've had many lost teenagers stay with us before," Sandra went on. "None of them have even tried at school. Most were too worried about scoring their next hit."

"I don't do drugs," Evie wanted to assure Sandra.

Sandra gave a smile, "I know that. What I don't know, is why you're running. What about your family? Surely they miss you."

Sandra noticed Evie's body tighten at the question, but Evie managed to maintain her composure as she turned to face Sandra and replied without emotion.

"They're dead."

Chapter 8

Sandra didn't say anything after Evie had so bluntly told her that anyone of any meaning in her life was dead. She held Evie close to comfort her for what seemed like forever. Sandra was such a caring woman. There she was comforting a girl she knew so little about, but acting as though Evie was her own daughter, as if it was Kelly she was cradling after a nightmare of epic proportions.

The embrace must have given Evie comfort she didn't realise it could, because she ended up drifting off to sleep in Sandra's arms. Sandra noticed Evie had fallen asleep and gently laid Evie back down on her pillow and pulled the covers up over her to keep her warm.

Quietly, Sandra padded out of the bedroom with one last look at Evie in her slumber, before gently closing the door and heading back to her own bed.

When Evie woke the following day, she was surprised with how rested she felt. It was as though she had had the best sleep in over a year and she didn't know what had changed.

As she sat up slowly in the bed, the sunlight trying to break through the small gap in the curtains, Evie remembered the events of the previous night. Images of her nightmare came flashing back to her, but what upset her most was how she had behaved with the Taylor family when she had woken them all in the middle of the night. She knew she owed them all an apology, especially Owen.

Evie hid her face in her hands and groaned at the memory of screaming at him. It wasn't his fault her life sucked and it wasn't fair on her to take it out on him. The problem was that in that moment the nightmare had been so fresh in her mind.

A single tear escaped the corner of Evie's eye and she quickly brushed it away. With a deep breath, Evie vowed to try harder for the Taylor's sake. She had to face facts she was stuck living with them for the next three months and it would make everyone's life easier if Evie could just be, well, normal. Acting differently could draw more attention to her than she wanted.

Maybe she would be okay. Maybe it would actually be a safe option for her, living with the Taylor's. Her hair was a different colour, she had a different name and a different family. She was a different person.

Evie thought about Owen. She really needed to get her emotions in check when it came to him. Owen couldn't help who he was and what he reminded Evie of. It wasn't his fault.

With a new look of life, Evie got out of bed and made her way to the bathroom which was free. She quickly had a shower to freshen herself up and get ready for school. Back in her bedroom, she hurried to get dressed. She didn't want Owen getting annoyed for having to wait for her.

As Evie came down the stairs, she was welcomed with a reassuring smile from Sandra who was sipping a cup of coffee. Kelly was at the kitchen table eating some cereal and Brian was drinking his own cup of coffee.

"About last night," Evie started, but Sandra cut her off.

"Don't worry about it."

"No, please," Evie continued on, "I need to do this. I need to apologise for my behaviour, not just last night but this past week. You have all been so kind to me, taking me into your home. I just want you to know that I do appreciate everything you have done for me and I will try harder from now on."

Sandra beamed at Evie, placed her coffee cup down on the bench and rushed to Evie's side to give her a hug. It made Evie genuinely smile, which surprised her.

When they pulled apart, Evie looked around noticing for the first time Owen was not in the kitchen.

"Is Owen still getting ready for school? I want to apologise to him too, for you know, screaming at him like I did."

Brian gave Sandra a knowing look and Sandra tried to cover it up with a gentle smile.

"Don't worry about Owen, he has thick skin," Sandra replied. "He actually had to get to school early today, so he's already left. I'll be driving you to school."

Evie nodded, understanding exactly what was going on. Owen was avoiding her, which she couldn't blame him for. Maybe she could find him at school and apologise to him there. She needed to give him back his notebooks anyway.

Sandra dropped Evie to school and Evie found her own way to her locker. As she swapped her books around and got ready for her first class, she continued to watch the halls for any sign of Owen, but she couldn't see him.

Sandra had told Evie that she would be driving Evie to school from now on, with some lame made up excuse that Owen had other commitments on. Sandra gave Evie some money to pay for the bus to get home in the afternoons and Sandra's phone number in case she got lost or something happened. Before driving away, Sandra reminded Evie she had to be home by five o'clock or her anklet would alert the police.

When Evie slammed her locker door shut, she jumped in surprise to see Harley leaning against the other locker waiting for her. Did this girl have no other friends, Evie wondered to herself.

"Harley, you scared me," Evie breathed.

"Sorry," Harley smiled apologetically to her. "So, word has it, Owen is your cousin or something?"

"Where did you hear that?" Evie asked, wondering how much she should say.

"Around," Harley shrugged.

The two girls started walking together down the hall towards their first classes.

"So, does Owen have a girlfriend?" Harley blurted out, taking Evie by surprise.

"Um, I don't know," Evie answered honestly. The truth was, she didn't know anything about Owen.

"Girl, you're meant to be my inside information," Harley exclaimed.

"Sorry," Evie apologised before realising she could use Harley to her advantage. "Hey, talking of Owen, you haven't happened to see him this morning? He left early for school and I have his notebooks for him," Evie half lied.

"No, haven't seen him," Harley shook her head but then pointed down a different hallway. "His locker is down that way though, number 238. Don't ask me how I know that."

Evie couldn't help but giggle at Harley's blatant crush on Owen. It wasn't hard to believe though, that Owen would have admirers. He was a very good-looking boy even Evie had to admit that.

"I might see if I can catch him before class," Evie announced, before waving goodbye to Harley and trekking off in the direction of Owen's locker.

Owen was closing his locker when Evie spotted him. Zane was with him, leaning casually against the row of lockers. Zane could have easily been modelling for a magazine with the way he was standing and of course the fact that he was very attractive. No wonder Harley was excited at the prospect of Evie knowing the boys.

Evie started to make her way towards the boys when Owen caught her eye. A frown furrowed at his brow, before he said something to Zane that Evie couldn't hear and walked off in the opposite direction before she could reach him. Zane looked over at Evie and shrugged his shoulders. Evie silently held out the pile of Owen's notebooks to Zane, who took them and after realising what they were, looked back at Evie confused. Evie gave a half smile before walking off in the direction of her first class. Zane hurried off after his friend.

Evie's shoulders slumped and she felt disheartened. It was obvious Owen was avoiding her, if only he would give her a chance to explain or at least apologise for screaming at him the way she did. She hoped she would have a chance to talk to him in Biology, one of two classes they shared.

Later that morning, Evie entered her Biology classroom to find Owen was not yet in class. She took the same seat she had had the day before next to Harley who greeted her enthusiastically.

As she sat down and opened her notebook and textbook to the required pages for the lesson, she looked up and saw Owen walk into the classroom, with Zane following behind. Owen sat down, without even looking in Evie's direction. Zane smiled and waved at Evie when he saw her then sat down beside his friend.

Evie began to feel even more discouraged at ever getting an opportunity to speak with Owen. More than anything, she wanted to apologise for her behaviour. He needed to hear it from her, not his mother or anyone else. Owen had been kind to her when he found her in the park the day before and then to lend her his notes from his classes.

At lunchtime, Evie found an abandoned table to eat outside, under the shade of a tree. It was a lovely sunny day and she really didn't feel like being stuck inside with everyone being loud and noisy. Outside it was peaceful, quiet and almost serene.

She ate in silence on her own and watched the commotion and activity going on inside through the big glass windows. Evie recognised the back of Owen's golden blonde head. He was sitting at a table inside by the window with a crowd of other students. Harley had said he belonged to the popular group.

Evie didn't notice she was staring at the group, laughing and talking animatedly together, until she saw someone sitting at the table watching her. His brown eyes smiled when he did and before she knew it, Zane stood up and walked away from the table.

Evie took a deep breath and shook her head to clear her mind. She had resolved to just talk to Owen at home, she didn't want to seem weird or desperate chasing him around school.

"Look at you with all your friends," came a familiar voice beside her, as they approached her table.

Glancing up from her food, Evie saw Zane walking towards her, a grin spread across his face.

Evie couldn't help but admire how he swaggered towards her in a cool guy kind of a way. His hands were in his pockets, as though he had no care in the world. Zane's hair was brushed back in a way that made his dark curls spring in the right way that made it look like he had spent the time on each individual curl. Realising she was once again staring Evie looked away and blushed slightly, turning back to her lunch.

"What? No hello?" Zane asked as he sat on the seat across from her, essentially blocking her view of the building, not that she cared.

Zane seemed to have a happy-go-lucky kind of personality that was infectious, but still, even Zane couldn't stop the anxiety from creeping up inside her. Evie tried to steady her nerves by taking a couple of long, deep breaths.

"Silent treatment again? Really?" Zane pushed further.

Evie played with the stem of her uneaten apple in front of her, avoiding his eye contact. Would she ever be able to have a proper conversation with a boy ever again?

"Okay, well anyway, I came out here to apologise for Owen's behaviour today," Zane said.

His statement took Evie by surprise and she looked up at him, confused.

"Excuse me?" Evie spoke for the first time.

"He's in some mood today. I don't know why. I'm sure he'll get over it."

I bet I know why, Evie thought to herself.

"And, the other reason was to make sure you're coming to the lake this weekend." Zane went on, oblivious to Evie's withdrawn behaviour.

"I'm sorry, what?" Evie asked.

"This weekend. The lake." Zane explained, as though Evie should know what it all meant.

Evie shook her head slowly in confusion.

"Owen didn't tell you?" Zane was surprised at the fact two people who lived in the same house had such a lack of communication.

"We don't really talk much," Evie mumbled, wondering how much Zane knew about who she really was, or was he like everyone else thinking they were cousins.

"Right then," Zane continued on, "This weekend, we're all heading out to the lake for a party; swimming, music, food. Just a way to kick back and relax before all the big exams and assignments start popping up next month."

"Uh," Evie tried to think of an excuse not to go, "I don't think I can make it."

"Why not? Owen will be there," Zane stated as though it made everything ok.

Evie glanced over Zane's shoulder and saw Owen laughing with another boy she didn't recognise, before her eyes made their way back to Zane who was waiting patiently for her responce. How could she get out of this? It's not like she could tell him the truth. It wasn't usually something you talked about, being under house arrest with an ankle monitoring system.

That would look real sexy, Evie thought to herself, bikini and police anklet to match.

"I'll think about it," she mumbled. It was all Evie could think to say that would placate Zane enough to stop bugging her about it and leave her alone.

"I'll tell Owen you're coming to the lake."

Zane winked at Evie as he stood up and started walking away. Evie left speechless, sitting on her own, or so she thought.

"Did I just hear Zane asking you personally to the lake party this weekend?" Harley exclaimed excitedly as she sat down beside Evie.

Evie rolled her eyes at Harley's infatuation and the fact Evie knew she now had to have an excuse to give Harley about why she wouldn't be going.

"I'm not going to go," Evie muttered, standing up and gathering her things.

"Excuse me?" Harley stumbled after Evie as she started to walk away. "No one in their right mind would miss this party. And to get a personal invite from one of the populars, even if you are related to one."

Evie shrugged her shoulders as she climbed the stairs to go back into the school.

"It doesn't interest me," Evie stated plainly and made her way towards her locker to get ready for the afternoon classes.

"Hot guys don't interest you? Are you a lesbian? Because that's totally cool if you are, but just to clarify right here and now, you're not my type."

"I'm not gay," Evie said exasperated, "I'm just not interested in going to the party. Why is that so hard to understand?"

"I don't think as a new person to this school, you understand the magnitude of this party. As your newly appointed best friend, I promise to make sure you don't make any social suicide decisions."

Evie frowned at Harley's enthusiasm for the party and worried about how close would be too close to let Harley get to her. Harley honestly seemed like a genuinely nice girl, it actually surprised Evie that Harley didn't seem to mention any other friends of hers. Evie couldn't allow herself to get caught up in any high school drama or get too close to anyone while she was there. In three months, she would be gone. It was the only safe option for everyone.

"We are going to that party together," Harley stated in a matter-of-fact tone.

Without another word, she waved goodbye and once again, Evie was left on her own, speechless and unsure of what had just been exchanged.

All Evie knew is she needed to find a way out of going to this party. Maybe she could ask Owen for his help, after she managed to apologise to him of course.

For the past year, all Evie had dreamt about, wished for was a life of teenaged normalcy once more. Now that she had it, she couldn't remember why it had been so important to her. Maybe life was simpler on the run.

Chapter 9

When Evie arrived at the Taylor's house that afternoon after school, no one was home yet. She knew she had until five to stay out, but she had decided to come straight home as there was nothing else she wanted to do and she didn't feel safe staying out in the open.

That plan backfired on her. The house was locked and Evie didn't have a key. Sandra obviously expected to beat Evie home or she was running late herself. It could have been a combination of both.

Feeling exposed out the front of the house, Evie pushed open the side gate and wandered into the backyard. The Taylor's backyard was pretty, lots of flower gardens everywhere. There was a medium sized oval pool fenced off towards the back fence.

Evie dumped her bag to the ground near the backdoor and wandered over to the pool, letting herself in through the gate. Evie took off her sneakers and socks, rolled up the cuffs of her jeans and sat down on the edge of the pool.

As she sat there, her feet dangling in the cool water, Evie studied the warped image of her ankle monitor beneath the water. A sigh escaped her lips as she wondered how things would have been different if the police hadn't caught her.

She would still be running, moving on each day, never staying too long in one place. Evie never would have had the opportunity to experience a mother's love again. The thought saddened her.

Hot tears welled in her eyes and started to run down her face, dripping off the end of her cheeks and into the pool. What had she done to deserve this life? A life of unknown and always running. A life with no family. A life without love.

Evie knew exactly what had caused her life to end up that way. At the time, nobody had known what was going to happen. There was no warning. Evie's life could have been so different, so normal, and it was all her fault.

Male laughter from inside the house brought Evie out of her thoughts. A glance towards the house, Evie saw through the back glass sliding door, Owen and Zane talking and laughing in the lounge room.

Quickly, Evie wiped her cheeks, running the tips of her fingers under her eyes, trying not to make her eyes any redder than they probably already were as she dashed away her tears. Standing up and collecting her shoes, Evie walked towards the house, collecting her bag along the way.

When she reached the back door, Evie rapped her knuckles against the glass panel, alerting the two teenaged boys to her presence. Owen looked up at the door and his wide smile suddenly vanished when he saw her. Still he stood up from his spot on the couch and unlocked the backdoor for her to enter.

"Thanks," Evie spoke quietly as she stepped inside, still unsure how to act around Owen and yet to apologise to him for her behaviour towards him the night before.

"Whatever," he mumbled only loud enough for her to hear, before he walked back over and resumed his position.

Zane however, either choosing to ignore the tension between the two or not noticing, wandered towards Evie with a welcoming smile.

"Hey, what are you doing out there?" he asked.

"Locked out," Evie murmured, just wanting to go to her room, but Zane was blocking her path.

Owen sat quietly with an agitated look on his face, watching the exchange between his friend and the girl he barely knew.

Zane nodded knowingly at her explanation, as his eyes grazed over her body, taking her in. Evie was standing there, bag slung over one shoulder, her shoes with the socks pushed into them in her other hand and the cuffs of her jeans rolled up to her knees. It was then he noticed the unfamiliar object fastened around her ankle, it took him a short minute to realise what it was, a glowing green light on top.

"Why are you wearing an ankle monitor?" Zane asked curiously.

Evie's face drained of colour and she immediately looked down at her own ankle. She had totally forgotten in her tormented state to roll the cuffs of her jeans back down to hide her monitor. Her eyes found Owen's instantly. He looked at her with, concern, she couldn't tell, but she hoped he would read the pleading in her own eyes, asking him to help her out.

"Zane," Owen commanded his friend's attention. "Leave her alone."

"Seriously, man," Zane pointed to Evie's ankle as if the monitor wasn't obvious enough. "Why is your cousin wearing a tracking device? What are you hiding, Evie?"

Zane had a joking tone to his voice but it didn't matter. Evie's heart was already pounding so fast she felt like it was going to run away without her. Her breathing picked up and she felt her anxiety creeping up to take hold of her. A panic attack was the last thing she needed at that point, but it wasn't like she could control when they happened.

"Evie," Owen's voice etched with concern, which surprised Evie, "Are you ok?"

Owen was by her side in a flash and managed to catch her as her body fell towards the floor.

Everything went dark, but Evie could feel Owen's strong arms around her, one of them behind her head. A cool breeze began to blow rapidly on her face. Opening her eyes slightly, Evie saw Zane with a car magazine fanning her. Zane's mouth was moving but she couldn't hear anything, only white noise.

Darkness took hold of Evie once more. She hadn't had a panic attack like this in a while. Normally she could control them better. This one had come on so fast and by something so simple, it scared her.

The darkness began to fade and Evie managed to flutter her eyes open. There was something cool and damp on her forehead. She could no longer feel Owen's strong arms surrounding her. Instead, she was lying on a something soft. Evie opened her eyes more and realised she was now lying on the couch, her feet resting up on the arm of the couch. Evie's eyes felt heavy and she closed them again.

Slowly she began to hear sounds around her, voices, still softly muted, but she could make out what they were saying.

"I'm sure she will be fine," an unknown female voice said, "It's likely she's had a panic attack of sorts. They can range from small to severe. Something must have triggered her body to shut down. You have my number, call me if you need to, but all she needs is quiet and rest for now. No stress."

"Thank you doctor," Sandra said appreciatively.

Nothing, then a door closed and footsteps.

"You did the right thing calling the doctor," Sandra stated.

"I'm sorry Mrs T, I didn't know," Zane apologised.

"It's not your fault, Zane," Sandra assured him, "These things happen. I'm glad you boys were here to help her when she needed you."

"So, what happens now?" Owen asked quietly.

"We just need to be supportive of her. There's obviously something that has happened in her life to make her react this way. Whatever it was, it can't be easy for her. And Zane, you need to promise," Sandra was cut off by Zane.

"It's okay Mrs T; the secret is safe with me. I'm actually surprised Owen didn't tell me the truth to begin with, but I get it."

The voices faded once more.

When Evie opened her eyes once more, it was dark, but she noticed she was now in her bedroom. Unsure how she got there, she slowly sat up in the bed. Looking out the window, she could see it was now dark outside.

Still dressed in the same clothes she had gone to school in, Evie was grateful no one had tried to change her clothes. It would have made all matters worse if they had seen her scar and asked her about it.

Opening the bedroom door, Evie could hear what she assumed was the television downstairs. She padded softly into the bathroom, needing to use the toilet urgently. When she was done, she washed her hands and opened the door to the hallway to go back to her room.

As she stepped out of the bathroom, she noticed Owen leaning on the doorframe of his own bedroom just down the hall. He was watching her intently, but not in a scary way. Wanting to thank him and still needing to apologise, Evie wandered down the hall quietly towards him.

Owen stood still, his arms crossed casually across his chest. He wore a white t-shirt that was just tight enough to show off his muscular torso, but not too tight that it looked like he was showing off. He also wore long blue pyjama pants that hung from his waist.

Once she was standing in front of him, Evie looked up at him shyly through her lashes. She met with his concerned eyes.

"Thank you," she managed to murmur, still unsure of what he might say or do, he was very difficult for Evie to read.

"Are you feeling better now?" he asked honest concern for her health. It touched Evie.

"I'll live," she shrugged, then after a moment's pause, "I'm sorry."

"You can't help what happened, it's not your fault," Owen replied.

"No, I mean yes," Evie stuttered, trying to find the right words, "What I mean is, I'm sorry for screaming at you last night. It honestly had nothing to do with you. I- I can't really explain it, but I just wanted you to know, I'm sorry."

Evie held her breath while she waited for his response. Would he accept her apology?

"Forget about it," Owen stated simply.

Evie nodded slowly, hoping he meant he would forget it ever happened too.

"I guess I'm going to go back to bed," Evie murmured, "Night."

Evie turned and started to walk away, back towards her room.

"Hey Evie," Owen called quietly after her.

Turning around at her bedroom door to face Owen once more, Evie saw Owen standing slightly more relaxed, his arms now uncrossed but still leaning against the doorframe.

"Sweet dreams, okay." Owen whispered, before giving her a half smile and going into his own room and closing the door behind him.

Evie smiled slightly at what she felt was Owen showing concern for her having more nightmares. Maybe, just maybe, the next three months wouldn't be so terrible living with him after all.

Chapter 10

Evie entered the kitchen the next morning to find the entire family sitting down at the kitchen table finishing off their breakfast. When Sandra saw Evie she immediately stood up, walked over to her and embraced her in a warm hug.

"How are you feeling this morning?" Sandra asked Evie, holding her at arms-length and studying her for any indication of something wrong.

"I'm fine," Evie murmured, still taken aback by how welcoming and caring Sandra was towards her.

Sandra eyed Evie suspiciously as though she didn't believe her, "Are you sure, because you don't have to go to school today if you don't feel up to it."

"Honestly, I'll be fine," Evie insisted.

Owen's chair scraped against the floor as he stood up from the table and grabbed his bag and car keys.

"Mum, leave her alone. She says she's fine." Owen exasperated, then to Evie said, "Come on, I'll give you a ride to school."

Owen nudged his head towards the door as an indication he was leaving and Evie should follow. Evie nodded and smiled politely at Sandra before hurrying off after Owen out the front door.

Evie had known the excuse of Owen having a commitment before school was all a lie. It seemed now that she had cleared the air with him. It was okay for him to give her a lift to school again.

Once they were in his car, Owen reversed it out the driveway then started down the street towards the school.

"Mum can be a bit full on at times but she means well," Owen explained, not taking his eyes off the road to look at her.

"It's okay," Evie shrugged, "It's kind of nice to have someone worrying about me. I mean, it's been awhile."

Owen just nodded as if her explanation made sense to him.

It was weird to Evie that they were talking how two normal people would do in a car while driving, but the relationship between Owen and Evie was anything but normal. She knew he didn't like her, though it seemed like he could now tolerate her presence.

They rode the rest of the drive-in silence, but it wasn't an awkward silence like it had been the first day Owen had driven her to school. It was more of a comfortable silence.

Owen parked the car and they wandered towards the school together without a word. Evie suddenly stopped walking and Owen turned to look at her in confusion.

"You okay?" Owen asked her, an eyebrow raised in question.

"What do I do about Zane and... you know." Evie looked down at her covered ankle before looking back to Owen for an answer.

"Don't worry about Zane," Owen replied cavalier, "He has been my best friend since kindergarten. He won't say anything to anyone."

"How do you know that?" Evie worried.

"Because I told him not to," Owen shrugged as though it was as simple as that.

Not wanting to argue with Owen or make things uncomfortable, Evie decided to put her faith in Owen and his trust in his friend to keep her secret. One of them.

They parted ways when Evie reached her locker. Owen told her he would wait for her in the parking lot after school to give her a ride home. She was grateful for his offer as the bus ride home the day before made Evie feel too exposed but she wasn't going to tell Sandra that.

When lunchtime came, Evie collected her food and was about to head outside to the comfort of her secluded table under a tree when Harley spotted her. Harley raced across the cafeteria waving at Evie and calling her name. Evie stood there wondering if she could possibly pretend she hadn't seen or heard Harley but knew that was impossible. The entire cafeteria had heard Harley and was watching her bound towards Evie.

"Hey," Harley greeted Evie breathless.

"Hi," Evie smiled slightly.

Harley wasn't bad. She was a friendly person and Evie appreciated the fact that if she had been a regular new kid to the school, Harley was willing to be her friend. Evie wasn't a regular kid and she needed to be careful who she allowed to get close to her. She didn't want anyone getting hurt on her behalf.

"Come sit with us," Harley offered, but not waiting for a reply, began to drag Evie by the arm while Evie balanced her tray with the other.

"Us?" Evie asked, confused and scared at the same time of having to talk to people she didn't know. All she wanted was to be alone and get through the school day.

"My friends," Harley smiled back at Evie, still pulling her through the crowd of students until they reached a table with a group of teenagers sitting at it.

Evie was surprised by the fact Harley had a group of friends. She had just assumed Harley was a loner, which didn't really make sense as Harley's personality was far from any type of loner.

"Everybody, this is Evie, the one I was telling you about," Harley introduced Evie to the group.

Evie tried to swallow the lump that had formed in her throat and could feel her anxiety creeping up. She took slow, deep breaths in an attempt to calm herself down.

The group of teenagers looked friendly enough, but Evie knew that looks could be deceiving. Just because someone looked nice, didn't mean that deep down they were. Evie of all people knew that.

"Evie, these are my friends," Harley went on, not noticing Evie's reluctance to join the group. "Marcus, James, Paige and Rebecca."

Every one of them smiled and waved when Harley said their names. Evie probably looked like a stunned mullet, not saying or doing anything.

Harley sat down on a seat and pulled Evie down to sit beside her. The group continued a conversation they had most likely already been in the middle of before Harley had run off to kidnap Evie.

Evie nervously looked around at the group before her and took them in.

Paige sat across from Evie at the rectangular table. Paige had long, mouse brown hair, blue eyes and a round face. She reminded Evie of a friend she had at her old school. Evie shook the thought quickly from her mind, not wanting to remember her past in that moment.

Next to Paige, with his arm slung casually across the back of Paige's chair was James. Evie could tell from their body language, how Paige leaned towards him that they were an item. James had dark brown hair that it was nearly black, styled messily that it made Evie wonder if he had even brushed his hair when he woke up that morning. His eyes were a bright blue and framed with thick, black rimmed glasses on his small face.

On the other side of James was Marcus, who looked like a want to be cool person, but wasn't. He had sandy blonde hair that was dishevelled and messy as if he needed a haircut and brown eyes the colour of chocolate.

Then lastly, there was Rebecca, sitting next to Harley on her other side. Rebecca's hair was dark blonde, almost a strawberry blonde. Her smile could light up the room and she was very pretty with her hazel eyes.

Evie tried to think up an excuse to leave before she got in too deep but the next thing she knew they pulled her into their conversation.

"You are coming, aren't you Evie?" Paige asked her excitedly.

"I'm sorry, what?" Evie had no idea what they were talking about because she hadn't been listening. She had been too preoccupied with thinking of how to get away.

"Of course, she's coming," Harley answered, "I've already told her she would be crazy to miss it."

James saw the look of confusion on Evie's face and felt sorry for the poor girl. He knew the girls in their group wouldn't stop talking long enough for her to catch up, so he decided to help her out.

"They're talking about the lake party on Saturday."

Evie filled with horror. Again, reminded she had to find an excuse to get out of it.

"I can't make it," Evie lied.

"What do you mean, you can't make it?" Harley looked at her suspiciously, "I know for a fact Owen will be there. So, if he can go, why can't you?"

Harley made a valid point, Evie thought. Her excuse needed to be a good one but she was struggling to think of something quickly.

All eyes were on her. Evie didn't like being the centre of attention. Once upon another time, maybe, but not anymore.

Colour started to drain from her face and she could feel the room starting to sway. Slow deep breaths, in and out. Evie tried to remain calm and bring herself out of the attack before it took hold of her. She hadn't had two so close together in such a long time. Normal life was proving harder than she thought.

"Evie," Harley said a little too loudly which caused people at the surrounding tables to look and stare too, making the situation worse, "Evie what's wrong?"

Without saying a word, Evie tried to get to her feet, knocking her tray of food to the floor with an almighty crash. She didn't care. All Evie wanted in that moment was to get out of there and away from all the watching eyes. Evie couldn't stand the feeling of being watched.

Evie spun around in a circle, looking every which way, trying to get her bearings so she could leave.

Harley's concerned voice rung out around her, but Evie couldn't make out what she was saying.

Suddenly there was a strong arm around Evie's waist, pulling her forward, forcing her to walk quickly to keep up. She stumbled slightly, but the arm kept her upright and, on her feet, moving forward.

Evie tried to focus on her breathing, in and out. Slow, deep breaths.

The warmth of somebody pressed up beside her made Evie realise someone was helping her escape her trauma, but she didn't know who. Everything was a blur.

A door opened in front of her and a bright light shone in her eyes as she felt herself stumble down some concrete steps. It wasn't a light, she realised. It was the sun. She was outside.

Who had Evie and where were they taking her? For the first time, Evie was grateful for the ankle monitor, knowing it had a tracking chip inside it, at least the police might have a chance to find her this time. Either way, she knew she had to fight. Evie refused to go down easy.

Using all the strength she could muster in her blurry and dizzy state, Evie pushed away from her kidnapper and tried to run away from them in the opposite direction. He called for her, a male voice, but she didn't stop. She stumbled and fell to the grassy ground beneath her, closing her eyes as a reflex, even though she couldn't see anything anyway.

Two strong hands touched her shoulders and she tried to move away but had no more strength to fight back. Evie wanted to cry. After all this time and all the running, this was the end.

"Evie," a familiar voice called to her in the distance as she lay on her back on the grass.

"Evie," the voice was closer now, clearer even.

"Evie, open your eyes," Owen's voice rang out through her ears, "Come on, look at me."

With what little strength she had left in her, Evie fluttered her eyes open once more, slowly, allowing them to adjust to the bright sunlight. A shadow fell over her face. Someone was leaning over her. Evie counted to herself; one, two, three, taking more deep breaths.

Slowly the fuzziness began to fade and things started to take shape around her. It was in this moment Evie recognised Owen leaning over her. At first, she tried to struggle to move, but he gently held her still.

"Don't get up yet, just rest," he instructed her. "Just take slow deep breaths."

Evie did as she was told. Slowly, the anxiety began to leave her body. The darkness in her head began to fade and she felt well enough to sit up. Owen hesitated to let her, but she pushed his arm away gently.

"I'm sorry," Evie muttered an apology to Owen, hoping he knew she was apologising for running away from him, but she couldn't explain to him why.

"Stop apologising okay," Owen replied gently, "Just rest. Zane's gone to get my car keys from my locker. I'm taking you home."

"I have History," Evie protested.

Owen laughed at Evie worrying about her next class.

"Trust me, History isn't going anywhere. It will all still be the same tomorrow. Nothing will change," Owen told her with a smirk on his face.

Evie just nodded and put her head between her knees in an attempt to get the last of the fuzziness in her head to go away.

Minutes later, Zane ran out to meet the pair, carrying Owen's car keys. Owen and Zane both helped Evie to Owen's car, even though she tried to tell them she was okay to walk on her own, they didn't listen, both holding onto one of her arms to support her.

Zane stayed at school, he was going to inform the office of what was going on, that Evie was unwell and Owen had to take her home. Evie was worried about Owen missing his classes on her behalf, but he assured her he would catch up easily enough.

Once home, Owen made sure to help Evie into the house, against her protests. When Evie was laying on the lounge, he went and got Evie a drink of cold water, before going into the other room to call his mother and let her know what happened.

Evie didn't want to worry Sandra, but Owen said it was the right thing to do and Evie didn't want to argue with him. After the phone call, Owen informed Evie that Sandra was stuck an hour away, but would be home as soon as possible. Evie really didn't think they had to make such a fuss, it was only a panic attack, she would live.

Owen sat down on the other end of the large modular lounge and turned the television on to find something for them to watch. It had been a long time since Evie had just sat down and watched something on television or seen a movie, so when Owen asked her what she would like to watch she didn't have a clue. Evie insisted Owen just pick something for them to watch and he settled on a movie she hadn't seen before and didn't know the name of, but she didn't care.

As the movie played, Evie found herself stealing glimpses of Owen. It was the second time in less than twenty-four hours he had readily jumped to her aide without question or reward. She could see another side to Owen now, different to the boy who had warned her off going near his room only a week before.

Evie smiled briefly at the thought that maybe they could actually become friends, but then she quickly reminded herself that was not a possibility in her world and her smile disappeared. She turned her attention back to the movie to see a car speeding down a highway as police followed with sirens on.

Chapter 11

"I promise I'm fine," Evie tried to convince Sandra for the umpteenth time, while sitting on a kitchen chair.

They had been discussing whether Evie should return to school the following day. Sandra was concerned about Evie having another attack at school and felt she should rest up after the last two. Evie on the other hand felt fine and would rather risk having another episode at school than stay at home all day alone, and left with her thoughts.

Evie was dressed and ready to go, Owen stood leaning against the kitchen bench not saying anything and Sandra paced worriedly around the kitchen.

"Maybe I could stay home with you," Sandra offered, stopping in front of Evie with a hopeful look that she had figured out a solution.

A day at home alone with Sandra wouldn't be relaxing, Evie thought to herself. Knowing Sandra, she would try to find out more about her. Evie would rather face Harley and her friends' questions again. Evie threw Owen a pleading look, but he looked away from her. Either bored of the conversation or didn't care what the result was.

"I might have to move some meetings and reschedule some things, but I could do a lot of my work from home," Sandra continued on, counting on her fingers as she listed things she could do.

Owen looked back over at Evie and saw her distressed face as she watched Sandra. With a roll of his eyes, he sighed and moved away from the bench.

"Mum, if Evie says she will be fine, let her go to school," Owen complained to his mother, slightly agitated at having to stand up for Evie. "I can keep an eye out for her."

Sandra studied her son and thought long and hard about his offer. Glancing back at Evie she could see by the look on her face that she was only stressing Evie out more. Relaxing her stance, she decided it was probably best to give in and trust Evie.

"Okay, you can go," Sandra stated finally.

Evie smiled and stood up from her chair, grabbing her bag and ready to follow Owen to the car.

"Just a second," Sandra stopped them, before dashing out of the room.

Evie gave Owen a questioning look and he just shrugged his shoulders in answer to her unspoken question. He didn't know what his mother was doing either.

Sandra bustled back into the kitchen with a small, flat, white object in her palm.

"Here, take this," Sandra ordered, handing the brand-new phone to Evie.

Evie stared down at the phone in her hand in astonishment; it was not a cheap phone. Easily a new design, not that Evie would know much about it, she hadn't owned a phone for a long time.

In the corner of her eye, Evie could see Owen's surprise at the gift his mother had given to a complete stranger who had been in their home for only a week. When he had asked for a new phone, his parents had told him he had to save his own money for it.

"I can't accept this," Evie protested, reaching out to give the phone back to Sandra, but she didn't take it from her.

"I want you to have it, it will put my mind at ease," Sandra explained, gently pushing Evie's hand away from her not accepting the phone back, "My number is programmed into it as an emergency contact. I've also put Brian, Owen and Kelly's numbers in it just in case."

"What?" Owen exclaimed, unsure he wanted Evie to have his number.

Sandra ignored Owen's small outburst and went on, "This is my condition if you want to return to school. Otherwise you can stay at home with me."

Evie sighed, giving in and stowing the phone into a side pocket of her bag.

The drive to school was silent and the only time Owen spoke to Evie was when they were getting out of the car. It wasn't even speaking to her, more ordering her.

"Don't you dare share my number with any of your little friends," Owen ordered, slamming his car door shut.

Evie frowned, confused by his sudden cold-shoulder towards her. She thought they had passed this. It frightened her, his abrupt and domineering personality. It was too close to home. She closed her eyes briefly, taking a deep breath to prevent any anxiety creeping over her.

"I don't have any friends," Evie replied plainly, looking down at the ground as they walked towards the school together, unable to look him in the eye.

Owen scoffed at her comment, "I'm talking about the blonde-haired chick that is always hanging around you and her crowd."

"Harley," Evie murmured her name.

"I don't care what her name is," Owen argued, grabbing Evie by the elbow and turning her to look at him, but she avoided his intense stare, "She better not be calling or texting me, or I will know she got my number from you. Got it?"

Evie just nodded, unable to speak.

Where had the caring Owen that had rescued her from her episodes gone? He was acting as if he didn't give a shit about her anymore and all hope of them being remotely like friends faded in Evie's mind.

Owen gave Evie a final glare, even though she wasn't looking up at him and stormed off into the building leaving her alone.

Evie would have loved to put the scene with Owen behind her and forget all about it, but that was hard to do when she had Biology first and he was in her class.

Thankful Owen wasn't in class yet; Evie hurried to the back of the room and took her seat, Harley joining her moments later. Harley chatted animatedly at Evie, but Evie wasn't listening, not that Harley noticed.

Evie watched the door from under her lashes, waiting for Owen to arrive. She didn't know why she was watching for him, she rationalised with herself it was so she wouldn't get a surprise when he did suddenly appear.

Owen sauntered into the room, Zane following him. He looked right at Evie, before taking his seat towards the front. Evie bowed her head down, pretending she hadn't been staring at the door or noticing he had arrived.

Running her fingers through her ponytail, Evie twisted the end around her finger absent minded. She doodled on the corner of her notebook while the teacher took attendance and started the lesson, letting her mind wander.

For the rest of the day, Evie just went through the motions mechanically. Evie was amazed at how quickly she had easily fallen back into the adolescent and mundane routine of high school. Oh, how she had missed normalcy. It almost made her wish that she could stay there forever, but she knew that wasn't possible. Evie was already pushing her luck staying as long as she had and there was still eleven weeks left of her sentence.

As it turned out, Evie shared her next class; English, with Rebecca and Paige. When Evie walked into the room, they called her over to sit next to them. Evie obliged but stayed cautious to how close she would allow herself to get to the girls.

The girls asked Evie if she was okay after what had happened the previous day, showing genuine concern for her.

Evie was touched by their compassion, but just passed it off as a once off thing that came on unexpected, that was a lie.

By lunchtime, Evie knew Harley and her friends were expecting her to sit with them again. Feeling slightly more prepared for the situation, she took a deep breath as she carried her tray over to their table.

When Evie sat down next to Rebecca, there was only James and Paige at the table too. Evie searched the cafeteria for Harley, suddenly feeling awkward that she was with her friends and she wasn't even there, but Harley was nowhere in sight.

As Evie turned around in her seat, she noticed Owen watching her with a furrowed brow. It wasn't that he was angry, more like just watching her carefully to make sure Evie wasn't handing out his number.

Evie had totally forgotten about the phone Sandra had given her and on impulse of remembering about it, she pulled it out of her bag to make sure Sandra hadn't tried to contact her at any point in the day. No messages. Evie placed the phone back in her bag and began to eat.

The chair next to Evie pulled out and she expected it was Harley, but instead noticed Marcus sit down beside her.

"How you doing?" Marcus nodded at her.

Was he trying to hit on her? Evie groaned inwardly, she did not need his unwanted attention. Feeling rude by doing so, Evie ignored him and continued to eat in silence, suddenly wishing she had gone to her private outdoor table where she could be alone. Harley wasn't even there, but it was too late to go.

Harley never showed up to the lunch table and Evie felt awkward sitting with a group she barely knew, not even really interacting with them.

Evie wandered into her final class for the day, History, which she shared with Owen and Harley. Evie was surprised to see Harley sitting in her chair, waving for Evie to join her.

"Where were you at lunch?" Evie asked Harley, as she sat down in the empty chair beside her.

"Mrs Franco kept me in all lunch for detention," Harley rolled her eyes, talking about her least favourite teacher of her least favourite subject, Maths.

"What did you do?" Evie asked, curious.

"It's what I didn't do," Harley answered, "I didn't do well on our test the other day and was meant to show my failed test to my parents to get their signature, but I didn't. I forged my mum's signature and they found out because I didn't realise Mrs Franco was calling parents to discuss my options to achieve a better grade before graduation."

"What are the options?" Evie wondered, noticing Owen enter the room, but she ignored him and focussed her attention on Harley.

"Getting a tutor and taking a make-up test," Harley groaned at the thought of having to do extra work.

Evie bit her bottom lip and wondered if she should offer to help her new friend when Mr Graham started the class.

To most people, Evie being as smart as she was and doing so well in Maths, it seemed like a no brainer that she should help Harley out. But Evie had had a bad experience when she last offered to tutor someone. Bad was putting it mildly.

It had turned her life upside down and made it a living nightmare.

Harley shared her notes from the lesson Evie had missed when she went home. Evie couldn't help but grin slightly remembering Owen's comment about how history would remain the same, even if she missed a class, he was right. Evie wondered if Owen would like Harley's notes too, considering he also missed class taking care of her.

When the bell rang out to signal the end of the day, everybody stood up and started filing out of the room at once. Evie watched as Harley collected her belongings, making them some of the last to leave the room.

Evie stewed in her mind about her moral dilemma, but she knew deep down it wouldn't be the same, not with Harley. The situation was completely different and Harley was a friend, wasn't she? Yes, she was, Evie told herself and without thinking, began to offer her services to her friend.

"Harley, if you want, I could tutor you," Evie proposed.

Harley looked up at Evie with a huge smile of appreciation on her face, "Seriously? Are you any good at Maths?"

"I know a thing or two," Evie smirked at her modesty.

"That would be so great! Thank you!" Harley squealed in delight, that the last few people still in the room looked at the two girls in confusion.

Harley pulled out her phone and asked Evie for her number. The truth was, Evie didn't know what number to give Harley. Sandra had given her a phone that morning, but never told Evie the phone number for her phone.

Thinking quickly, Evie replied, "Give me your number and I'll send you a text so you will then have mine."

Evie took out her phone and fumbled her way through the applications before managing to open a new text message. She added Harley's name and number then composed a message simply stating her name "Evie".

Harley's phone pinged alerting of a new message received.

They walked and out of the classroom together, Harley hugged Evie appreciatively before saying goodbye and wandering off in the direction of her locker.

Evie smiled, feeling good about putting herself out there to help someone else. She almost felt normal and forgot about her reality.

She turned on her heel to walk off in the opposite direction and saw Owen standing a few feet away, leaning against the nearby wall, arms crossed over his chest and scowl across his face. He wasn't happy, Evie could tell that right away, but why she had no clue. Still his stance and glare frightened her and in an instant her euphoria was gone and overtaken by anxiety, a feeling she had come all too familiar with and she hated it.

"Did I just see what I think I saw?" Owen growled and stalked towards Evie.

The hallway was emptying fast, everyone eager to get out of school and go home for the day. Being alone with Owen and his mood scared Evie to the bone.

"Wha- what?" Evie stuttered. She had no idea what Owen meant.

"Did you just give your friend my number, after I specifically told you not to this morning?"

Evie's body began to shake slightly at Owen's intimidating stance over her.

"No!" Evie blurted out, "I gave her my number. I offered to tutor her in Maths because she's failing. I wouldn't give her your number, I swear."

Owen stayed silent, looking intensely into Evie's eyes, studying her.

"You better not," was all he said before turning around and walking off down the hall in the direction of the parking lot.

Evie took a few steadying breaths, trying to calm herself down, before hurrying down the hall after Owen for her lift home.

Chapter 12

Evie sat on her bed, doing her History homework, her textbook opened on the bed in front of her crossed legs and her notebook in her lap. She tapped the end of her pen on her bottom lip while she read the textbook page, taking notes as she went.

It was such a normal thing for a teenaged girl to be doing on a school night, but for Evie it was more monumental than anyone would understand. The simple task of doing her homework was not an activity Evie had taken part in for over a year.

One tragic event, followed by a chain reaction of other events, meant Evie spent her life on the run. Running away.

A knock on the bedroom door, brought Evie out of the Second World War and into the present.

"Come in," Evie called out, as she looked up and waited.

The door opened and Sandra poked her head in to see Evie. When she saw Evie doing her homework, she smiled with delight and entered the bedroom. Closing the door behind her, Sandra walked over to the bed and sat down on the end.

"School work?" Sandra asked, peering over the opened page of the textbook.

"History," Evie replied.

"So, you're settling in at school then?" Sandra probed, not looking Evie directly in the eye.

Evie shrugged, looking down at her notebook, not sure what to say.

"Owen mentioned you've made some friends," Sandra went on, watching Evie this time for a reaction.

Evie looked up at Sandra in surprise. She didn't know what surprised her more; that Sandra had been talking to Owen about her or that Owen had mentioned Harley to Sandra.

"Are you going with them to the lake party this weekend?" Sandra continued asking questions, even though Evie wasn't answering anymore.

"Not likely," Evie muttered, looking back down at her notebook, pretending to read her notes.

"Why not?" Sandra asked quietly.

"You have to ask?" Evie blurted out rudely, giving Sandra a look that she was crazy.

Sandra just sat patiently and waited.

"Where should I start," Evie put her pen down on her notebook, "I have an ugly ankle monitor that sticks out like a sore thumb and would look very attractive in a bikini. Which leads to the fact I don't have any swimwear of any kind but not that I care anyway. Those friends Owen told you about I hardly know and they certainly know nothing about me. And to round it all off I doubt very much Owen would want me anywhere near him and his friends."

Evie panted as she caught her breath after having her rant, staring long and hard at Sandra, she waited for her to just get up and leave the room.

It was for that reason it didn't surprise Evie when Sandra stood in silence and walked to the bedroom door, opening it. Sandra stepped out the door, Evie waited for her to close it behind her, but she didn't. Instead, Sandra called out Kelly's name and waited.

Evie watched on in confusion. She didn't know what was going on.

Kelly wandered down the hallway from her room after her mother's call and found her standing outside the guest bedroom, which had become Evie's bedroom while she stayed with them.

"Yeah?" Kelly asked.

"Can you get me some of your swimming costumes that might fit Evie," Sandra asked her daughter, "She needs something to wear to the lake party."

Kelly wondered what was going on, but had learned not to ask questions and just do as she was told, it made life easier. With a simple nod, Kelly returned to her bedroom, in search for some nice bikini selections for Evie.

When Evie heard Sandra's request of her daughter, her mouth fell open. Did Sandra not hear anything Evie had just said to her? There was no way she was going to the lake party.

Kelly returned with three sets for Evie and Sandra gave a smile in appreciation, before going back into Evie's room and closing the door.

"What are you doing?" Evie asked in bewilderment.

"You said you didn't have anything to wear." Sandra replied simply, "Now you have a choice of three."

Sandra laid the three options out on the end of the bed for Evie to peruse.

The first set was a tankini in white with green trim and dark pink hibiscus flowers on the material. It had triangular shaped breasts that tied up with green straps in a halter style. The material was lined, likely so it wouldn't become see through when wet.

The second set was a bikini with a round neckline that went on like a bra, with a clasp at the back. It was a mix of deep red, navy and teal green in an Aztec like pattern.

The final was plain black and a little sexy in Evie's opinion. It made her wonder why Kelly, who was nearly fifteen, had such a revealing costume and Sandra allowed it. Evie immediately knew she herself wouldn't be caught dead in that bikini.

Evie gazed up at Sandra who was watching Evie carefully. Evie swallowed. It wouldn't matter which she picked, she wouldn't be going while she had the ankle monitor on; she refused to.

Then there was the other issue, the one Evie had not even mentioned to Sandra and wouldn't as it would open too many questions. Questions she didn't want asked and didn't want to answer. Evie would not reveal her scar to anyone, least of all to the entire year level of her school. The ankle monitor was one thing, but her scar was her deepest secret of all.

Without a word, Evie just pointed to the tankini as it was the only option presented to her that would hide her secret.

"Right then," Sandra collected the two discarded choices, "That's one problem sorted. Leave the others to me."

Without another word, Sandra got up and left the room.

Evie eyed the tankini on the end of the bed and closed her eyes, willing it to disappear. When she opened them, it still lay there, taunting her. Letting out the breath she had been holding, Evie closed her books, placing them down on the floor beside her bed. She kicked the swimming costume off the bed to the floor with her feet, turned out the light beside the bed and laid down to go to sleep.

Friday morning, Evie did her best to avoid Sandra in order to evade any further questioning or encouragement on her socialising at the lake party. She waited until the very last second to descend the stairs and walked right past Sandra and Kelly in the kitchen, Brian was already at work. Owen stood by the doorway and watched in shock as Evie passed right by him and headed for his car. Sandra stared in confusion and Owen looked to his mother for reassurance. She just nodded, to which he followed Evie out to the car.

Owen drove his Jeep down the street towards school and looked to his side briefly at Evie before training his eyes back on the road.

"What was that all about this morning?" Owen asked, still watching the road.

Evie gazed out her side window, not facing Owen and stayed silent.

"Whatever my mum has said or done, I'm sure she has done only with the best for you in mind," Owen defended his mother's actions not knowing what they were.

Evie smiled slightly at Owen's unwavering support of his mother, before she quickly pushed it away.

"There is no best for me," Evie stated, wrapping her arms tightly around her as if to protect herself.

Owen glanced over at Evie once more and saw a scared teenaged girl who thought little of herself. He wondered for a moment what had happened in her life to make her feel this way. He shook his head, not wanting to give it another thought as it might show he cared in some way and turned his attention back to the road.

Owen pulled the car to a stop in the school parking lot. Before the engine even turned off, Evie had grabbed her bag and climbed out of the car, heading into the school building. Owen frowned at Evie's abrupt departure, knowing something had obviously upset her. What had his mother said?

Evie went straight to her locker and swapped her books around. She had no idea what she was going to do. In only a week, everything had changed so dramatically. Evie knew she had become lazy and too relaxed. How easily she had fallen into a normal routine of a normal life. She couldn't do that. It was too risky for her and everyone around her. Just being at school, she put all the students at risk, every single one of them.

Teenagers laughed and talked as they went about their business; getting ready for classes, discussing their plans for the weekend or sharing notes about some television show they had watched the night before. Everyone was so oblivious to the danger that one girl, the new girl, could bring to all of them just by being there. She had seen it happen before and she refused to see it again.

Evie slammed her locker shut, leaving everything in it and storming off down the hallway empty handed. She pushed past students, who stopped and glared at Evie as she went on not caring.

Evie turned a corner and headed for some double doors that lead to the back of the school. She had no plan of where she was going, just that she needed to get out of the school. As long as she stayed in the school precinct her monitor shouldn't go off, but she wasn't going to waste her time going to classes. In three months, all the studying, tests and classes were going to mean shit. In just eleven weeks, she would be out on the streets again, running.

Pushing the large door open with both hands as the first bell of the day rung out behind her, Evie pressed on, out into the yard. As she did so, she banged into another student, not looking or caring, Evie continued.

"Evie?" came the familiar voice of Zane, "Hey, Evie!"

Not looking back, Evie kept moving, ignoring Zane.

Footsteps running, followed Evie and she turned quickly and on impulse swung a fist to hit. She hadn't intended to hit Zane, but the sound of someone following her, while she was lost in thought and in a trance, brought Evie back to the life she knew all too well of being stalked.

Zane flinched backwards, dodging the hit and catching Evie's wrist as he did.

"Wow, Evie," Zane was surprised by Evie's reaction.

Still not thinking straight, Evie lifted her other arm, but Zane caught it too. Evie cried at the thought of losing, of failing. Her legs collapsed beneath her and she cried harder, defeated. Zane caught Evie in his arms and together they fell gently to the grass. Zane cradled Evie in his arms while she sobbed into his chest.

Chapter 13

Zane continued to hold Evie while she cried and slowly managing to calm herself down. He didn't talk, he didn't move, he just held her close, comforting her. Even when his phone buzzed in his pocket, signalling a received message, he didn't look at it, he just ignored it.

The bell sounded out in the school, signalling the end of first session. Zane's phone began to buzz insistently, but he remained focussed on Evie. Evie however took one last deep breath and pulled from his embrace.

Zane held onto Evie, his hands on her arms, gently touching her. His eyes searched her now red and puffy eyes for an explanation of what was going on, but he never asked her aloud, he waited for her to say something in her own time; Evie was grateful.

Sitting on the ground in silence, another bell rang out; it was the start of second session. Evie didn't care about her own classes but she worried about Zane missing his.

Not two minutes later, Zane's phone buzzed again, quickly followed by another.

"You should really check that," Evie spoke softly, indicating to his phone.

Zane let out a sigh and pulled his phone out, looking at the screen there were missed calls and text messages all from one person.

"Shit!" Zane exclaimed, startling Evie slightly. "It's okay, nothing to worry about," Zane reassured Evie while he quickly wrote a text on his phone.

Evie stood up and dusted herself off, dashing away the last of her tears.

"Zane, you should go to class. I'm fine. I swear. I just need to be left alone."

Not waiting for a response, Evie walked off towards the school oval. Once there, she made her way over to the bleachers and climbed the metal frame all the way to the top. Taking a seat, Evie leaned forward and rested her head in her hands.

Ten minutes later, the sound of someone walking up the metal staircase made Evie jump, her eyes looking up quickly to see if there was a threat. Owen climbed towards her and sat down beside her in silence.

Evie clasped her hands tightly together, her breath caught in her throat and her heart began to pound rapidly. Anxiety crept up inside her, scared of what Owen was going to say. How did he know she was outside?

Then she remembered; her first two classes of a Friday would have been History and Biology; the two classes she shared with Owen. He would have noticed she wasn't in class, which then meant Zane wouldn't have been in Biology either. It had been Owen who was messaging and phoning Zane, that's why Zane had reacted the way he had when he looked at his phone.

"First week at school and already skipping class," Owen said casually while he looked out across the oval.

Evie said nothing.

"You know if you don't show up to class, the office contacts your parents to tell them," Owen went on to explain.

Evie's eyes widened, Sandra. Pulling the cuff of her jean up Evie glanced down at her ankle monitor, the light was still green.

"Don't worry, I told Mum you were with me," Owen noticing Evie's sudden fear that Sandra would call the police if she wasn't at school.

Evie's eyes moved up to look at Owen who was now watching her. What was his angle? Why did he care what she did? Why didn't he let his mother call the police?

"What's going on?" Owen asked. "Is this to do with Mum and you avoiding her this morning?"

"She's pushing me to go to the lake party tomorrow," Evie finally murmured, just above a whisper.

Owen's brow furrowed in confusion.

"And you don't want to go?"

"Not you too," Evie groaned.

"Well, what's the problem?"

"Beside the fact I have an ugly tracking device on my ankle?" Evie replied sarcastically.

"Okay, so you want to keep it hidden. Is that the only thing stopping you?"

Evie stared at Owen in bewilderment, was he seriously implying she should go?

"There's no valid reason for me to even go," Evie retorted, "I don't know anyone and I doubt you want me hanging around you."

Owen looked out across the oval once more, processing what Evie had just said. Instead of answering, he changed the topic back to his mother.

"You know Mum is only pushing you because she cares," Owen explained.

"I'm sure she will get over it once I'm gone and find someone else to fuss over and bring into your home."

Owen's eyes found Evie's once more.

"Is that what you think?" Owen sounded bewildered by her comment, "Sure Mum has brought other troubled teenagers home with her, but normally they stay one night, two at the most, before social services find them something more permanent. The fact you have been a week and will be with us for the next couple of months; proves that Mum cares."

Evie didn't know what to say. Why was Owen telling her this? It was obvious he wasn't happy with the arrangement of Evie staying at his home long term. She looked back down at her hands, her fingers fiddling with one another trying to calm her anxiety that seemed to be bubbling gently at the surface like a kettle ready to boil.

Silence stretched out between the pair. Owen watched as Evie sat nervously beside him. He didn't want to upset her in anyway, his mother wouldn't be happy if he was the reason for her having another panic attack, but he felt she deserved to know the truth.

Sure, he wasn't keen on Evie being around, especially for an extended length of time, but there was nothing he could do about it. Never before had Owen even spoken to his mother's cases she brought home, he tried his best every time to just stay away. Sandra had told her son that Evie had no family and pleaded with him to help her watch out for Evie. Owen justified with himself that that's all he was doing; keeping his word to his mum.

"Zane tells me you took a swing at him," Owen smirked as he said it.

Evie's eyes looked up at him, unsure.

Still, Evie remained silence once more.

Owen let out a sigh, "Zane is a good guy. He's just trying to help you."

Evie couldn't stand the nice guy act anymore. Owen had no idea of her life was really like. She couldn't let Sandra, Owen, Zane or anyone be close to her in any way. It was too dangerous.

"I just want to be left alone." Evie pleaded with him to leave.

"But," Owen started but Evie cut him off.

"Thank you for looking out for me, but everyone would be better off if they just left me alone. It would be safer for everyone," Evie shouted at him, then realising what she had just said her hand flew over her mouth, eyes wide in fear.

"Why would it be safer for us?" Owen quizzed gently, suddenly concerned for his family and even Evie.

"Just forget it," Evie stated, standing to her feet, "Forget about me."

Without another word, she galloped quickly down the metal stair case, leaving Owen standing at the top, watching her go. Evie raced across the grass towards the school. She passed Zane who was leaning casually against the wall outside the door. He called out to her, but she kept running, pushing through the door and down the empty hallway, thankful everyone was in class at that moment. Turning a few corners, Evie found a female bathroom and made her way inside, locking herself in a cubicle. At least in there she knew Owen and Zane couldn't follow.

Evie lost track of time, sitting on the closed lid of the toilet. Bells rang; girls entered the toilets and left again. It wasn't until the end of lunch time, that Harley entered the bathroom, calling Evie's name. Evie looked at the locked cubicle door and remained silent. The bell had sounded once more to signal students to move onto their next class.

"Evie, is that you in there?" Harley's voice called through the door. "Come on, open the door."

Evie said nothing, willing Harley to give up and leave.

"Fine, I'm not leaving until you come out and talk to me," Harley stated and Evie believed Harley had the stubbornness to wait her out.

Letting out a sigh, Evie unlocked the door slowly and walked out of the cubicle. The bathroom was empty, only the two girls were there.

"Owen's going frantic looking for you," Harley explained, leaning against the basin, arms crossed over her chest. "I've never seen Owen like this, you must be close cousins."

Evie frowned, not saying anything in relation to the lie about why Evie was at the school.

"Not that I'm complaining," Harley gave Evie a smile and a slight eyebrow wiggle, "It meant he initiated talking to me for the first time ever. You should have seen Rebecca, I swear she was jealous."

"I just want to be alone," Evie tried to explain, "I just need everyone to leave me alone."

"Yeah well that's not going to happen," Harley replied, "Owen and Zane are outside waiting for me to bring you out."

"So, tell them you didn't find me in here," Evie complained.

"Not happening," Harley stated matter-of-factly, "I've been in here for nearly five minutes now. If you're not in here they might think I've been on the toilet all this time. No way am I letting the two hottest guys in school think I have a bowel issue."

"Say you were doing your make-up then," Evie suggested.

"Do you see my bag with me?" Harley held her arms out wide to show Evie they were empty.

Evie's shoulders slumped in defeat. There was no other choice but to face them. Why couldn't they just leave her alone?

Harley led the way out the bathroom door and Evie followed unwillingly after her.

Owen was standing across the hall, arms crossed. Zane leaned casually against the locker behind him, playing on his phone. The hallway was empty, minus the one or two final students doing the mad dash to their class.

"Here she is," Harley purred at Owen, batting her eyelashes at him.

"Thanks," Owen acknowledged Harley briefly, his eyes trained on Evie.

Evie looked at the ground, not bringing herself to make eye contact with him.

"Evie let's go," Owen growled in a low voice, grabbing her by the elbow and leading her down the hall.

Harley watched on, sulking at the fact her interaction with Owen was over. Zane stood up and followed after his friend casually without any acknowledgment to Harley, she may have well been invisible for all he cared.

"Where are we going?" Evie asked, scared of what the answer might be.

"Home," Owen stated, his eyes trained ahead, "We've missed half the day of school already and I don't trust you to go to your last classes on your own, so instead of chasing you all over school, as much fun as that is, I'm taking you home where I can keep an eye on you until Mum gets home."

Evie tried to swallow the lump in her throat. She took deep breaths, trying to stay calm. What she was afraid of most she didn't know; Owen taking her home in what seemed like a foul mood or Sandra finding out that she skipped school today. The latter seemed like an easier fate at that point in time.

Owen stopped past his own locker to collect his things and then did the same for Evie to collect her things from her own locker.

The drive home was silent. Zane had joined them, resolving he had no issue in missing his Maths and Chemistry classes. Zane had insisted Evie sit in the front seat, while he sat in the back behind Owen. Evie watched the passing houses in a blur.

Once home, Evie walked straight to her room, closing the door behind her, flinging her bag to the floor and flopping down on her bed; her head buried in her pillow.

Evie heard a gentle knock on the door, but she ignored it. Why couldn't they just let her be alone? Was it so hard?

The door opened slowly and then closed again. Owen had simply peeked in to see Evie face down on her bed. Resolving to give her the space she wanted, he left and headed back downstairs to watch television with Zane. He sent a simple message to Sandra letting her know they were all home, there was nothing wrong and he would explain later when she got home from work.

While the movie played, Owen wondered about the lonely teenaged girl upstairs in his family's guest room. There was something about her he just couldn't understand.

Most kids his mother brought home were happy to have a second chance at a normal life, rescued from the streets. The biggest issue some of them would have sometimes was being addicted to drugs. They were the ones Owen hated because they usually went into his room and stole money or objects they could trade for drugs.

Evie was different, Owen thought. She didn't want their money. She didn't even want their hospitality. All she wanted was to go back to her life on the streets and be on her own once more. Why would anyone possibly want that sort of a life?

Chapter 14

"Evie," Sandra called up the stairs when she came home, "Could you please come here for a moment."

Evie slumped her shoulders, knowing she was about to get in trouble for skipping a whole day of class. She tried to tell herself she didn't care but she knew deep down she didn't like to disappoint Sandra.

In the kitchen, Evie found Sandra with a man she recognised, but couldn't understand why he would be there.

"Evie, do you remember Jack?" Sandra smiled brightly when Evie joined them.

Evie looked between Sandra and Jack, then back to Sandra again, confused. Jack was the man who had fitted Evie's ankle monitor the weekend before.

"Evie," Jack nodded in greeting, "If you would take a seat please."

Jack motioned to the nearby kitchen chair and Evie sat down reluctantly. She knew there would be consequences for running off during school, but it wasn't like she had run away. Evie feared that Sandra would no longer even allow her to go to school and Evie would be house bound for the remainder of her sentence. The thought made her ill. At least school was a semi escape for her. Not allowed to leave at all would make her all the more vulnerable.

Jack knelt down in front of Evie as she pulled up the cuff of her jeans. Opening his special tool kit, Jack set to work doing his job. Evie sat sullenly the entire time, not watching him, but eyeing Sandra. Sandra just continued smiling. Evie wondered why she was smiling.

Owen and Zane walked to the kitchen from the lounge room, standing either side of the arched doorway, watching the scene before them. Evie avoided meeting their eyes, still ashamed and upset about how the day had played out.

Evie felt a sudden release around her ankle, looking down she saw Jack packing her ankle monitor away in his kit and standing up.

Evie's eyes met Sandra's with question and confusion. What was going on?

"Thanks Jack," Sandra smiled and led Jack to the front door.

Evie stared in astonishment at her bare ankle. It was gone. Jack had removed her monitoring system all together. Every nerve in Evie's body wanted to jump for joy and run while she had the chance, but something stopped her.

"So, what do you think?" Sandra's voice broke into Evie's thoughts and Evie looked up at her, standing slowly to face her.

"I don't understand," was all Evie could muster to say still confused by the whole situation.

It then dawned on Evie that maybe it was Sandra's way of telling her she was free. That Evie was free to leave and run away yet again. Evie felt a pang of sadness in the pit of her stomach. All she had wanted was to keep moving, stay out of danger and keep danger away from everyone else. Now that she had that handed to her, she found it difficult to move.

"I spoke to a judge today, a friend of mine, called in a favour," Sandra started to explain, "I told him about your situation. He agreed to remove the device on one condition."

Evie held her breath, waiting for Sandra to continue.

"You have to continue to live with us for the remainder of your sentence, but you can do it tracker free," Sandra clarified, "You will need to let me know where you are at all times. No leaving school to go to the shops or anything. But if you break this agreement and try to run away again, the anklet goes straight back on and you will see yourself living here until you graduate at the end of the year."

Internally, Evie laughed at the example Sandra gave of Evie ditching school to go shopping. Evie couldn't think of anything worse so there was no chance of that happening. If Evie broke the conditions, she would see herself here for the rest of the year; that was eight months away. Evie knew she couldn't risk running away and getting caught again. Her only option was to continue her sentence and play it out for another eleven weeks.

Sandra didn't wait for Evie to agree, she knew it was the only choice she had.

"Now that also means you have no more excuses to not go with the boys to the lake party tomorrow with the rest of your senior class," Sandra beamed at Evie.

Evie's stomach dropped and her eyes dashed to the two teenaged boys watching on. They were probably thinking she had planned it all along, but Evie didn't want to go. It was too risky. Neither of them gave her any clue to how they felt about her being a burden to them.

"But..." Evie started, turning back to face Sandra, but Sandra cut her off.

"Evie, you are a teenager, you need to start acting like one, stop feeling like you have the weight of the world on your shoulders," Sandra declared, "The boys have said their happy for you to go with them."

Evie's head whipped round to face the boys in surprise. Zane gave Evie a beaming smile as if he was happy about the idea. Owen just stared back at Evie for a brief second, not giving anything away, before turning on his heel and walking back to the lounge room.

The following morning, Evie rose early to an eager Sandra's voice calling her. It seemed to Evie that Sandra was excited about the lake party, as if Evie should have been but wasn't. All Evie felt was anxious and scared.

Collecting the tankini Kelly had loaned to her, Evie got dressed pleased she was right in choosing it as it covered her scar perfectly. Selecting a pink top to go over the top and some denim shorts Sandra had presented her with the night before. Since being at the Taylor's, Evie had only ever worn jeans as to cover her monitor. Now it wasn't an issue, it would be the first time anyone in the family had seen her in such little clothing. The thought unnerved her slightly.

In the kitchen, Owen and Zane waited patiently on kitchen chairs, while Sandra hovered around the base of the stairs.

"Mum," Owen pleaded, "Please, stop pacing."

Sandra glanced at her son, feeling thankful that she had raised such a caring and gentle young man. She knew he may not have acted it all the time, he had a reputation to protect like most boys his age, but deep down she knew she could rely on Owen to protect Evie if need be.

Sandra hadn't told her children the truth about Evie. Brian had told her to keep it between them. Not even Evie knew how much Sandra and Brian knew. Even though she didn't know everything, she understood enough to know Evie needed protecting. Brian was still cautious about the whole idea and the situation Evie presented by being in their house, but he also supported his wife.

The night Evie had a nightmare; Evie disclosed some facts about herself to Sandra, not a lot, but enough that Sandra could use to do some research back at her office the next day. Although the search only told her bits and pieces, Sandra felt she had a fairly, good idea where Evie was from. It all seemed to fit into place like a puzzle. There were a few pieces still missing, but Sandra hoped that in time, with more trust, Evie might open up to her.

In the meantime, Sandra swore to help Evie live a normal teenaged life. She deserved that much, school, friends and parties. Sandra was going to make sure Evie got a glimpse of what her life should have been, what it still could be. Evie had already proven she was an intelligent student and could go far if given the opportunity.

Evie started to walk down the stairs, the three in the kitchen all hearing her footsteps turned their heads to look. Owen and Zane both stared in shock. It was the first time they had seen Evie's legs; she was normally always wearing pants or jeans. Sandra just smiled at the sight of seeing Evie ready to go to the party.

"Wow," Zane breathed, snapping Owen out of the stare and who, hit his friend in the chest as a warning to watch himself.

"Let's go," Owen grunted, trying to shake an unfamiliar feeling that was brewing inside him.

The boys stood up and headed out the front door to Owen's car, leaving Sandra alone with Evie in the kitchen.

"Have fun."

Sandra emphasised the word fun to Evie before embracing her in a quick hug, then pushing Evie out the front door to join the boys.

It took them thirty minutes to reach the lake. Zane explained from the front passenger seat on the way to Evie that the lake was the chosen location for the senior party that year as their friend Cassie's parents owned a lake house, or mansion as Zane put it. Cassie's family were rich, her father was some fancy cosmetic doctor.

Cassie volunteered to host and organise the senior party, and was going to be providing all the food, drink and hiring a popular DJ to play music. Owen was quick to mention the drink selection was both alcoholic and non-alcoholic, watching for Evie's reaction in the rear-view mirror.

"I don't like to drink alcohol," Evie replied honestly.

It was the truth. Sure, in her old life, she may have had the odd drink at parties, but when everything changed, Evie never touched it again. She wanted to know she had a clear head at all times. She couldn't risk getting drunk and losing her inhibitions.

When Owen pulled his car up at the lake house, the party down by the lake's edge was already in full swing. Teenagers were everywhere. Evie anxiously looked around, nervous to be in the middle of nowhere.

Owen turned to face Evie, "Have you got your phone?"

Evie nodded, pulling it from her shorts' pocket to show him. Owen took it from her and started typing.

"If you can't find me and want to leave, call me. You have my number," Owen handed Evie back her phone, "Now you have Zane's number too. Don't go anywhere on your own with anyone else."

Zane winked at Evie, "Call me."

Owen rolled his eyes at his friend's comment and climbed out of the car. Zane and Evie followed.

"What do you want to do first?" Zane asked Evie, as the two of them followed Owen down to the lake's edge where the party was set-up.

"Don't say go home," Owen said from in front of them, "Mum would kill me if I showed up home with you so early."

Evie smiled at how Owen feared his mother's wrath. Evie had no idea what she wanted to do. Going to the lake party hadn't even been her idea.

"Evie! You came!" Harley's voice rang out across the lake as she pushed her way past dancing teenagers.

Harley hugged Evie while Owen and Zane watched on. It was obvious Owen was not a fan of Harley and it made Evie wonder why.

"Hey Owen," Harley flirted.

"Catch you later, Evie," Owen ignored Harley, "Don't forget what I said."

With that, Owen and Zane sauntered off into the crowd.

"Come on," Harley grabbed onto Evie's hand and started pulling her into the crowd, "The rest of the gang is over here."

The girls found Harley's group of friends; Paige and James were standing with arms wrapped around each other, and Marcus and Rebecca talking with drinks in their hands. When they saw Evie and Harley approach, the four of them greeted Evie with enthusiasm, which made Evie feel a little more at ease with them and with being at the party.

Marcus approached Evie with a smile, "Evie, do you have a drink? Can I get you one?"

Evie nodded, "Thanks, not alcohol though."

"Sure," Marcus smiled and wandered off.

Evie spoke briefly with Harley and the other two girls, more listening than talking on Evie's behalf.

Marcus returned and handed Evie a punch drink. Evie sipped the sweet liquid and continued to stand awkwardly while the friends talked adamantly around her.

It was a warm day and Evie was thankful for Marcus refilling her drink. Two hours in and Evie had begun to feel loose. She started to dance with Harley to the upbeat music the DJ played and laughed. It was the first time in over a year, Evie felt like a teenager again, young and carefree.

Owen watched Evie from afar, playing the protective cousin role to a tee. At least that's what he tried to convince himself. Zane kept telling him to loosen up, that Evie would be fine, but there was a niggling thought in the back of Owen's mind that he couldn't shake; he knew he had to watch her.

Evie was swaying to the music, not a care in her mind when suddenly a girl close by screamed at the top of her lungs. Evie's head whipped around so fast, looking for the danger, wondering which way to run, then another scream from someone else.

Evie started to panic. Her heart raced. Evie searched the crowd around her. People began running and squealing. That's when a hand grabbed her wrist and started to pull her away from the crowd.

Chapter 15

Harley held Evie's hand tightly, pulling her away from the crowd. Suddenly, a blast of cold water hit Evie square in the back. Evie couldn't help but scream in the panic of it all. Then Harley was hit she squealed but laughed at the same time.

Evie swung her head around as Harley continued to pull her away from the commotion. That's when Evie saw it. About ten boys with large water guns and were spraying everyone at random, drenching them in the cool water.

Evie couldn't help but smile, thinking about how silly she had been for thinking there was an actual threat. It was all a big game. It was fun. A simple teenage experience.

Harley kept on dragging Evie along with her, even though now she had some resistance. Suddenly, they were wading into the lake and they both tripped, falling into the water.

Evie spluttered and tossed around in the water until she found her footing. Pushing herself out of the water, she stood up in the knee-high water, now saturated from head to toe. Harley stood also, looking equally the drowned rat that Evie felt. Both girls laughed at the irony; they were running from water, only to end up worse off in the lake.

"Oh no," Evie exclaimed, "My phone!"

Evie reached into her pocket of her wet shorts and pulled out her phone. She knew it was an expensive and brand-new model of phone, the last thing she wanted to do was have to tell Sandra she drowned it in the lake. Even if it was Sandra who pushed Evie to go to the lake party in the first place.

The phone looked like it was still working, which surprised Evie, knowing how it had been fully submerged. Harley looked over Evie's shoulder at the phone.

"Not to worry," Harley said in a breezy tone, "Those new phones are water resistant."

Evie breathed a sigh of relief at Harley's comment.

Once it looked as though the water fight had ended, the two girls made their way out of the lake and up the shore. Evie giggled when she saw Zane in the distance, looking like he had not survived the water attack either. When his eyes met hers, he gave her a wave as he laughed at how drowned Evie looked.

Harley pulled off her red sundress and rang it out, draping it over a lawn chair to dry in the sun. All Harley was left wearing was a blue and white striped bikini set that looked amazing on her. Evie tugged her top off and did the same, but chose to keep the denim shorts on. As her shirt came off, Evie felt the tankini top rise on her stomach. She reached down as fast as possible and held it down; worried someone may have noticed her scar.

When they met up with Harley's group of friends again, Marcus readily handed Evie another large cup of punch, to which she thanked him. With her drink in one hand, the four girls of the group began to dance around again to the music. James and Marcus watched on, sitting in lawn chairs talking.

Hours passed and Evie felt tired and her head was feeling dizzy. She put it down to the heat of the day and her slight anxiety about being at the party still sat in the back of her mind. The sun was starting to set, a bon fire lit down on the shore of the lake and many lanterns lit around the foreshore.

"I think I need to sit down and rest for a bit," Evie called out over the pulsing music to Harley.

Not getting a response from Harley, she stumbled away from the girls and nearly landed in Marcus' lap. James laughed at her misfortune and went off find Paige amongst the crowd. Marcus held Evie by the hips, helping to steady her as he stood up next to her.

"You okay?" he asked in concern, leaning close to Evie's ear so he could hear her.

Evie nodded, "My head is spinning and I feel hot. I need to sit down."

"Come with me," Marcus instructed her, "We can go inside the house and cool you down."

Marcus slung one of Evie's arms around his shoulders and he leaned into her, one of his own arms around her waist to help her walk. Evie was appreciative of Marcus helping her out. She didn't like how she was feeling one bit and the fact her barriers were down at the party scared her. Just thinking about it frightened her even more, anxiety started to cloud her mind further.

"Owen," Evie mumbled.

"No, I'm Marcus," Marcus reminded Evie, laughing slightly.

"I need Owen."

By now, her head swayed as the dizziness increased. Evie feebly tried to push Marcus away, to walk back towards the crowd at the party, to look for Owen. Marcus, however, held Evie tighter reassuring her she would be okay with him, that he was going to help her.

Owen saw Evie stumbling, Marcus' arm around her waist. He frowned at the sight. Evie looked him in the eyes and said she didn't drink, yet at that point he would have sworn she was drunk. Not only was she intoxicated, it looked like Marcus was keen to take advantage of Evie.

"Zane," Owen called to his friend.

Zane looked up at Owen from where he was sitting chatting to Charlotte, a brunette with legs up to her waist and in Zane's Geography class. Owen nudged his head in the direction of the lake house and Zane spotted a silhouette of two people walking away from the crowd. Zane knew Owen was indicating he wanted Zane to join him.

While Zane apologised for leaving Charlotte, Owen started making his way quickly towards the swaying Evie, closing the distance between them quickly. Zane followed a few meters behind his friend, not as fast, unsure of what they were actually doing in that moment.

"Evie!" Owen's voice called out.

The couple stopped in their place and Marcus looked behind him.

"Clear off Taylor," Marcus called over his shoulder, "She's spoken for."

Owen could never tolerate men taking advantage of drunken girls, but the fact that this particular girl was Evie made Owen red with rage. He justified his actions with that his mother would kill him if he let anything happen to Evie, but deep down, Owen knew it was more than that. He pushed the thought to the side as he approached Marcus and Evie with clenched fists.

Owen shoved Marcus in the back, forcing him forward. Evie slipped from his grasp, stumbling to the side slightly. She tried to take deep breaths to steady herself. Evie didn't like how she was feeling one bit. It was one of her worst episodes ever and she wanted it over.

"What the fuck, Taylor!" Marcus yelled as he scrambled to his feet, ready for a fight.

"Evie's leaving with me," Owen growled at Marcus, not wanting to get into an actual fight with Marcus.

"Go find one of the other sluts around here," Marcus spat back, "I'm sure Harley would give you a go."

Owen didn't hold Harley to high regard and usually tried to avoid the girl whenever she tried coming on to him strongly, but that was no excuse for Marcus to refer to her as a slut, or for that matter, Marcus was in a way saying that Evie was a slut too.

With a clenched fist, Owen swung at Marcus' face and hit him square in the jaw. Marcus fell backwards to the ground with a thump.

Evie screamed at the blurry image of Owen punching her friend Marcus to the ground, when all he was trying to do was help her during one of her attacks.

"It's okay," Owen assured Evie, reaching for her, "Come with me. Let's get you home."

"No!" Evie screamed again in fear.

Evie tried with all her might to push her anxiety away to be able to run to safety. Stumbling slightly, Evie raced away from him.

Almost immediately, Evie ran into Zane who was walking towards the lake house.

"Help me," Evie pleaded with Zane, gripping the front of his shirt in her hands.

"What's wrong?" Zane asked, "What's happened?"

Zane looked to his best friend who was walking back towards him. He could see on the ground behind Owen was Marcus, cradling his face in his hands. A few onlookers nearby watching in interest, but not getting involved.

"He's after me," Evie screamed, tears starting to run down her face.

"Who?"

"There's no time, we have to go," Evie screamed in fear as she tried to pull Zane to make him start moving.

"What's going on?" Zane asked, not budging.

"Zane, please!" Evie pleaded once more, "We need to find Owen and get out of here."

This statement confused Zane even more.

Owen approached them carefully, watching the scene unfold with his friend and the troubled teenaged girl.

"Evie?" Owen spoke gently.

Evie turned to see Owen, but to Evie he wasn't Owen, he was an image of her past. Evie screamed loudly, though no one down close to the party heard her, her scream drowned out by the music.

Evie screamed.

It seemed Zane wasn't going to be much help to her in that moment, Evie decided she had to fight back. She fought against her dizziness and fear and lunged forward to attack.

Owen was surprised as Evie pounced towards him and actually got a good hit at him, right in his left eye. It wasn't enough to bowl him over, but enough that a searing pain shot into his skull.

"How did you find me?" Evie yelled at him, before grabbing Zane's hand, trying to pull him with her using all of her strength.

Evie's right hand throbbed in pain from the punch she just threw, but the pain kept her going. It would help her survive and she had been through worse before.

Zane shot his best friend a worried and confused look.

Owen touched his eye with his palm, his head already starting to pound. He knew something was not right with Evie and all he wanted was for her to get home safe.

Thinking fast, Owen pulled his car keys from his pocket and chucked them towards Zane, who caught them easily with one hand.

"Get her home," Owen called, "I'll find another way home."

Zane nodded, understanding.

Evie was still freaking out, trying to pull Zane away.

Zane pulled Evie close to him and whispered into her ear, "It's okay. I'm going to take you home."

Evie felt instant relief by his words.

Zane helped Evie back to Owen's Jeep and into the passenger seat, before getting in the driver's side and starting the car. Pulling the car away, Zane started to drive back towards Owen's house.

Evie sat beside him. She was shaking all over. Her head was still spinning and she felt like she couldn't breathe.

Owen watched as his best friend drove his car away with Evie inside. He knew then that maybe what had happened to Evie in the past was actually a lot worse than he first thought. He needed to get home and talk to his mother, so Owen set off to find his friend Mark for a lift home.

Chapter 16

Zane pulled Owen's car to a stop in the Taylor family's driveway. He turned to look at Evie, concerned with the events that had transpired that evening, one hand still on the steering wheel and the other resting casually on the back of Evie's chair.

"Are you okay?" Zane asked.

Evie swayed slightly, she felt dizzy and fear had taken hold of her emotions. Her hand throbbed from the punch but she was scared. All their lives were now in danger. It was what Evie had been trying to avoid the entire time.

"I'm going to be sick," Evie announced, reaching for the door handle and scrambling out of Owen's Jeep.

Zane rushed around the front of the car to help Evie, but she was already vomiting on the grass when he got to her. He stood beside her and held her hair back out of the firing line.

Sandra looked out the window as the car pulled up. Owen had called her to explain, or at least attempt to explain, what had happened at the party. He didn't understand what was going on, but for Sandra it was another piece of the puzzle she called Evie.

Sandra watched as Evie stumbled out of the car and fell to her knees, before retching on Sandra's front lawn. Running out the front door, Sandra went to check on Evie, finding Zane, now beside Evie, holding her hair as she continued to vomit.

"Mrs T," Zane looked worried when he saw Sandra approach, "I don't know what happened. We warned her about the alcohol but it seems she didn't listen."

Evie's stomach stopped regurgitating and Evie looked up at Sandra. The last thing she wanted now was for Sandra to be angry with her.

"I didn't drink," Evie tried to explain, "I swear. I only had the punch."

Zane rolled his eyes at Evie's innocence. Everyone knew the punch had alcohol.

Sandra helped Evie to her feet without a word and began to lead her inside.

"I should probably go back for Owen," Zane started to walk back towards the Jeep.

"Don't bother," Sandra called after him, while helping Evie towards the house, "Mark's bringing him home, he'll be home soon."

"Owen," Evie mumbled, "Is Owen okay?"

Sandra gave Zane a confused look, who only shrugged in response.

"She wasn't making any sense," Zane replied.

"I'm not safe here," Evie spoke softly, "I need to leave. If I stay, you will all be in danger."

"It's okay, sweetheart," Sandra reassured Evie, "Let's get you inside and fixed up. We'll discuss it in the morning."

Zane helped Sandra to get Evie up the stairs and into the bathroom, then left the two alone and went back downstairs. When he reached the kitchen, Owen came in the door. Owen's eye had already begun to swell and darken in colour.

"How is it I managed to evade her swing when she's sober, but you get hit by the girl when she's drunk?" Zane teased his best friend.

Owen walked to the fridge and pulled a bag of frozen peas out of the freezer. He sat down on the kitchen chair beside Zane and placed the peas on his eye to help stop the swelling.

"Shut up," Owen replied, "I wasn't expecting her to do it."

"And I was?" Zane laughed.

"Where is she?" Owen asked, changing the topic.

"Your mum is with her in the bathroom cleaning her up," Zane nudged his head towards the stairs, "You're lucky, she waited until she was out of your car before vomiting."

Upstairs, Sandra assisted Evie in getting undressed, the shower turned on. Vomit had splattered up on Evie's clothes and regardless of Zane's best attempt to hold her hair back, some had gotten in her hair too. Sandra reached to pull up Evie's tankini top, and Evie feebly tried to stop her.

"No," Evie cried out.

"It's okay Evie," Sandra assured her, "It's nothing I haven't seen before. I've had to help Kelly out on occasion."

As the tankini top came up, Sandra saw what Evie had hoped to hide. A large scar on Evie's stomach stood out against her skin. Sandra's worried eyes met Evie's and Evie closed her eyes as though she was in pain.

"Come on," Sandra spoke softly, "Into the shower and wash off. I'll go get you some clean clothes."

Sandra left Evie in the shower and left the bathroom, closing the door behind her. She leaned back against the door and wondered what piece of the puzzle she had just uncovered. What was it that Evie feared? How did she get that scar?

Evie stood under the streaming warm water, sobbing. The tears washed away as quickly as they came with the water from the shower running over her face. Evie knew the lake party was a bad idea. Evie knew she had to do whatever it took to protect the Taylor family. She wouldn't let them end up in the same fate as her own family had.

Sunday morning, Evie woke with a pounding head. She couldn't remember much of the previous day, it was a blur mostly. She knew she didn't feel safe anymore and that fear washed over her once more. Evie's chest began to tighten and her heart pounded, tears threatened.

Evie felt paralysed. She didn't want to get out of bed. She feared the outside world. Pulling the covers up over her head Evie decided to hide, at least for a little bit.

Sandra looked at the clock, concerned.

"Maybe I should," Sandra started to stand.

"Sandra, leave her," Brian warned, "She will come down when she's ready."

"But Brian," Sandra began to protest.

"It's only nine o'clock," Brian argued, "Any normal teenager would sleep in past nine after a party."

"She's not a normal teenager," Sandra shot back.

Owen and Zane, who had stayed over the night, came down the stairs and walked into the kitchen. Owen's eye had turned purple, swollen from Evie's right hook.

"Mr and Mrs T," Zane greeted his best friend's parents, grabbing a muffin from the plate on the table.

Zane had grown up with Owen. The Taylor's house was his second home, Sandra and Brian were his second parents. He was at ease in their house, like it was his own.

"I'm going to check on her," Sandra stated and dashed up the stairs before her husband could argue otherwise.

Brian shook his head, he knew his wife meant well.

Sandra slowly opened the bedroom door to Evie's room a slight crack and peeked inside. On the bed, she saw a large lump; it was obvious Evie was under the covers, head and all. Opening the door wider, Sandra entered the room, closing the door behind her and walked over to the bed.

"Evie," Sandra spoke softly, not wanting to startle Evie if she was still asleep.

Silence.

Sandra bit her bottom lip then reached out and gently pulled the covers back. There was Evie, looking up scared at Sandra. Her face was wet and puffy from crying. Sandra said nothing, just pulled Evie into a strong hug. Evie hugged Sandra back while sobbing into her shoulder.

After some time, Evie pulled away, wiping away the last of her tears. Sandra brushed a lock of Evie's hair back behind her ear.

"I know what I promised," Evie whispered, her voice shaking slightly from crying, her eyes looking down, avoiding Sandra's, "But I can't stay here."

"Yes, you can," Sandra assured her, "You are safe here. We can look after you."

Evie shook her head, "I'm not safe anywhere."

"Seems like you can look after yourself," Sandra explained gently, "You hit Owen."

"Owen?" Evie looked up at Sandra, trying to figure out what she was saying.

Evie couldn't believe what Sandra had just said. Why would Evie hit Owen, she was looking for Owen?

"Yes," Sandra smiled slightly at the thought of a girl hitting her son, "You ran from Owen after hitting him and he now has a black eye."

"But I thought," Evie's voice trailed off.

The thought that she had hit Owen flooded Evie with guilt.

"You were very drunk," Sandra explained further.

"The punch," Evie thought aloud, realising now in her sober state that Marcus had been giving her punch that was spiked. How could she be so naive?

"Sadly, some teenaged boys can't be trusted." Sandra spoke gently, "That's why you should always get your own drinks at parties."

Wait until the next time I see him; Evie thought to herself but then realised, she would unlikely see anyone at school ever again. It wasn't safe anymore, it never was.

"I told you I didn't want to go," Evie complained.

"Well, the positive from this situation is you're still safe here, with us."

Evie's eyes darted to Sandra. Sandra had no idea what she was talking about, Evie thought.

"I'll never be safe anywhere," Evie said with vindication, "Especially not staying in one place for so long."

"You need to tell me everything," Sandra told Evie, "Some things I've managed to find out for myself but there are some pieces missing from the puzzle. Please will you tell me?"

Evie frowned at Sandra's request. Sandra was actually asking Evie about her past, about who she really was. Evie was dumbfounded. Sandra said she already knew some parts. What did she know? The thought scared Evie.

Then Evie wondered, maybe it would be a good thing to get it all off her chest. To confide in someone and share the burden of her past. Sandra had shown nothing but love and support to Evie since she first found her that night only a week ago out in the rain on the side of the road.

No. She couldn't do it. The more people knew, the more danger they would be in, Evie couldn't be selfish. It was her burden to bare, nobody else's. Biting her lip, she closed her eyes. No one could know her secret.

After a few seconds of silence, which felt like longer, Evie pulled the bed covers up over her head as she laid back down, her back to Sandra. Blocking out the world.

"Evie," Sandra pleaded once more, but Evie ignored her.

Letting out a sigh of defeat, Sandra stood up and left the room.

Chapter 17

When Sandra entered the kitchen, she indicated to Brian with a nudge of her head that she needed to talk to him in private and together they left the kitchen, leaving Owen, Zane and Kelly sitting at the table.

"What do you think is going on?" Kelly asked her older brother and his friend who sat silently, oblivious to the events that had been happening over the previous week. "What happened at the lake party? And why do you have a black eye?"

Zane looked to Owen, waiting for him to answer. When he stayed silent, avoiding both sets of eyes on him, Zane just offered Kelly a half smile.

"Fine," Kelly moaned, sick and tired of being treated like a baby in the family, she was a teenager, nearly an adult, and they still treated her like a child. "Don't tell me. I'm sick and tired of being left out of everything. I'm going to Melissa's."

Without another word, Kelly stood up from her chair in frustration and headed towards the front door. The boys watched in silence as Kelly stormed out of the house, letting the door slam close as she did.

Sandra heard the bang of the door and rushed back into the kitchen, with Brian close behind her.

"What happened?" Sandra asked as she looked around the room, "Where's Kelly?"

"She went to Melissa's," Zane replied, watching Owen sit uncharacteristically quiet beside him.

"Mum, what's going on?" Owen questioned his mother, standing up and walking around the table to face his parents, "Something is going on with Evie that you're not telling us."

"Don't use that tone with your mother," Brian warned his son.

"It's complicated," Sandra spoke gently, a hand resting on her husband's arm to calm him, "Evie is a complicated case, I don't know exactly what."

"I still think we should be contacting the authorities," Brian turned to face his wife while ignoring the confusion on the two teenaged boys' faces.

"That's something we need to discuss with Evie," Sandra replied quietly. "I just need to gain her trust enough for her to open up to me, she obviously has no care for the authorities, I've seen that for myself. Let's just give her some time. We are all probably just overreacting to nothing for all we know."

"What about the safety of our family," Brian argued back at his wife, indicating a hand towards the boys, "Our children?"

"Why would we not be safe with Evie being here?" Owen enquired, lost in confusion, not knowing exactly what his parents were saying. He had believed there was more to Evie than what he knew, but he never thought it would be serious enough that his father would be concerned for their safety or a need for the police to be involved.

"Her right hook seems pretty dangerous to you," Zane joked from where he still sat at the table, but stopped smiling as soon as he registered the serious looks on everyone else's faces around him.

"Does this have anything to do with her freaking out last night?" Owen turned his attention back to questioning his parents.

"For now, all you boys need to know is Evie needs your support and keep her close," Sandra explained.

"What do you think we've been doing for the past week?" Owen exploded, "I've missed many classes because of Evie. What more do you want from me for some stranger you found on the side of the road and decided to adopt?"

Owen had never spoken to his parents in such a way, but the secrets and tension in the house was getting too much, all because of a girl. Evie was hiding something and it seemed his parents weren't letting on how much they knew. His father was concerned for their safety, was Evie dangerous? What had she done in the past two years? What bothered Owen more is the feeling that he actually felt protective of Evie.

Evie came out of her room to head to the bathroom. She opened the door quietly, not wanting to draw attention to herself. Eyes still puffy and swollen from all her crying. Evie could hear voices coming from downstairs. It was Sandra and her family talking, Evie wondered if it was about her.

Deciding she didn't want to know, Evie dashed across the hall to the bathroom.

Returning to her room, Evie suddenly heard Owen's voice clearly from downstairs. He sounded frustrated, speaking louder than she had heard him ever talk.

"What do you think we've been doing for the past week? I've missed many classes because of Evie. What more do you want from me for some stranger you found on the side of the road and decided to adopt?"

Evie stilled in the hallway, just outside her room. He was upset because of her, because she was living with them. Her head bowed in acknowledgement of how much she was ruining the lives of those around her.

For the remainder of the day Evie stayed locked in her room, refusing to even leave for meals. Sandra tried her hardest to coax her out, but Evie politely declined. She never mentioned she had overheard part of their conversation that morning, keeping that to herself.

Monday morning, Evie rode to school in Owen's car in silence. She could feel his inquisitive gaze but avoided it by watching out her side window. Evie had resigned to keep her distance from Owen and everyone else. She would complete her obligated time and then leave without a backwards glance.

Once at school, Owen mentioned briefly how he would meet her at the car after school and all Evie did was nod in response, before heading off in the direction of her locker.

After collecting her books for her morning classes, Evie slammed her locker door shut and jumped back in surprise.

Standing silently in front of her was Harley. She had a knack for doing that Evie found. Harley smiled her usual happy smile at seeing Evie, but Evie was unsure of what Marcus had told Harley and her friends about what had happened at the lake party. Evie didn't say a word and started to walk off towards her first class, Harley following beside her.

"What happened to you on Saturday?" Harley inquired, as they walked together down the hallway, "We were dancing then you just left."

Evie shrugged her shoulders, avoiding Harley's eyes. She didn't want to be rude or mean to Harley, but after the weekend events, Evie had resolved to remain secluded from everyone else and not get involved with anyone. It was the only safe thing to do.

Harley watched Evie intently, waiting for her to answer the question. They soon reached Evie's maths classroom, so Harley stepped in front of Evie and blocked her way into the room.

"What's going on with you?" Harley asked, "Is everything okay?"

Evie let out a breath, "I'm fine."

Harley frowned, thinking about how blunt Evie's answer had been. Recognising the lesson Evie was about to attend, it reminded Harley of Evie's offer to tutor her to help her grades.

"When can we meet up to do our first tutoring lesson for Maths?" Harley requested, "I'm free every afternoon this week. Which suits you?"

"Um, actually..." Evie bit her lip nervously, trying to think of an excuse to get out of it yet feeling guilty at the same time. She wanted to help Harley, she honestly did, but Evie knew it was more important that Harley was safe than anything else.

After everything that had happened over the weekend, Evie had vowed to herself to keep her distance from everyone and keep her head down.

"I don't actually think I'll be able to tutor you after all, sorry."

"Since when?" Harley balked at Evie's sudden reluctance to help her out.

"It's just not a good time for me," Evie blabbed, her mind blank of an explanation, "I'm sorry."

Evie quickly stepped around Harley, leaving her looking stunned, and dashed into her own classroom to take her seat just as the bell rang.

Owen strode towards his first class for the morning when he noticed Marcus walking towards him. Taking deep breaths, Owen tried to calm himself, his right hand clenched in a fist by his side.

"Hey Taylor," Marcus called out as he approached, stopping in front of Owen.

Marcus' face bruised along his jaw and his lip blistered from where it had split, results of Owen punching him in the face at the lake party on Saturday night.

"Listen, about the party, I'm sorry. I had no idea Evie was your cousin. I think my drunken state of mind clouded my judgement. I didn't mean what I said," Marcus apologised.

Owen glared at Marcus. His half-assed attempt to smooth things over was pitiful. Leaning in slightly, Owen spoke forcefully and quiet, enough to scare Marcus.

"Stay away from Evie. If I catch you even look at her, what I did to your face at the party will be nothing compared to what I will do to you next."

Without another word, Owen continued on his way to class. Marcus breathed a sigh of relief, watching Owen walk away, thankful he was still in one piece after their encounter.

At lunch, Evie quickly collected her food and avoided Harley's enthusiastic wave, calling her over to the table she sat at with her friends. With her head bowed and cap pulled down, Evie walked outside and took up residence alone at the same table she had sat at the week before.

Inside the canteen, Harley sat back down in her chair confused by Evie's sudden withdrawn manner. She looked around at her friends who were speaking animatedly together about their weekends and especially the party.

"What happened to your face, man?" James asked Marcus across the table, "And don't say you fell over, we know that's a lie."

"Taylor punched me for something I said in my drunken state," Marcus lied feebly, brushing it off, "It was a misunderstanding."

Marcus couldn't bring himself to confess to his friends the truth of what had happened the night of the party. He would have to explain trying to take advantage of Evie while she was highly intoxicated with punch he had been giving her all night, after she had asked him only for non-alcoholic drinks, or to admit he had referred to one of his own friends as a slut. Marcus knew the girls in the group would hate him instantly and James would stand by his girlfriend. It wasn't an option.

It was another student, who had come to Marcus' aide at the party after Owen had hit him and left, that reminded Marcus of Owen's family relationship with Evie. It allowed Marcus the chance to try and attempt to smooth things over with Owen before the story of what really happened spread through the senior class.

"Does anyone know if Evie is okay?" Harley queried her friends, "She's become extremely distant with me today and won't even look at me."

"We had English with her just before," Rebecca answered nonchalantly, shrugging her shoulders as she picked at her food, "but she didn't sit with us, didn't even acknowledge us. Just went to a seat in the back."

Harley frowned. It seemed like her friends didn't care about her new friend. It may have only been a week, but Harley didn't like the idea of just forgetting all about Evie. It wasn't in her nature.

Abandoning her lunch on the table, Harley strode with determination across the cafeteria towards the popular table, towards Owen and his friends.

Owen sat with his back towards the large windows, talking and joking around with his friends like normal. His laughter wasn't as high spirited as it would normally be and he knew it, but it was the why that bugged him.

Owen had watched as Evie collected her lunch and then left the canteen on her own. Zane had nudged Owen's side and nodded towards the window, indicating that Evie was eating outside, but Owen refused to look and ignored his friend's gesture. Still, Owen didn't like how the idea of Evie sitting on her own outside made him feel.

As Mark finished telling his joke and the table laughed together, Owen noticed Harley making her way towards their table, an unusual sight. He frowned and looked down at his food, hoping she wasn't coming to speak to him and it had nothing to do with Evie. He didn't care what she did. At least, that was what he tried to convince himself.

"Owen," Harley's voice broke through the laughter at the table, which instantly stopped.

Sighing, Owen glanced up slowly to meet Harley's eye.

"What?" he muttered; bemused with her presence.

"Can we talk?" Harley asked gently, "It's about Evie."

"What about her?" Owen leaned back in his chair uninterested; making it obvious he wasn't about to go anywhere alone with Harley, he didn't want to give her any ideas.

"Has something happened?" Harley pushed for answers, "She has suddenly stopped talking to me."

"That's her choice," Owen replied with a shrug of his shoulders.

Everyone else at the table sat silently, pretending not to be listening. Zane was the only one watching, leaning forward with his elbow on the table beside Owen, his eyes flicking between the two.

"Why do you not care about her?" Harley asked in disbelief at Owen's lack of concern for his cousin. He may have been hot, but in that moment, Harley couldn't believe she had a crush on him all that time.

"What I feel is none of your business," Owen answered, standing up to stare Harley straight in the eye, "And if Evie has chosen to do something else with her time than hang out with you and your poor choice of friends, then I think she's made the best decision she could."

Without another word and before Harley could recover from her stunned state, Owen walked off and out of the canteen.

Chapter 18

"What's with you ditching Harley?" Owen questioned Evie on the way home from school that afternoon, his eyes trained on the road.

They had been driving in silence for five minutes before Owen spoke suddenly. It surprised Evie, as well as his question. She eyed him cautiously, turning from looking out her passenger window. Not saying a word in response, she returned to looking out the window.

"It's going to be a lonely three months for you with no friends," Owen continued on when Evie didn't answer. "Don't think you can hang around with Zane and me-"

Owen didn't get a chance to finish, Evie cut him off.

"Don't worry about me," Evie spat back, cutting Owen off, yet not looking at him, "In less than three months I'll be back on the side of the road where your mum found me."

It was in this moment that they arrived home. Evie wanted to unbuckle her seatbelt and jump out of the car for dramatic effect, but her fingers kept slipping past the button in her haste. She frowned at herself as she tried to concentrate harder, frustrated she couldn't complete the simple task, yet she was upset with Owen's comment. It was because of him, what she overheard him saying on Sunday, that she realised how much she was risking, she had to pull away, from everyone.

Tears began to brim in her eyes. Keeping her head down, Evie stilled when she felt Owen's fingers touch hers. He held her hand gently in one of his and unbuckled her with the other.

Confused once more by Owen's whiplash in demeanour, Evie didn't know what to do. Only minutes before he was being heartless and insensitive, then suddenly his caring and gentle nature shows. Glancing up at him through her eyelashes, Evie met with concern in Owen's eyes.

"Thank you," Evie whispered, almost too quiet for Owen to hear.

Retrieving her hand from his, Evie grabbed her bag at her feet and exited the car, walking to the house without a backwards glance.

For the remainder of the week and the four weeks following, Evie went into auto pilot mode. She kept her distance from Owen, and Harley, and their respective friends. Evie attended school, went to her classes, handed her assignments in and took her exams. At home, she did her homework and confined herself to her bedroom. Sandra tried profusely to coax her out, but the only time she would budge was for meals.

By the fifth week, Sandra had had enough with Evie's behaviour and didn't want her to fall deeper into bad habits for the remainder of her stay with them. She was half way through her term of house arrest, what would come of her in another six weeks if Sandra allowed her to continue down the same path?

Sandra gently knocked on the bedroom door.

"I'm studying," Evie called from inside the room.

With a turn of her hand, Sandra opened the door and walked into the room. There was Evie, lying on her bed, just staring at the ceiling. Sandra rested her hand on the knob, just watching Evie, who sat up suddenly on her bed when Sandra walked in.

"Interesting way to study," Sandra murmured, closing the door behind her and sitting on the foot of Evie's bed.

"I was taking a break," Evie muttered in response, her legs crossed on the bed.

"And your books just magically put themselves away in your bag?" Sandra prodded, noticing Evie's books were nowhere in sight.

Evie rolled her eyes, knowing that Sandra wasn't going to let it go. Over the past month and a half, Evie had taken to pushing Sandra away. She didn't want to, more than anything she wanted to hold Sandra close as she would have her own mother if she was still alive, but Evie knew if she wanted to protect Sandra and the rest of her family, she needed to keep them at a distance.

"Is there a reason you are here?" Evie rudely replied.

Sandra took a deep breath and smiled at Evie as though the way she had just spoken to her hadn't hurt her a little. Sandra knew though that it was all a façade and Evie was acting tougher than she felt inside.

Evie was pushing the Taylor's away and not only the family. Owen mentioned weeks before that after the doomed lake party weekend, Evie had stopped speaking with her new friends she had made at school. She stuck to her own while at school, not even speaking to Owen unless necessary during their drives to and from school. Evie didn't join in the family conversations at the dinner table, only answered with simple yes or no, and the occasional whatever. Evie was like a hermit in her own shell and Sandra was determined to get her out of it.

"Get dressed, you're going out," Sandra announced standing up from the bed but crossing her arms across her chest to demonstrate she wasn't taking no for an answer.

"What?" Evie frowned, confused by Sandra's sudden declaration, "No I'm not."

"It's not negotiable," Sandra explained, not backing down, "Either get yourself dressed or I will dress you. You have ten minutes to be downstairs, or I will come back and drag you out if I have to."

Sandra turned on her heel and opened the door, leaving the room. As she closed the door behind her, she poked her head through the closing gap, "Ten minutes," Sandra warned Evie once more before closing the door.

Evie let out a deep sigh of frustration and leant back against the bed head. There was no point fighting Sandra.

Whatever she had planned wasn't going to solve anything. With reluctance, Evie climbed off her bed and got dressed to go out.

Wearing some dark jeans and a comfortable red top, Evie tied up the laces on her sneakers, grabbed her zip up hoodie, cap firmly on her head and headed downstairs; exactly ten minutes after Sandra had left her room.

In the kitchen, Sandra sat at the kitchen table talking to Zane. Evie paused at the bottom step, looking from one to the other, her brow furrowed.

"What's going on?" Evie asked.

"I told you," Sandra beamed at her, standing and walking over to where Evie stood on the stair, "You're going out. Zane has come over to take you to the movies, get ice cream; do regular teenage stuff for a Saturday night."

Evie stared at Sandra in disbelief, how could she have done this? It was too dangerous for her to be out in public just walking around for all to see. To put Zane in danger too, what was she thinking?

"I'm going back to bed," Evie stated and turned to ascend the stairs to her room, but Sandra caught her arm and pulled her down into the kitchen against Evie's resistance.

"No," Sandra declared, "You are going out with Zane. No arguments."

Zane stood up silently and waited by the bench while Sandra convinced Evie, fiddling with his car keys in his pocket. He felt slightly unsettled about the situation. It had been his idea after all to take Evie out. Zane hadn't mentioned it to Owen; he knew his friend wouldn't have been keen on the idea of him taking Evie out on a semi-date. Owen had made it clear to Zane that he didn't want anything to do with Evie. Instead, Zane had approached Sandra only half an hour earlier about the idea, hoping she would agree it would be a good idea.

"What about Owen?" Evie inquired, looking over to Zane, who avoided her eye when she asked.

"He's out with Mark and a few other friends," Sandra replied looking over at Zane and then back to Evie. "Go and have fun. Remember what it's like to be a teenager; you only get to be one once. Don't throw it all away out of fear."

Evie thought about what Sandra said. Was she right? It was true. You only live once.

Nervously, Evie bit at the inside of her bottom lip. Debating internally what she should do. She knew Sandra wouldn't take no for an answer and she was starting to get cabin fever being inside whenever she wasn't at school. Taking a deep breath to calm her beating heart and steady her breathing, Evie silently nodded.

Sandra clapped her hands together in glee and ushered Evie to the door, Zane leading the way.

Outside in the cool evening air, Evie slipped her arms into her navy hoodie and zipped it up half way. Zane held the passenger door open and Evie climbed in, Zane shutting the door behind her. Sandra stood in the front door way waving, before going back inside and closing the door behind her.

Zane got in and started the engine, backing his car out of the driveway. Evie looked around the car, taking it in. She didn't think he had a car, that's why Owen did all the driving.

Yet, there she was, sitting in the front seat of a small white coupe car, only a few years old by the look of it too.

"Nice car," Evie murmured, breaking the silence and speaking to Zane for the first time in five weeks.

"Thanks," Zane smiled, feeling a little more confident in his decision to take Evie out for the night. "It's actually my mum's. I'm trying to fix up my sports car from scratch, so that's why Owen usually drives me places."

At the mention of Owen's name, Evie became silent again, she didn't know why. Zane must have sensed it, quickly changing the topic.

"So, the movies," Zane said cheerfully, "What sort do you like?"

"Anything," Evie replied, "Just not any horror or thrillers."

The last thing Evie needed was a reminder of her everyday life.

"Comedy it is then," Zane smiled, looking over at her.

Evie returned his smile, only not as brightly, grateful for his understanding. Still she wondered how much did he know about her situation. Evie still didn't know how much Sandra knew. Had Owen confided in his best friend with details?

Fifteen minutes later, they arrived at the cinemas. Zane parked in a spot just down from the entrance, leaving them only a short walk to the cinema. Still Evie found herself in old habits, as her heart began to race; her eyes darted around, looking at all the faces as they passed.

It wasn't until after Zane had purchased the tickets, some popcorn for them to share and two drinks, and they were settled in their seats that Evie managed to slightly calm her anxiety. Still, with each group of people who entered the darkened cinema, Evie was watching, taking them in.

When the movie started, Evie relaxed slightly. It had been nearly two years since Evie had last been to see a movie at the cinema. It was the night her life changed and would lead her to where she was now.

As the movie went on, Evie found herself forgetting about what was going on around her and enjoying the movie. Even loosening up and laughing at the comedic nature of the movie.

Evie took a sip of her drink then reached for some more popcorn from the bucket between her and Zane, her eyes trained on the screen, waiting to see what happened to the main character as he found himself in a hilariously embarrassing situation.

Her finger touched the salted, buttery popcorn half way down in the bucket. As she began to scoop a few popped kernels with her fingers, another hand touched hers. Upon touching Evie's hand, Zane quickly removed his hand and the pair looked at each other embarrassed, neither had been paying attention to what they were doing.

Evie's heart thrummed in her chest and not from anxiety, which surprised her. She pushed the feeling aside, offering Zane a reassuring smile as she removed her hand from the bucket and popped some of the popcorn into her mouth, looking back to the movie on the screen.

When the movie ended, Zane dumped their rubbish into the bin at the door and Evie followed him outside, onto the sidewalk, taking a deep breath of fresh air to clear her mind.

"Feel like getting some ice cream?" Zane asked; his hands stowed deep in his pockets nervously.

"I'm actually full from the popcorn," Evie replied, blushing at the memory of their hands touching while reaching for the buttery treat.

"What would you like to do then? It's your choice."

"Honestly," Evie spoke gently, "I would like to go home now, if that's okay. I'm still not all that keen on being out for so long and around lots of people in public."

Zane nodded, understandingly. He didn't want to push the matter, he had managed to get her out of the house for a couple of hours as he had promised Sandra, and the last thing he wanted was to do was bring on one of her debilitating anxiety attacks. He knew it would take small baby steps.

Zane placed a hand on the small of Evie's back and guided her in the direction of the car, removing his hand after a minute. Evie felt tingles where his hand had been and tried not to think anything of it. She put it down to the fact it had been so long since she had had any type of date and it was normal teenage hormones. She cursed her body for betraying her.

On the drive home, the pair spoke enthusiastically about the movie they had just seen, reliving their favourite parts and what they would have done, if had they been faced with certain situations. They discussed how the story line had plot holes and parts of it were unbelievable but that was what added to the humour of the movie.

When they reached the Taylor's house, Zane parked the car in the driveway and got out to walk Evie to the front door. They walked side by side still laughing about the silliness of the movie.

Once they reached the steps that lead to the front door, Zane paused and Evie turned to face him, smiling. It felt good to smile, she thought to herself. It had been a long time since she had felt genuinely happy and at ease. She owed it to Zane and was grateful to Sandra for pushing her into going out with him.

"Thank you for tonight, Zane," Evie smiled up at him, "I actually enjoyed myself, which I didn't think I would."

"It was my pleasure," Zane smiled back, "Whenever you need cheering up, I'm just a phone call away."

Evie giggled at Zane's enthusiasm for helping her out. Zane was legitimately a nice person.

Any normal girl would be flirting and swooning for Zane to kiss them by this stage, but Evie kept her distance. It wasn't like that for her. Sure, she had felt the usual rush in the heat of the moment when they touched, but deep down she knew Zane was just a friend to her. She wasn't going to get involved with anyone while in her situation, there was no point. In six weeks, she would be leaving again.

"Well, thank you," Evie said again, "I guess I will see you at school on Monday."

Leaning towards Zane, Evie embraced him with a grateful hug and he returned the gesture.

"Whatever is bothering you," Zane whispered in her ear, still in the embrace, "Just know that we are all here for you. Even Owen. He just doesn't know how to show it."

Evie gave a slight smile.

"Thank you," Evie murmured, "I wish it was that simple."

Evie pulled back away from Zane's touch just as the front door opened. The pair of teenagers looked to the door to see Owen standing there with his mouth open in shock.

Chapter 19

Evie's heart was racing, and not in the good way, her breath felt tight in her chest.

"What the..." Owen was the first to speak, "What's going on?"

"Owen, what are you doing home already?" Zane asked casually.

Zane felt guilty for not having told his best friend his plans to take Evie out for the night. All Zane had wanted to do was get Evie out of the house. After Owen had mentioned to Zane that Evie stayed locked up in her room the entire time unless she was going to school. Zane knew Evie had been avoiding all contact with people at school; she had deserted her new friends after only a week and if Zane approached her, she would make up an excuse to leave suddenly.

Owen descended the steps quickly and stood with Zane on the bottom, Evie a step above them in the middle. His eyes grazed over Evie and then back to his friend, waiting for an answer.

"Owen, stop," Evie pleaded grabbing his arm and attempting to pull him away from Zane, a sense of déjà vu blanketing her, "Nothing happened. Don't punch him, please."

Owen and Zane both looked at Evie in confusion.

Evie's heart was pounding so fast she feared it would jump out of her chest. It was just as she remembered. Was history repeating itself?

"I wouldn't hit Zane," Owen replied, watching Evie intently, "He's my best friend."

Silence extended over the three. Evie glanced between the two boys in front of her, their confused yet concerned faces made her feel a little more at ease. With a steadying breath, Evie tried to calm her heart to a normal rate.

"Oh, I know, I just meant," Evie stumbled for an excuse for her behaviour, "Never mind."

Evie took a step up towards the house, the boys still watching her as she went. She turned and looked at Zane, trying to ignore the analytical look Owen was giving her.

"Thank you, Zane, for tonight. I had fun."

With a small smile in appreciation, Evie retreated into the house, closing the door behind her, leaving the boys to talk on their own. Once inside, she dashed upstairs to her room not wanting twenty questions from Sandra, closing herself inside and taking a deep breath to calm her nerves and anxiety.

In the short moment when Owen found them, it had felt like her life was on repeat. She could never escape her past. Evie closed her eyes, standing against the door and concentrated on her breathing and calming her entire body down.

Outside, Owen turned back to look at Zane when Evie closed the front door.

"What happened?" Owen interrogated his best friend, arms crossed over his chest. He had a good idea after finding the Zane with Evie on the doorstep of his house, but he needed to hear it from Zane himself. "What were you doing out with Evie?"

"We just went to a movie, that's it," Zane replied earnestly, his hands held up in surrender.

"You told Mark you couldn't come out with us tonight because you had a date," Owen pushed, "Please don't tell me you're trying to hook up with Evie."

"No, I just thought she needed to get out of the house, be a normal teenager," Zane explained.

"She's not a normal teenager. You and I both know that and there's something off about her. You can't get attached to her."

"You're telling me that you don't care about Evie?"

"Exactly," Owen exclaimed, "She's just another runaway, another one of Mum's charity cases."

"Listen nothing happened, it was just one friend helping out another."

"She's not our friend."

"Ever since Evie arrived you've been all tense," Zane accused his friend, "You can't tell me you don't feel sorry for her."

"I've been tense because I don't like it when my mum brings complete strangers into our home and we know nothing about them. She'll be gone in six weeks," Owen said bluntly, "What do I care?"

Zane raised an inquiring eyebrow at Owen.

"I don't care about her," Owen huffed, "And neither should you."

"I don't think she's like all the other's your mum has brought home," Zane explained, "She's different. Has she taken advantage of living with you? Has she stolen anything from you?"

Owen scoffed at his friend's rationalising, "That's what makes it all the more suspicious. She's hiding something, so I don't trust her."

Zane didn't respond. It was obvious Owen wouldn't relent on his thoughts about Evie. It still didn't prove to him that Owen didn't feel something deep down. Zane knew that Owen wouldn't have helped her out all those times if he didn't feel something, it wasn't like him to go so out of his way for someone he didn't feel for in some way or another. He wondered too, if that was the reason Owen was upset that Zane had gone out with Evie after telling Mark he was on a date. Was Owen jealous of Zane taking Evie out?

"I'll see you tomorrow," Owen mumbled to his friend, not wanting to get any further into an argument with his best friend and say something he'd regret.

Zane watched his friend leave before climbing into his car and heading home. He knew he had hit a chord with Owen. It was obvious he had feelings on some level for Evie, but what Zane couldn't work out is why Owen wouldn't admit it.

Owen trudged up the stairs haunted by what Zane had said. He tried to push it aside, but he knew Zane was right. He had been fighting a feeling deep down about Evie, maybe she had a secret he didn't know, but for some unknown reason he felt a need to protect her.

Walking down the hallway, Owen found himself stopping outside Evie's door. He raised a hand to knock on her door; he just wanted to check she had returned to her room. It wasn't true though, he wanted to check that she was okay, she had looked shaken up when he came outside after discovering Zane and Evie out the front of the house.

Letting out a sigh, Owen dropped his hand and moved on to his own bedroom, shutting himself inside.

Midmorning the next day Evie paced back and forth in her room, stopping every now and then to gaze out her front window. She felt trapped and anxious but at the same time didn't feel safe leaving the house. It was a flurry of emotions in the pit of her stomach.

With every passing car, Evie would watch carefully. She had stayed too long. She knew that. Her new family were at the highest risk of being hurt or killed and she couldn't bear the thought.

Thoughts and plans on how to run away once again without Sandra catching her crossed her mind. She knew the first thing she would need to do is leave the state. While she stayed in the same state as the Taylors, Sandra had a chance of finding her in the system and bringing her home again.

Evie let out a sigh, tormented by her inner turmoil.

A knock at the door pulled Evie from her thoughts, "Who is it?" Evie asked, turning away from the window and looking at the door.

The door creaked open slowly and Kelly's head popped in, "Just me."

Evie smiled weakly at Kelly. Kelly had been so welcoming and helpful in Evie's short stay, yet Evie had rarely spoken more than a couple of words at a time to her. She felt guilty inside.

"My friend, Melissa is over and we're about to go out back for a swim in the pool and sunbaking. Want to join us?" Kelly offered, still standing only halfway in the room.

"I'm fine thanks," Evie refused kindly.

"It's a lovely day," Kelly pushed on, "It would be a shame to waste it inside. I can lend you some swimmers again."

Evie studied Kelly's pleading face. There was something more going on, but she couldn't figure out what.

"I don't feel like swimming or sunbaking."

Kelly didn't say anything else, but sent Evie a pleading look, Evie nodded, finally agreeing.

"I'll come down and study in the gazebo while you sunbake and swim," Evie suggested, grabbing her Modern History textbook from her bag and following Kelly out the door and downstairs.

While Kelly and Melissa set up their towels on the grass in the sun and set to baking their already tan bodies in the sun, Evie positioned herself on one of the two lounge chairs under the gazebo in the shade. The shrubs and bushes around the sides and back of the gazebo meant Evie's only view was of the crystal blue twinkling water of the pool and the small, grassed area where the girls were sunbaking.

After thirty minutes in the sun, Kelly and Melissa decided to sit on the edge of the pool and dangle their legs in the water while gossiping about the boys in their classes. Evie lay back on the lounge, her text book leaning on her bent knees and open on World War Two.

Listening to the giggles of the teenaged girls by the water's edge, Evie smiled slightly at the normalcy of the situation, reminding her of a simpler time in her life. Reminding her of her best friend, Casey. How the two of them would gossip about the boys they liked and hatch plans on how they could start conversations with them. Casey's idea was for them to take their watches off and ask their crush for the time. It never worked though because they could never get up the confidence to ask such a simple question.

The sound of the house's side gate latch opening brought Evie out of her thoughts, followed by the laughter of what sounded like a few teenaged boys laughing. Evie's heart stilled and her breath hitched in her throat at the sound of the intruders. She knew it was likely Owen and Zane, but she could tell by the amount of voices it was more than just the two of them. The bushes around the gazebo hid her from view.

Owen unlatched the gate and opened it for his friends, leading them into his backyard. They had been out playing football with a group of friends from school, when they had decided to cool off with a swim in Owen's backyard pool.

Zane walked through the gate first, laughing at something Mark had said who followed him. Four other friends Lucas, Jensen, Tyler and Xander followed after. Owen brought up the rear, closing the gate behind him. Jensen was attempting to re-enact a pass he had made during the game when Lucas stuck out a foot, tripping him over which to they all laughed.

Walking towards the pool, which Owen saw occupied by his younger sister and her best friend, Melissa. They sat on the edge of the pool, wearing skimpy bikinis, dangling their legs in the water as they talked to one another. The bikinis were a little to revealing for Owen's liking, especially on his own sister. The protective big brother in him wanted to wrap her up in layers of clothes away from any male's eyes.

"Wow," Xander exclaimed, looking in the same direction as Owen, "Check out the talent by the pool."

Owen whacked Xander in the shoulder as warning, giving him a glare as Xander rubbed his shoulder.

"That's my little sister," Owen warned, he also felt protective of Melissa, whom he had watched grow from a little girl too and was like another sister to him.

"Can't blame the guy," Lucas agreed, admiring the scene, "He's got eyes."

"Well, if he wants to keep them, he'll watch himself," Owen stated firmly.

Owen didn't bring his larger group of friends home often, so the last time they saw Kelly she would have been younger and to no interest of them. Now though, she had grown up she was starting to attract the opposite sex, Owen knew his job as the older brother was about to get tougher.

The group of teenaged boys entered the pool area and the girls' eyes looked up and smiled at the sight. Owen rolled his eyes at the notion, knowing too well he was going to be spending his time keeping the two groups apart.

Owen moved past the group heading to the opposite end of the pool, where the gazebo was. It was then he saw Evie, sitting up straight on one of the lounges, watching Owen's group of friends with unease. He noticed Evie was fully clothed, unlike his sister, wearing a shirt and some denim shorts. On her lap was her history textbook, closed.

When Evie noticed Owen looking at her intently, Evie suddenly felt very unsure of herself and the situation. Zane walked up behind him, with a smile at seeing Evie was there. Evie realised the boys were obviously still on friendly terms, but she didn't want to be there any longer than she needed, especially with the larger group which made her feel uncomfortable.

Standing up, Evie moved to leave the pool area. Not looking Owen in the eye, she quickly moved past him and Zane, heading towards the pool gate.

"Excuse me," Evie whispered as she went past them, having to step closer towards the pool.

"Watch out!" Mark yelled out, but it was too late.

Jensen couldn't stop himself from running into Evie, who was suddenly in his path. Lucas had knocked into him as they were joking around, which created a domino effect. Jensen tried to stop himself when Evie walked in front of him, but it was too late. He collided with her, knocking both of them into the pool.

Evie's eyes were wide in shock as she fell backwards into the pool. She noticed Owen step quickly towards her with Zane, Owen's hands reached out to grab Evie, but she was out of reach.

The water enveloped Evie and she was very aware of Jensen in the water beside her. Turning her body, she kicked around to right herself and got her head above the water. Jensen stood beside her, a sheepish apologetic look on his face.

"Are you alright?" Jensen asked in honest concern, "I'm so sorry. It was Lucas' fault for pushing me." Jensen shot Lucas a dirty look.

"I didn't expect you to tackle the girl and take her down with you," Lucas shot back in defence.

"Evie, are you okay?" came Zane's concerned voice, as he leaned down at the pool's edge.

"My text book," Evie murmured, looking around for it.

"Yeah, it drowned," Jensen held it up from the water.

Evie shook her head in disbelief, how was she going to study for her upcoming test now?

Pushing through the water, Evie moved to the edge of the pool to climb out. As she rested her hands on the edge of the pool, a hand reached out for hers from above. Looking up to the owner, Evie saw an anxious Owen waiting for her to accept his waiting hand. Wanting out of the entire situation as quickly as possible, Evie took his hand and Owen helped pull Evie out of the pool.

"Thanks," Evie muttered, looking at Owen, whose eyes were looking down at her body and wide in surprise.

Evie looked down, noticing her shirt had come up slightly over her stomach, revealing her scarred stomach. She quickly pulled her shirt back down, before anyone else could see and gave Owen a pleading look to keep quiet. Sandra was the only other person who had seen it, but now Owen had too which gave her a very unsettled feeling.

Anxiety started to take over Evie's body, she could feel her heart quicken and the fog taking over. Not wanting to explain to Owen, especially while they had a crowd of people watching them, Evie pushed passed Owen and dashed towards the gate, leaving the pool area with many confused faces.

"Good on you guys," Kelly told off the group of boys, arms crossed over her chest, "I had managed to convince her out of the house and you come in and ruin it."

Zane turned to Owen, who was still watching the back door to the house where Evie had disappeared. Owen's mind was lost in thought, how and why did Evie have such a large scar on her stomach? He knew she was keeping something from them, now more than ever he wanted to know what it was.

"Want me to go check she's okay?" Zane offered.

Owen frowned at his friend's proposal, pushing away the reasoning to why he didn't like what Zane was suggesting, he couldn't be jealous over a stupid runaway girl.

"No," Owen replied, "Just leave her alone."

Chapter 20

After having dried herself off in the bathroom, Evie changed into some dry clothes and stowed her wet ones in the wash basket. Coming out of the bathroom, she ran into Zane, causing her to jump in surprise.

"Hey," Zane greeted her happy he had found her. "You okay after your swim?"

Evie smiled at Zane poor attempt at humour, but he achieved his goal with her smiling at him.

"Safe to say I won't be joining the Olympics Swimming Team any time soon," Evie replied, stepping around Zane and heading back to her room.

"Evie," Zane called after her.

Evie turned in her doorway to look at him. Zane was unsure of himself, unsure what to say to Evie. He didn't want her to become withdrawn around him again, he had just managed to get her out of her shell again.

"About last night," Zane started.

"Forget about it," Evie smiled reassuringly at him.

Not wanting to discuss it any further, Evie gave Zane a small wave goodbye, before disappearing into her room and closing the door.

Sitting down on the edge of her bed, Evie noticed the mobile phone Sandra had given her. She had played with an idea but talked herself out of it every time, scared and unsure if she wanted to know the answer.

Over the previous six weeks, while hauled up in her room or alone at lunch times, Evie had wondered if maybe she was still running for no reason. Maybe it had all been pointless. Evie had never thought before to search for her past, she had just assumed the worst.

Biting her bottom lip, Evie suddenly decided to go for it. She snatched up her phone and opened the internet browser. Holding her breath, she Googled a name she wishes she could forget. News articles popped up, going all the way back to the beginning. The headlines of each article taunted Evie with her past and her heartbreak. Tears began to swell in Evie's eyes reading the words that had shaped her life.

Quickly, Evie closed her phone off and threw it to the opposite end of her bed, as if it had given her an electric shock. Glaring at the phone through tears, Evie closed her eyes and took slow, deep breaths in an attempt to calm her.

Minutes passed and Evie opened her eyes slowly, wearily. There was her phone, still face up on her bed with a black screen. Taking another deep breath to give her courage, Evie reached out slowly and collected her phone once more. With another deep breath, she opened the internet browser once more.

Not wanting to be overwhelmed once more, Evie flicked swiftly through the headlines and found nothing. One headline caught her attention though. Unable to help herself, Evie opened the article and skimmed through.

Evie's shoulders slumped. It was all speculation. No one knew the truth. Only her.

Closing her phone once more, Evie ran her fingers through her hair in frustration. She was helpless. In her mind, she did the right thing running. The police stated they had no leads. There was no escaping except for running.

Looking out the bedroom window from where she sat on her bed, Evie thought about how she had been in the same place for six weeks at that point. Once she had decided to run, she had never stayed anywhere longer than twenty-four hours. Yet, here she was, safe; or so she thought. Evie holed up in her room. It was as if she was giving herself away.

Evie stood up with determination. If she was going to be in the Taylor's house, she needed to be prepared. Evie knew she couldn't just sit around waiting. She needed to be fit.

Evie grabbed some sneakers and put them on and quickly texted Sandra to let her know she was going out for a run. Flipping her phone back onto her bed, Evie skipped down the stairs and out the front door.

It had been awhile since Evie had last worked out and she soon discovered how unfit she had become sitting around for six weeks. She panted tirelessly but pushed herself to keep going. A stitch began to develop on her right side and forced her to stop, taking slow deep breaths in a bid to get rid of the pain.

Continuing to pace along the footpath, Evie found herself at a familiar park. She soon recognised it as the one she had run off to after her first day of school and getting into an argument with Sandra. That meant Evie had done a circuit and was nearly back at the house. Not wanting to return so soon, Evie wandered over to the swing, and like the last time, sat down and allowed herself to sway gently back and forth.

Zane emerged from the house after going inside to use the toilet, but Owen knew he just wanted to check on Evie. A sense of jealousy washed over Owen, but he ignored it and returned to his other friends that were swimming in the pool.

Zane stopped and talked with Mark for a couple of minutes before he approached Owen and stood by him at the side of the pool, neither one of them looking at each other, just at the others in the pool. Owen's arms crossed over his chest as he made sure his friends kept their distance from his younger sister and her friend.

"How is she?" Owen asked, still not looking at Zane.

Zane looked at Owen, surprised by his question. He realised Owen would have seen through his lame excuse to use the toilet, but Zane had to check up on Evie, even if Owen wouldn't.

"She seemed ok."

Owen nodded in response.

"Man, when are you going to admit you care about Evie?" Zane demanded.

"I don't," Owen replied, turning to scowl at Zane.

Over Zane's shoulder, Owen noticed a flash of someone running through the house. Frowning, he moved past Zane and out of the pool fence, watching the house the entire time for more movement. The sound of the front door closing, made him stop for a second in surprise. Jogging over to the side gate of the house, Owen saw the moment as Evie ran off down the street.

"What is it?" Zane asked, running up behind Owen, but when he looked over the fence, he saw nothing.

"Stay here," Owen ordered, "Make sure those guys keep their hands to themselves."

Without another word, Owen opened the gate and headed off in a jog down the street to look for Evie, afraid she was attempting to run away again.

As he jogged, Owen wondered why he cared if Evie ran away. He tried to reason with himself that if Evie left, his life could go back to normal. No more running around worrying about her, no more giving up his social or school life to look after her. His life could get back on track. Yet here he was, running after her to bring her home.

Owen was nearing his house again after going around the block. He slowed to a walk, had all but given up when he saw a figure sitting on the swing in the playground. It was Evie. He wondered what she was doing as he wandered over to her.

"Evie?" Owen spoke gently, not wanting to frighten her off.

Evie's head looked up, startled but when she saw Owen, a small smile crossed over her lips.

"Owen? What are you doing here?" Evie asked, looking behind him expecting to see Zane or any of his friends with him.

"I came looking for you," he replied, stopping to stand in front of her, grabbing hold of the swing's chains and stopping her from swaying. "Why were you running away?"

Evie baulked at his notion of her running, although agreed it was a fair assumption on his part.

"I wasn't running away," Evie shook her head, looking up at Owen, "I was just going for a run, to exercise, well, tried to. I realised how unfit I was instead."

Owen cocked his head to the side, trying to understand what Evie was saying then smirked a little. Letting go of the chains, Owen moved out from in front of Evie and sat on the swing beside her.

"What's with the sudden decision to go running? Getting ready to make your escape?" Owen joked, but upon seeing Evie's face regretted what he said.

Evie considered Owen's words, looking away from his eye contact and down at the ground.

"I'm sorry, I didn't mean..." Owen let his voice trail off.

Silence fell over the pair.

"Are you okay?" Owen finally spoke, Evie gazed up at him. "After the whole pool dunking incident thing, I mean? You know Jensen didn't mean to run into you."

Evie smiled. She could see that deep-down Owen cared for her, worried about her, but he tried so hard to fight it. The thought touched Evie, but scared her too. She couldn't afford for another person to care for her, it was too dangerous. As quickly as her smile appeared, it went away. Evie stared down at her feet again.

"I know," she mumbled, "They were just being teenagers, having fun and mucking around with their friends."

"You can do that too you know," Owen suggested, allowing himself to swing back and forth slightly on his seat.

Evie frowned in confusion at Owen's words, looking at him sideways.

"Be a teenager," Owen continued, "Zane mentioned you had fun at the movies last night. You have a chance to be one while living with us, what else do you have to worry about?"

Owen waited for Evie to react. He had seen the scar; he knew there was more to her story. Maybe he could find out from Evie.

"How about being unable to study for our upcoming Modern History test since my textbook drowned?" Evie replied, seeing through Owen's attempt to get her to open up to him. That wasn't an option.

"Right," Owen breathed, "Well, you can always borrow mine or we could study together."

As soon as he said it, Owen surprised even himself. His brow creased in thought, he cleared his throat as he thought of something else to say.

"Owen, what are you doing?" Evie asked softly.

"What?" Owen stared at Evie in wonderment.

"Why are you being nice to me?"

"I just thought..."

Before Owen could reply, which in one way he was grateful, as he didn't know what he was going to actually say to Evie, a car horn beeped incessantly to gain their attention. A car full of teenaged boys, the ones Evie recognised at Owen's friends drove past. Yelling and cheering from the windows, before speeding off down the street.

Evie jumped slightly at the sudden blast of the horn, snapping her head to face the road. Her eyes wide and heart racing, which slowed to a normal rate when she realised there was no danger.

Owen watched as the car disappeared down the road then looked back at Evie. He realised in that moment that at some point in their conversation, he had moved in closer to Evie and at the same time pulled her swing slightly towards him. They were mere inches from one another.

Evie's eyes raised slowly to meet Owen's blue ones. Her heart began to speed up at the intensity of Owen's eyes fixed on hers. She tried to swallow the lump in her throat.

Owen's eye studied Evie's. What was she hiding from him? How did she get that scar on her stomach? Why was she so intriguing to him? For six weeks, he had struggled internally with himself; pushed down feelings that tried to surface. He had kept his distance, and thankfully, she had kept hers, but when he had found her standing on his front step the previous night with his best friend, he had to fight back feelings of jealousy.

"Owen?"

Evie's soft voice broke Owen from his thoughts. Blinking, he let go of her swing and allowed his own to sway back away from her.

"We better get home," Owen stated standing up and holding a hand out to Evie.

Evie looked at his awaiting hand and wondered once more, what Owen's motive was.

Not taking his hand, Evie stood and started walking back towards the Taylor's house, Owen right behind her.

Chapter 21

The next day at school, as Evie wandered into her Modern History class, the final lesson of the day, she walked straight up to the teacher's desk. Owen's eyes watched her from his desk in the middle of the room, but Evie ignored him. After their conversation in the park, Evie had become confused towards Owen. More than ever, she needed to keep her distance.

"Mr Mason?" Evie addressed the teacher.

Mr Mason, who was sitting at his desk checking his emails on his laptop, looked up to see Evie standing awkwardly before him.

"Yes?" he mumbled, trying to rack his brain for the name of the new student.

Even though she had been there for a couple of weeks, she remained quiet in class and he was yet to remember her name. He recalled she was a relation to Owen Taylor in some way, or was she staying with the family? Something had been mentioned at a staff meeting, but Mr Mason admittedly wasn't paying attention at the time, more focussed on getting home to mark the junior classes' assessments.

"Um, I was wondering if there was a spare textbook I could borrow?" Evie asked timidly, placing her dried out but water damaged textbook that had met its end in the pool. "Mine accidently got wet."

Mr Mason took the book and studied the pages. Some were stuck together, others crinkled and mostly unreadable all together. Not thinking about it, he threw it into the bin next to his desk.

"Unfortunately, that was the spare," Mr Mason informed her, "You will have to ask someone to study with you, perhaps Mr Taylor."

Mr Mason nodded his head in Owen's direction, who looked up from his book at the mention of his name. Evie's shoulders slumped in despair.

"I'm sure the two of you can work something out," Mr Mason said, before essentially cutting off the conversation by turning back to his emails.

Evie let out a sigh, wandered to the back-corner desk and sat down, pulling out her notebook. She flipped through the pages of her notes, wondering if she could get by on those alone, still wondering why she was so worried about good grades when she would be gone in a few weeks anyway.

The screeching sounds of a table pulled across the floor snapped Evie to attention. Owen moved the table close to Evie's, and sat down in it. Without a word, he placed his textbook on the table between them and opened it to the page they were looking at that lesson.

Evie glanced up at Owen, unsure of what to say but grateful for him once again rescuing her even though she refused to ask for his help. Behind him, across the room in the back row was Harley, watching on with interest. Evie blushed. As far as everyone in the school was concerned, Evie and Owen were cousins.

The class dragged on, Evie felt herself holding her breath and peeking glances at Owen beside her. He never once looked her way, focusing on what the teacher was lecturing, taking notes and reading from the book.

When the bell rang, signalling the end of the day, the students all began to collect their things. Owen felt his phone vibrate in his pocket, pulled it out to glance at the text and grunted slightly in response.

"I need to swing by my locker to get something for Zack," Owen spoke, looking at Evie for the first time. "Meet you at the car."

Not waiting for a response, he grabbed his notebook and textbook, pushed his table back to its original spot and stalked out of the classroom.

Evie took a deep breath, finally feeling at ease once Owen had left the room.

"Evie?" a quiet voice asked cautiously from behind Evie as she began to leave the room.

Evie turned around and came face to face with Harley. The two hadn't spoken in weeks. Evie had avoided Harley and her friends since the Lake Party. Harley had persisted for the first week but then gave up, letting Evie be.

"Hey, how are things?" Harley queried, testing the water.

Evie eyed Harley, wondering why she was suddenly speaking to her again.

"Good," Evie answered.

Evie continued to walk down the hall and Harley followed alongside her.

"I know it's been awhile since we spoke last but I want you to know I'm here if you ever need a friend," Harley offered. "I noticed you don't have a textbook anymore and I'm happy to share mine, we could study together even."

The entire reason Evie had avoided Harley was to keep her safe from any harm. Before that, Evie had agreed to tutor Harley in Maths but then reneged on her offer wanting to keep Harley at a distance.

"Owen's lending me his," Evie replied.

It wasn't a lie, Owen had suggested they study together, but Evie had never accepted. Harley didn't need to know that though.

The two girls walked in silence for a few minutes, passing the many teenagers in the hall trying to get out of school eagerly.

"Um, so I was wondering," Harley started, breaking the silence, "Owen's party..."

Evie immediately stopped in her tracks, confused.

"Party?"

Harley's brow furrowed slightly at Evie's bewilderment.

"His birthday party in two weeks," Harley explained, "The party every senior is talking about."

Evie's face paled as the blood drained from her face. The thought of another party made her feel ill.

The fact she knew nothing about the upcoming event surprised her too. Sandra hadn't mentioned anything, but then again, Evie had been locking herself away in her room. She didn't even know it was Owen's birthday soon.

Trying not to give the fact that his supposed 'cousin', who lived with him, knew nothing of the occasion, Evie lied and began to walk in the direction of the carpark again.

"Oh, that party. I didn't realise it was public knowledge."

"Everyone's been invited," Harley commented, continuing to follow her.

Evie just shrugged in response.

"Well, anyway," Harley went on, not seeming to notice Evie's apprehension. "I was hoping to make a bit of a statement, you know, dress to impress. I would really love to get Owen's attention. What do you suggest?"

Evie frowned slightly at the thought of Harley and Owen together making her jealous, but it subsided when she remembered Owen's lack of interest in Harley. Owen showed more annoyance than tolerance where Harley was concerned.

"I don't know."

"Come on," Harley insisted, "You're his cousin. You live with him. You must have some idea."

"We don't really have that kind of a relationship," Evie replied honestly.

The pair reached the front of the school, the car park in view. Evie noticed that Zane was leaning against Owen's car, but Owen was nowhere.

They stopped on the front stairs and Evie turned to face Harley.

"What are you wearing?" Harley asked, genuinely interested.

"I'm not going to go," Evie replied.

Up until five minutes earlier, Evie hadn't even known about the party. Yet even knowing about it didn't change the fact that she didn't think it would be a good idea.

"What do you mean you're not going?" Harley was alarmed. "It's going to be the biggest party of the year!"

"You said something similar about the lake party," Evie moaned at the memory of the lake.

"And I also promised you to make sure you didn't do anything that would cause you social suicide."

"I don't care what people think."

Evie looked down at the ground. Part of her wished that she could be a normal teenager again; going to parties, flirting with boys, but that wasn't her reality anymore. It wasn't an option.

"I've got to go," Evie mumbled quietly, wanting to end the conversation and skipped down the stairs and hurried towards Owen's car.

Zane smiled as he greeted Evie with a wave, but Evie kept her head down and stood to the back of the car, not wanting to converse with anyone at that point.

Zane glanced back at the steps and saw Harley watching them briefly, before turning on her heel and heading off in the other direction.

"What did she want?" Zane asked, poking a thumb in Harley's direction as she disappeared.

"Nothing," Evie muttered, not making eye contact.

It was clear that Evie was just getting in the way of everyone's lives. She had known nothing of Owen's party, now she had to depend on him to study for history, which didn't matter in the long term anyway, because school wasn't important. In six weeks, she would be gone, everything she had worked for in school all this time would mean nothing on the streets, running for her life again.

"I find that hard to believe," Zane laughed, trying to get Evie to loosen up. "Hey, what's up? You can tell me."

Silence fell over them in the car park, and for a brief moment Evie felt like opening up the can of worms called her emotions she held down deep inside.

"Sorry I took so long," Owen's voice startled Evie, stopping her from saying anything. "Ran into Mark and got talking."

As Owen unlocked the car, Evie dove into the back seat, avoiding answering Zane's questioning. She knew he wouldn't ask with Owen there, she was grateful for that.

Owen pulled the car out of the student car park and they drove home. It seemed like a ritual that most days Zane would accompany Owen back to his house to study, before going back to his own home.

Evie found it comforting in a strange way, having Zane there. She may have felt awkward being alone with Owen and she was always unsure how to act or what to say around him. He reminded her so much of her past and his mood swings kept giving her whiplash.

While the boys sat in the front and discussed various topics that had absolutely no interest to Evie, she started to wonder what the point of it all was.

Evie had grown comfortable living with the Taylor's; too comfortable for her liking. She knew she needed to get fitter if she ever needed to fight off an attack. It was as though she was of two minds about her situation. Does she risk sticking around and being discovered, because she stayed or maybe she's safer, because it wouldn't be expected of her to stay in the one place? Would she be safer on the run? Just as she had been before being pulled into this life as Evie? Would everyone around her, especially the Taylor's be safer with her gone?

Anxiety began to fill Evie's veins and her heart rate quickened. Pulling out the mobile phone Sandra had given her; Evie quietly sat in the back of the car and started to search the internet once more for any new information. A quick search brought up no new results. She bit the inside of her cheek as she searched her old name, her real name. There was nothing different there either.

Evie was still at a crossroads of what to do, but her anxiety calmed ever so slightly at the idea that no news was good news. Maybe everything would be okay. There would be no way to track where she was if there wasn't a single lead she could find. Then it hit her like a tonne of bricks and anxiety began building once more inside of her.

Creating a new search, Evie typed in what she feared might be her undoing. She clicked on the first result and there staring Evie in the face was a clear picture of herself. She was smiling, looked like she was a normal teenager; nobody would think anything of it normally. Evie's fingers trembled as she realised that even though it was a photo of her with different coloured hair and a different name, there was still every chance for her to be recognised.

All Evie had typed in was her new name: Evie Taylor. The first result was a student run blog for the school. That particular blog story was about the Lake Party and how even Owen Taylor's cousin, who was a new student to the school had enjoyed the event. Of course, being associated with Owen would get her noticed, as Harley had so happily pointed out many times, he was one of the most popular guys in school.

Alarm gripped at Evie's throat like a bow tie pulled too tight. In that moment, all she wanted to do was run, but Evie knew she had to be smart about it, otherwise Sandra would just find her again. If that happened, Evie would be wearing the ankle-monitor once more and stuck living with the Taylors until graduation, which was not an option for Evie.

Owen pulled the car into the driveway and Evie tried her hardest to act as normal as possible and head inside. She needed to get to her room and plan her escape. She needed to figure out how to keep the Taylors, a family who she had come to care about like her own, safe.

Chapter 22

Evie locked herself in her bedroom, threw her backpack into the corner and sat on the bed with her phone clasped in her hand. Taking a deep breath in an attempt to settle her nerves, Evie opened the search browser once more, looking at the school blog page where she had found the photo of herself as Evie Taylor, Owen's cousin.

With a quick glance over the page, Evie noticed through the various photos from the blog that people were able to comment on the photos. There was a photo of Owen with Zane and some of their other friends; students, mainly girls, had been commenting on how hot the boys were or who they would date.

Scrolling back to the picture that featured herself and Evie studied it carefully. She was dancing with Harley, Paige and Rebecca; looking like any typical teenager. Evie looked at the comments for the photo. The comments were from students, commenting on if they had a class with one of the girls, very normal given the circumstances, Evie thought.

Sighing with some relief, Evie closed her phone off as a knock came at her door.

"Come in," Evie called and the door opened slowly.

Owen's head poked in hesitantly, when he saw Evie sitting on her bed watching him, he entered stopping a few feet from Evie. In his hand, he held his Modern History textbook, Owen now feeling unsure of himself.

Evie waited quietly for Owen to speak first, wringing her hands in her lap nervously.

"Uh," Owen tried to remember why he had even come up to Evie's room. His clasp tightened uneasily on his textbook, drawing his eyes down to his hand, he held it out to Evie. "I thought you might want to borrow this to study."

Evie reached out and took the proffered book. She held it on her lap and her eyes grazed the cover before trailing back up to look at Owen.

"Thank you," Evie whispered, feeling the awkwardness between them filling the room like heavy smoke.

Owen lingered, not making any move to go. He wanted to ask Evie how she was but didn't want to overstep any of her boundaries. How did Zane manage to talk with Evie about her emotions so easily? Owen wondered if he should have just sent Zane up how he had offered to do.

"Was there something else?" Evie found her voice, feeling restless having Owen standing in her room, towering over her, watching her.

Owen cleared his throat before talking, "I was wondering how everything is, you know, with you?"

Evie eyed him suspiciously, wondering what Owen's angle was.

"You seemed upset when we came home and, in the car, you looked stressed out."

Owen shuffled on his feet, waiting for Evie's response.

Evie's eyes flittered down to where her phone lay on her bed, taking a deep breath to keep her nerves intact and not to show Owen any of her fear. It surprised her that Owen had even noticed her mood in the car.

"I'm fine," Evie lied quietly, avoiding eye contact with Owen, fiddling with the corner of the textbook he had given her.

"Are you sure? Because the last thing I would want is for you to have one of your, you know, attacks."

Evie's brow furrowed at Owen's suggestion, still acting as though the corner of the book was the most interesting thing to her in that moment.

Silence ensued.

Owen looked around the room for any clue of Evie being upset. He noticed her backpack dumped on the floor, not on the chair in the corner like usual. He sighed, trying to convince himself that he didn't care about her, but that niggling feeling that he did attempted to claw its way out once more.

"So, I hear your birthday is coming up," Evie suddenly announced out of nowhere, springing Owen's eyes back to hers.

Shocked herself that she brought it up, but Evie wanted to redirect the conversation from her current state of emotion and it was the first thing that came to her mind.

Their eyes met across the room, Owen's studying Evie, wondering how she knew. Maybe his mum had said something to her, although unlikely as Evie had been keeping to herself for the past few weeks.

"Did Zane say something?" Owen inquired.

"No," Evie replied. Not wanting to bring Harley up knowing how Owen felt about her she lied, "The school is buzzing about your upcoming party."

Owen rolled his eyes. His birthday beach bash had blown out of proportion by the entire senior student body. Originally, it was for Owen and his group of friends, but then Mark invited Danielle, the girl he is currently seeing. Danielle didn't want to come alone, so invited her best friend Vanessa to keep her company. Vanessa didn't want to play third wheel to Mark and Danielle, so decided to invite their two other friends Kasey and Sharon. It just exploded from there.

"It's not that big of a deal," Owen palmed it off then a thought struck him. Before he could overthink things, he said, "Did you want to come?"

"Excuse me?" Evie stunned by his invitation.

"Uh, my party, you're welcome to come if you would like," Owen mumbled.

Evie furrowed her brow and looked away from Owen's gaze. The phone lay taunting her on the bed, a reminder of how easily she could lose everything once more. Owen's birthday party was too big of a risk to her and to Owen and his loved ones.

"I don't think it's a good idea," Evie murmured, so softly Owen barely heard her.

Owen shrugged nonchalantly and tried his best to tell himself it made no difference to him, he was only asking as a courtesy.

"The offers there," Owen replied and silently left the room, closing the door behind him.

Owen headed back downstairs to where Zane waited. It seemed he had abandoned the table with their books and retreated to the couch in front of the television. Owen sat down beside him and put his feet up on the coffee table in front of them.

"How is she?" Zane asked, taking a handful of buttery popcorn from the bowl in his lap. "Did she say anything?"

"She heard about my party," Owen mentioned, his eyes on the television but not really watching what was on.

"That must have been what they were talking about."

Zane popped another kernel of popcorn in his mouth.

With a raised eyebrow, Owen turned his eyes on his best friend, "Who?"

"I saw Evie talking with Harley after school," Zane explained, "Afterwards Evie seemed upset. Guess she was upset about not knowing about the party. Not being invited."

"I just invited her then and she refused."

"Did you invite her or ask her to come?" Zane enquired, grabbing more popcorn and filling his mouth.

"What's the difference?" Owen asked, confused.

Zane shook his head at his friend's denseness.

"One is a passing invite like everyone gets and the other is saying you would like her to come."

Owen baulked at Zane's explanation.

"I don't care if she comes or not," Owen stated matter-of-factly with a shrug.

"Sure, you don't," Zane laughed, "I'm getting something to drink. You want something?"

Zane stood up, passing the half-empty bowl of popcorn to Owen, who shook his head in response as Zane walked to the kitchen.

Owen wondered if Zane was right, that he did want Evie to come to his party. It was a ridiculous thought; Evie was just some random girl his mother had brought home to stay with them while she was on house arrest from getting into trouble with the police one time too many, just another delinquent like all the rest.

Letting out a sigh, Owen ate some popcorn. He knew he was kidding himself. Evie wasn't like the rest of them and the fact he cared scared him.

The following morning, Evie descended the stairs and found the kitchen empty, the usual family breakfast non-existent. Evie looked around the room, hoping to find a clue of where everyone was.

"It's just us," came a deep voice from behind her on the stairs.

Evie jumped as she turned, a small squeal escaping her lips.

There was Owen dressed and ready for school. He held his hands up in surrender, an apologetic look on his face.

"Sorry, it's just me. Didn't mean to scare you."

Owen stepped down from the bottom stair and stood in front of Evie.

"You okay?" Owen asked concerned. "You look like you've seen a ghost."

Evie blinked a couple of times to pull herself out of the trance. Her heart was racing from the sudden appearance of Owen behind her. She mentally talked her anxiety down, telling herself she was safe with Owen.

"Uh, I – uh," Evie stumbled on her words.

Owen stepped forward, realising Evie was in a state of shock, why, he could not understand. Worried she might be on the brink of an anxiety attack, Owen took her by the arm and led her over to the kitchen table and assisted her in taking a seat. He rushed to the sink and took a clean glass, filling it to the top. In a few short steps, Owen was back at Evie's side, handing her the glass, encouraging her to drink.

Evie took a sip from the glass, watching Owen carefully. He looked genuinely concerned about her. Feeling calmer after a few more deep breaths, she placed the glass down on the table.

"I'm sorry," Evie murmured softly.

Owen sat down on the chair next to her, studying her to check she was okay.

"Should we skip school today?" Owen asked gently, pulling his phone from his pocket. "I can message my mum and let her know what's happening."

"No, don't do that," Evie said in panic, reaching out to Owen, touching his hand so he would not send a text message.

Owen's eyes moved to her hand touching him, the feeling of her skin against his warmed him more than he wanted to think.

Evie retracted her hand quickly, realising her action.

"Sorry."

"Stop apologising," Owen instructed her, his fingers caressed her cheek, he couldn't help himself.

Colour filled Evie's cheeks at Owen's touch. Her eyes met his. Evie could feel her heart starting to pound once more, but this time for a very different reason. She felt confused. Evie wanted to run but at the same time, she didn't want to break Owen's contact with her.

Owen looked over Evie's face. What was he doing? A part of him wanted to lean in and kiss her soft lips, but he held back, telling himself he wasn't thinking straight. He dropped his hand from her face and cleared his thought, trying to figure out what to say to Evie.

A shrill ringing came from Owen's phone. He looked at the screen and saw Zane's name on the screen. Owen cleared his throat and sat back in the chair to answer the call.

"What's up Zane?"

Evie bit the inside of her lip and looked away, collecting her backpack from the ground. She indicated to Owen she would wait outside for him at his car. Not looking back, she disappeared out the front door.

Chapter 23

The end of the week rolled in and Evie was grateful to enjoy a relaxing Friday night without the concept of having to go to school the next day. It had been a long week and Evie had tried her hardest to continue keeping to herself.

Harley had managed to weasel her way back into Evie's good graces, but Evie continued to keep her at arms' length where she could.

She spent her lunch times outside on her own away from the noise of the cafeteria. Through the windows, Evie could see Owen and Zane with their large group of friends laughing and enjoying their breaks. Every now and then Evie would feel eyes on her, and when she would look up she would find Owen's curious eyes on her. Their eyes would meet briefly before he would allow himself be distracted by those around him.

Evie sat on her bed looking over her Maths notes from the week. Next week was full of exams and Evie's old self returned, wanting to make sure she did well, even if it would mean nothing when she left again.

Numbers and symbols were swirling around in her head by half past nine and so Evie slammed her notebook and textbook shut. As she went to store them in the bag she used for school, Evie noticed Owen's Modern History textbook in her bag. She had had it all week, studying most nights with it. In class, Owen would sit beside her but never once did he ask for it back. Guilt flowed over Evie that she hadn't returned it to him yet with the exam looming.

With the borrowed textbook clutched tightly to her chest, Evie walked out into the hallway to return it to Owen. As soon as she stepped out of her room, she could hear music blasting in Owen's closed room down the hall. She wandered slowly to his room and paused in front of the closed door. Suddenly feeling unsure of herself.

Taking a deep breath, she quickly rapped her knuckles gently on the door, but loud enough so Owen would be able to hear it over his music.

"What?" Came an annoyed shout from inside.

Evie bit her bottom lip nervously, now feeling like she had overstepped some imaginary line. Every part of her told her to leave quickly and return to her room, but as the book dug into her tightly clenched hand, Evie reminded herself it was important that she return it to Owen.

"Uh, it's, um," Evie stammered, "It's Evie."

Owen didn't respond. Instead, almost instantly, the music was turned right down, and Owen opened the door, a remorseful look across his face.

"Sorry," Owen apologised gently, "I thought you were Kelly coming to bug me. She's been pestering me to borrow money all afternoon."

Owen's bedroom door was slightly ajar. Evie couldn't see inside but it made her realise how she had never seen inside his bedroom before and her curiosity spiked at the thought. Owen leaned casually on the doorframe, Evie still standing in the doorway clutching the Modern History textbook to her chest as though it would protect her in some way.

"I just wanted to return your textbook." Evie held out the book to Owen and he took it from her. "I'm sorry I've had it for so long."

Owen shrugged at her apology.

"No big deal. If you still need it..."

"Please, if I read anymore I think I will start to think there are Nazi soldiers coming to get me," Evie laughed then frowned as she realised how poor taste her own attempt at a joke was. There was someone coming to get her, maybe not Nazis but an evil dictator all the same.

"Plus, the exam is on Tuesday. You should really study yourself."

"Yeah, I guess," Owen nodded looking down at the book in his hand.

"Uh, well, goodnight," Evie spoke softly and turned to return to her own room.

"Evie, wait," Owen called after her.

Evie turned on her heel and faced Owen, who had stepped forward closing the distance between them.

Owen opened his mouth to talk and then shut it just as quickly when he heard voices coming up the stairs. He knew immediately they belonged to Kelly and her friend Melissa. Without thinking, Owen reached out and took Evie's hand, pulling her into his room with him and shutting the door behind them.

Evie startled by the suddenness of Owen whisking her into his room. She felt nervous for some strange reason, being in his room, but also a sense of curiosity to snoop around and find out more about what makes Owen tick.

On his walls were posters of cars, bands and one of a scantly bikini clad model on the beach. His bed wasn't made, yet it looked like the doona had been spread over it in haste in an attempt to do so. His bedroom window looked out over the backyard, giving a view of the pool lit up by garden lights during the night. On the bedside table was a small speaker hooked up to a phone dock. There was a desk on the opposite side of the room to the bed; a study lamp was on shining down on an opened maths textbook.

Evie smiled slightly to herself, noting how Owen had been doing what she had been doing only moments before she had disturbed him.

"Sorry about that," Owen apologised, "Didn't want Kelly to see me and start annoying me for money again."

Owen noticed Evie taking in the sight of his room and he felt self-conscious having her in there. It had always been a standing rule that his mother's charity cases weren't allowed in his room. He didn't trust them to not steal his stuff and sell it for drugs or whatever it was they were into.

Evie was different to all the others and he knew that, even if he tried to deny it. It was becoming more apparent to him that he had feelings for Evie, exactly what he felt he was still trying to work out. On paper, she was his cousin, but Owen knew his feelings extended further than concerned family.

"I wanted to talk to you about my party," Owen explained, Evie's eyes skipping to his at the mention of his birthday.

"What about it?" Evie asked uneasily.

"It would be great if you came," Owen blurted out before he could stop himself.

He had debated internally all week with what he should do, what he wanted to do and how he should do it. None of it began with him dragging her abruptly into his room late on a Friday night.

"I don't think it would be a good idea," Evie replied, shaking her head.

"You've said that," Owen acknowledged, "But I think it would be good for you to get out and have some fun."

"Owen, you of all people know it's not that easy for me. Look at what happened at the lake party," Evie exclaimed, wandering over to the window, she looked down at the pool, wanting to avoid Owen's watchful gaze.

"Okay I get that," Owen agreed, "But that was because some dickhead got you drunk. I won't let that happen this time."

Evie's eyes narrowed slightly as she thought about what Owen had just said, before looking back over at him leaning against the edge of his desk, arms crossed over his chest.

"And how would you do that?"

"By keeping an eye on you."

"Owen, that's ridiculous, are you listening to yourself? It's your party. You can't waste all your time hanging around me. It would be so much easier if I just don't go at all. There's no reason for me to go."

"But I want you there."

Evie stared at Owen in amazement and Owen's eyes widened in realisation of what he had just said. It was the first time he had said anything of the sort aloud, especially to Evie herself. He knew if Zane had been there, he would have teased him with an "I told you so" speech.

Silence surrounded them.

A knock at the door broke the tension hovering in the air.

Owen regained his composure first, went to answer the door as it creaked open at the same time.

"Honey, have you seen Evie, she's not in her room and I'm worried that..." Sandra's worried voice brought Evie out of her trance.

"Yeah, she's in here," Owen replied instantly, "We were just discussing our Modern History exam on Tuesday."

The door opened wider and Sandra looked further into the room and noticed Evie standing awkwardly by the window.

"Oh, there you are," Sandra smiled, relief flashing across her face.

"I was just leaving," Evie lied, but she wanted to get out of there as quickly as possible and with as little questioning as possible.

Evie started to the door, passing Owen on the way, Sandra watching on in interest.

"Thanks again for lending me the textbook," Evie mentioned on her way out, before disappearing down the hallway and closing herself back into the safety of her own room.

When Evie's door closed, Sandra turned to her son with an inquisitive look.

"Normally I wouldn't be fond of you being closed up in your room with a girl, you know the house rules," Sandra began.

"Mum, don't," Owen warned her to stop where he knew her train of thought was going.

"I was just going to say thank you," Sandra explained before her son could dismiss her like a typical teenager. "I know you've been looking out for Evie a lot and knowing you're helping her with keeping on track at school, it really warms my heart."

Owen simply shrugged in response.

"I'll let you get back to your studies."

Sandra smiled as she leant over and planted a soft peck on Owen's cheek, before leaving and closing the door behind her.

Owen let out a deep breath and ran a hand over his face to try clear his head, a space suddenly full of so many different thoughts, most of them about Evie.

Chapter 24

Saturday morning, Evie wandered down the stairs dressed to go for a run. Sandra and Brian sat with their coffees at the table talking quietly amongst themselves, stopping when they heard Evie coming.

"Off for a run again?" Sandra smiled up at Evie as she entered.

"I won't be long," Evie answered walking towards the front door with a wave.

"We may not be home when you get back," Sandra called after her, following her half way to the door. "We're taking Kelly and Melissa to the movies and thought we would catch one while we are there." Sandra paused then asked, "Would you like to join us?"

"No thanks. I've got exams coming up I want to study for."

Sandra beamed at Evie's interest in her studies.

"We'll bring dinner home with us," Sandra commented as Evie waved goodbye again and headed outside.

She had already stretched in her room, so Evie started out as soon as she got out of the house, warming up with a gentle jog. It had been a week since she had begun running again. Already Evie was feeling more athletic and found it easier.

After ten minutes jogging, Evie moved into a faster pace, her feet pounding on the footpath concrete. She focussed on her breathing and began to relax the further she ran. There was a type of euphoria in running, releasing endorphins that gave Evie a high every time.

Before Evie had become Evie, when she was a normal teenager, Evie had loved running. Casey, her best friend, had always groaned when Evie would suggest that Casey join her on her daily runs, but still she would tag along, all the while complaining.

Evie smiled briefly at the memory of Casey's complaints. She would have given anything to hear Casey whinging about a stitch in her side or a cramping leg muscle just one more time. A tear ran down Evie's cheek, which she hastily wiped away and pushed through her emotions.

Her thoughts changed to those of Owen. He had been acting differently around her lately and then to say he wanted her to go to his party. Evie was confused. She liked Owen, he had been kind and looked out for her, but she knew he was only doing it all as a favour to his mother, so why would he say he wanted her to go to his party? Evie could only guess his mother had told him to say that.

Feeling dismayed by her assumption, Evie wished that Owen had asked her because he really did want her there, as an actual friend. The realisation of this thought scared her.

She couldn't develop any strong feeling for Owen or anyone, reminding herself she would soon be leaving and they would all just become a memory like her family and Casey were. At least this time, the Taylor's' would be alive.

It wouldn't have mattered if Owen had wanted her at his party anyway, Evie thought, it wasn't safe for her to be out socialising. What if someone took another photo of her and posted it online. It was bad enough there was one out in the internet universe already. No, Evie couldn't take that risk.

Thirty minutes into her workout, Evie slowed down and just walked along, trying to catch her breath.

Looking around she noticed she had gone further from the Taylor's home than she had ever run previously. With one hand on her side to support herself, Evie turned around on the spot to take in her surroundings. She had been so focussed on her breathing and the many millions of thoughts scrolling through her mind, she hadn't been paying attention to where she was going and, in that moment, didn't know where she was.

Evie wandered along the footpath, hoping to recognise something or anything that would tell her where she was. Nothing. It was foreign to her. Houses for as far as she could see.

Heart pounding, Evie began to panic. Sure, she had lived on the streets for so long, but in those many months of running, she was prepared, she had her backpack, she was on a path.

In that very moment, Evie had nothing on her, not even her phone. She hadn't taken her phone with her as she enjoyed listening to the surrounding noises, she never wanted to distract herself with music in her ears that she wouldn't hear someone coming.

Stress levels began to rise and anxiety gripped its ugly hand at Evie's throat as she hurried along the path in the direction she thought would take her home. Palms sweating and shallow breathing, Evie powered on. Evie hadn't had an attack in weeks. Fearing she might black out in any moment, she quickened her step.

A faded old blue car drove by, slowing down after it passed her but not stopping. Still it was enough to scare Evie into a jog in the opposite direction. She breathed a sigh of relief when she saw a corner store further up the road.

Rushing inside, Evie couldn't help but check behind her. No sign of the car she saw earlier, which relaxed her slightly. Dashing towards the young man behind the counter, he looked up at her exhausted and panicked face.

"Are you okay, Miss?" the man asked, concerned and alert.

"I've gotten lost while I was out running and I don't know where I am or how to get home," Evie declared, visibly upset.

"Would you like to borrow our phone to call someone?" he offered kindly.

Evie cowered, "I, uh, I don't know their number."

Evie mentally vowed to revise and memorise all the Taylors' numbers for emergencies like the one she found herself in currently.

"Right, um," the cashier studied Evie, thinking for a moment. "Could we look it up online somehow?"

"I don't know," Evie shrugged but at that point, she was willing to try.

Inviting Evie behind the counter, the two looked on the store computer, opening a browsing window and beginning a search for the Taylors'. They managed to stumble across the home number of the Taylors' but none of the mobiles.

Evie's heart sank, knowing Sandra, Brian and Kelly had gone out for the day and wouldn't be home. Her only hope was that Owen was awake and still at home.

Dialling the number on the screen into the store phone, the cashier went to serve another customer at the register giving Evie some privacy. She bit her bottom lip in angst while listening to the phone ring; once, twice… on the fifth ring it picked up.

"Hello?" Owen's voice sounded out of breath, Evie figured he had had to run down the stairs to answer the phone in the kitchen.

"Owen?" Evie responded, "It's me, Evie."

"Evie?" Owen sounded surprised and alarmed at the same time. "Are you okay?"

"Um, I went for a run and kind of lost my way and now I don't know how to get home."

"Where are you? I'll come get you," Owen offered without hesitation.

Evie breathed a sigh of relief, "Really? I'm at some corner store called Sam's."

"I know the place," Owen replied, "You did go a fair way. I'll be there in ten minutes."

After hanging up, Evie went to wait just inside the store's door, too afraid to wait out in the open. The car earlier had frightened her, reminding her how careful she needed to be.

True to his word, Owen arrived ten minutes later. When Evie saw his black jeep coming down the road, she waved and called out a thank you to the cashier man, whose name she had found out was Tim. She then dashed out to Owen in his car before he had even pulled to a complete stop.

"Thank you so much, I'm sorry for making you do this, I really appreciate it."

Evie's words came tumbling out like a tidal wave as she climbed into the passenger seat and closed the door behind her.

Owen smirked at her rambling, "I'm glad you felt like you could call me when you needed help."

Evie eyed him. He was being the kind and caring Owen again. She didn't want to push her luck, but this was the Owen she liked and had hoped would come to her rescue. Not the one who found it a chore and treated her as if she got in the way, although he hadn't done that for some time.

Evie had begun to feel so much more at ease with Owen around. He no longer reminded her constantly of her past, there were brief moments but nothing that left her speechless and caught gasping for air in panic.

Owen drove them home in silence, neither one of them sure of the other or what they should say.

When they reached the house, they both climbed out of the car and walked together towards the house. It was then Evie found her voice, stopping on the step to face Owen.

"Owen, I would appreciate it if you didn't mention this to your parents. Sandra has been so good to me. I would hate her to think I was trying to run away or anything."

"Well, technically you were running," Owen winked at her, "Of course, I won't say a word."

"Thank you," she smiled in appreciation, "And again, for coming to find me."

"Anytime," Owen said with all seriousness, "I mean that."

Owen's eyes stayed on Evie's for a minute longer and Evie felt like she couldn't breathe again, but this time for another reason. It wasn't the first time that week Owen had winded her with an intense stare. Her heart fluttered and Evie had to shake her head to clear it.

"I'm going to take a shower," Evie whispered, overwhelmed by the emotions buzzing through her body in that moment. "Thanks."

"You've said that already," Owen smiled at her, his eyes still on hers.

"Yes, well, um, I..."

Evie didn't know what to say, so instead she turned to the front door that Owen had unlocked already and headed upstairs to the bathroom, leaving Owen on his own on the front door step.

Owen stood watching where Evie had departed through the house and up the stairs. He knew in that moment, that at some point in the previous two months since Evie had arrived, he had fallen for her. He hadn't meant for it to happen, in the beginning he was simply doing what his mother had asked him to, by watching out for her. Owen knew though, there was something different about Evie. He might not have known her whole story, but he did know he would do anything for her.

Chapter 25

Evie had hauled up in her room for most of Saturday studying, except for a short break to make herself a sandwich for lunch. By six o'clock, her brain was fried, and she was debating calling it quits for the day when there was a knock on her door. She knew it was Owen as the rest of the family had not come home yet.

"Come in," Evie called.

Owen stalked into the room and wandered over to the chair in the corner of the room and sat down facing Evie where sat. He took in her opened science textbook on the bed.

"Studying still?" he wondered aloud.

Evie closed the textbook and looked up at Owen.

"Finished for the day actually," Evie replied.

"Mum rang," Owen announced. "They've decided to have dinner out with Melissa's parents and the girls. That leaves you and me on our own for dinner. I've ordered us some pizzas, they should be here soon. I hope that's okay."

"Yes, of course," Evie smiled appreciatively, "Thank you."

As if on cue, the front door bell rang.

"That will be our dinner," Owen proclaimed, standing up and going to answer the door.

Evie followed Owen downstairs. While he went to pay for the pizzas, Evie found some plates and filled some glasses with coke.

The smell of hot, fresh pizza wafted into the kitchen as Owen returned with two square boxes.

"Why don't we watch a movie while we eat?" Owen suggested.

Evie nodded and went to collect the plates and drinks to take them into the lounge room.

"Don't worry about the plates," Owen said, nudging his head in their direction, "We can just eat out of the boxes."

Evie smirked at his suggestion and left the plates on the table, carrying only the large glasses. She placed the drinks down on the coffee table in the middle of the room. Owen placed the pizza boxes on the floor and sat on the ground, leaning against the couch.

"What do you want to watch?" Owen asked, reaching for the remote.

Evie settled on the floor on the other side of the boxes, crossing her legs underneath her.

"I don't mind. You choose."

"That's a trick, isn't it?"

"What is?" Evie giggled at his assumption.

"You say you don't care, but if I choose wrong you will sit there disinterested the entire movie or complain. All women do it. Kelly is the worst for it."

"Honestly, I don't care what we watch. I wouldn't even know what's out now to pick from."

"How about a comedy?" Owen suggested selecting from the menu on the television screen.

"As long as it's not a horror or suspense."

Owen eyed Evie, wondering if her statement was just a passing comment of her movie preferences or if it had something to do with her past.

Opening both boxes between them, Owen waited for Evie to choose a slice first.

"There's a pepperoni and a chicken," Owen indicated towards the pizzas.

"What, no pineapple?" Evie mocked as she reached for a slice of the chicken pizza.

"You don't put pineapple on a pizza," Owen said with all seriousness as he took a slice of the pepperoni.

"It adds some sweetness," Evie replied, taking a bite of her slice.

"Fruit does not belong on pizza," Owen stated once more before eating his own slice.

"Tomato is technically a fruit," Evie pointed out.

Owen looked over and smiled at her. She returned his smile, with a mocking sweet smile.

They watched the movie and ate in silence. It wasn't a movie Evie had seen before, but she recognised some of the actors, and even found herself laughing at times.

Owen watched Evie from his peripheral vision. It was the first time he had heard Evie laugh and it was a beautiful sound. Her face lit up and she became a different person. It suited her, Owen thought to himself. He wished he could make her happy for real all the time.

After the movie, Evie and Owen worked together to clean up the empty pizza boxes and glasses. Evie leaned against the kitchen counter facing Owen.

"Thanks for tonight, it was good to have a break and not be studying," Evie expressed her gratitude to Owen with a small smile. "It's been a long time since I've studied like this."

"It's important to not burn yourself out," Owen warned her, his concern showing.

"I won't," Evie smiled at his consideration for her. "I actually always enjoyed school, probably because I was good at it. I missed the consistency of it, but I did not miss the long hours of studying."

Evie narrowed her eyes as she thought about what she had just admitted to Owen.

"If you loved it so much, why did you leave?" Owen asked gently.

It was the first time he had ever asked Evie a personal question about her past. Owen wasn't sure how much Evie was willing to share but the seemed to be connecting in that moment. He held his breath slightly in hopefulness that Evie might open up to him.

Evie eyed Owen carefully, what did he want to know? The entire truth of why she was on the run? She couldn't tell him. He had just started being the kind and caring Owen. If he knew she was putting his family at risk just by being there, he would never forgive her. Just for a few more weeks. That was all she needed, a few more weeks of Owen's friendship and a sense of normalcy before she returned to her life on the road.

"We're home!" Kelly's voice rang out through the house as the door to the garage opened.

Sandra was the first into the kitchen though, with a skip in her step. She smiled brightly at Evie then embraced her in a breath-taking hug. Releasing a stunned Evie, she moved on to Owen, who seemed to roll his eyes as his mother wrapped her arms around the waist of her tall son.

"You two seem to be getting along," Sandra beamed.

"Mum, stop," Owen groaned.

"Someone had a few drinks at dinner tonight," Kelly explained entering the room, her father following behind her.

"I only had two or three..."

"Bottles," Kelly finished for her.

"Oh, shush you," Sandra slurred.

"Come on, Sandra," Brian beckoned her, taking Sandra's hand in his and pulling her towards the stairs. "Let's get you showered and into bed."

Brian cast the three teenagers a bemused look as he assisted his inebriated wife up the stairs.

Evie giggled at the sight of Sandra, one she had not seen the entire time living with the Taylors. She had always seemed so straight forward, not one to lose herself in a few wines.

"Your mum is great," Evie commented, looking back at Owen who was shaking his head in embarrassment.

"Easy to say when she's not yours," Owen mumbled, but a smile danced fleetingly on his lips.

"What's your mum like?" Kelly asked Evie innocently as she closed the fridge and opened a bottle of water, taking a sip.

"Kel," Owen growled at his sister, giving her a glare.

Evie's stomach dropped instantly at the question, though she tried to hide her emotions. Blinking a few times to stop any tears from falling, Evie swallowed and searched for the right words.

Kelly shrugged innocently, "It's not like she doesn't have a mum. Everyone has one. She didn't appear out of thin air."

"I'm sorry Evie," Owen apologised for his sister's blatant disregard for understanding the situation. "My sister doesn't always know when to shut her mouth."

"I think I might go to bed," Evie managed to croak, "Good night."

Evie ascended the stairs to her room and once he heard the bedroom door close, Owen turned to chastise his sister.

"Get a clue, Kelly."

"What?" Kelly asked, totally unaware she had done something wrong.

"You can really be a blonde sometimes," Owen retorted, pushing away from the counter and heading up the stairs.

He paused outside Evie's room, listening for any hint of a noise from inside the room. Owen's hand was frozen in the air to knock but he couldn't bring himself to do so, worried he was the last person he wanted to see in that moment, well after Kelly that is.

Dropping his hand, Owen padded quietly down the hall to his own room.

Inside Evie's room she sat on her bed, tears rolling down her cheeks as she quietly sobbed. She knew Kelly had not meant to upset her. She was right after all; Evie did have a mum, once upon a time.

Evie missed her mother every day, along with her father and brother. What hurt the most when she thought about them was that it was all her fault. They were dead because of her. The many times she had wondered if she had just done something differently, they might still be alive and they would still all be together; happy and normal.

Fresh tears streamed down her face and Evie hid her face in her pillow, muffling her soft cries so nobody would hear her.

Chapter 26

The sun peeked its way through a crack in curtains, a streak of light crossing Evie's pillow stirring her.

Evie groaned at the thought of waking up and facing the world, especially Owen and Kelly. She knew she had made a fool of herself running off to her room the night before to cry herself to sleep. She had been so exhausted from the tears she had fallen asleep without a shower and still in her clothes.

With a stretch, Evie rolled out of bed and decided to make her way to the bathroom for a shower. She grabbed a fresh change of clothes and headed out into the hallway.

The bathroom door was closed and Evie was still half-asleep, so when she tried the knob and it turned, indicating it wasn't locked, Evie pushed the door open.

Inside the bathroom was a flash that suddenly woke Evie up with wide eyes of shock. Along with the flash was a yelp from someone else.

"Evie?" Owen's startled voice brought Evie out of her sleepy trance as he rushed to wrap and tighten a bath towel around his waist.

"Oh my... I'm sorry, it was unlocked, I didn't," Evie stumbled on her words as she backed out of the bathroom in lightning speed, shutting the door as she went.

Leaning her back against the door, Evie closed her eyes trying to go back in time and change what happened. Her face was flushed with embarrassment and her heart pounded wildly in her chest, but not from an anxiety attack.

Without warning, the door behind her opened and Evie fell backwards, a pair of strong arms caught her instantly. Looking up, Evie found herself staring into Owen's blue eyes, slight amusement danced across his face.

"Bathroom's free if you want it now," Owen announced, righting Evie up on her feet. "Be careful though, the door lock is playing up."

Evie felt the blood rushing to her cheeks once more. Owen was still dressed only in a wrapped towel and it made Evie's stomach flip, an unsettling feeling she was not accustomed.

Owen gave Evie a wink and headed down the hallway to his room. It took Evie a few more seconds to focus and then she hurriedly shut herself in the bathroom, locking the door and testing it several times before pushing the washing basket up behind the door for good measure.

After a very quick shower, too scared that someone might walk in just as she had done to Owen, Evie dried herself and dressed in clean clothes for the day.

Evie headed downstairs to have some breakfast, expecting to find Owen telling the rest of the family about her walking in on him, but Owen wasn't even downstairs yet. Kelly was nowhere to be seen either.

Sandra was slumped over the table, a full cup of coffee in her hand, but her other arm shading her face from the sunlight. Brian was at the stovetop cooking bacon and eggs, toast popping up out of the toaster.

"Good morning," Evie greeted the pair as she wandered to the fridge to pour herself some orange juice.

A groan escaped Sandra's mouth, but her head continued to lay on the table.

"Good morning, Evie," Brian returned her greeting, "Sleep well?"

Evie simply nodded as she took a sip of her drink.

"Want some bacon and eggs for breakfast?"

"That would be great, thanks."

Evie sat down at the table with her juice, opposite Sandra and smiled when Sandra briefly looked up over her arm.

"This is not the example I wish to set for you," Sandra mumbled, "If you could please forget this ever happened..."

"Sandra, you're allowed to let loose and enjoy yourself too. You keep telling me to do that, so maybe you should take your own advice," Evie replied gently, reaching across and patting Sandra's hand.

"Does that mean you're coming to my birthday party then?" Owen's voice broke in, Evie looking up at him.

The sight of Owen fully dressed for the day made Evie blush slightly once more, recalling the events earlier that morning in her mind. She quickly looked away again without answering his question.

Owen stalked over to his father, stealing a bit of crispy bacon right out of the frypan and then pouring himself a glass of orange juice. He sat down between his mother and Evie and chuckled at the sight of Sandra.

"Dad, you got to fix that bathroom door. The lock is playing up again," Owen announced, giving yet another cheeky wink to Evie.

Evie dropped her eyes to the table and took another sip of her juice.

"How about you kids knock before entering?" Brian offered as his solution.

Owen glanced over at Evie with a shrug, her eyes widened, praying he wasn't going to tell them what happened.

"What if Kelly was in the bathroom and one of my friends was over and accidently walked in..."

"You know, you're right," Brian cut Owen off. "I will head to the hardware shop this morning."

A smug smile crossed Owen's lips and Evie mouthed a thank you to him, he just gave her a nod in response.

After breakfast, Sandra retreated to the lounge room to watch movies and recover from her hangover, lying spread out on the couch. Brian left right away to go to the hardware store, bent on fixing the lock on the bathroom door, scared after Owen's suggestion. As it turned out, Kelly had gone out early with Melissa to the beach.

Owen and Evie offered to clean up the kitchen for Brian. Owen stacked the dishwasher, while Evie cleared the table and wiped it down.

"Thank you for not saying anything," Evie smiled bashfully at Owen as she handed him some plates.

"You need to stop thanking me for every little thing," Owen joked, nudging Evie gently with his elbow.

"About this morning," Evie began, passing him the two coffee mugs his parents had used.

"I'll do you a deal," Owen stated as he closed the dishwasher and turned it on, before turning to face her as he leant against the counter. "What happened this morning will stay between us, but in return you will come to my party."

"You're blackmailing me?" Evie frowned at Owen.

"No, no, no," Owen lost all confidence and stepped towards Evie, afraid he would scare her away from him, taking her hand in his. "That came out wrong. I'm not going to say anything to anyone, I swear. I just want you to consider coming to my party."

Owen looked right into Evie's eyes; it sent a shiver down Evie's spine. She had never had this reaction to a boy before.

Evie took a step back to create some distance, but stumbled slightly. She could feel herself falling backwards, but Owen still held her hand. He pulled her towards him to stop her from falling, catching her in his arms.

Evie's face was flush against Owen's hard chest; she could feel the rise and fall as he breathed. She could hear his racing heart, matching the rhythm of her own. Raising her eyes, Evie found Owen looking down at her. Her breath caught in her throat, she swallowed.

Owen couldn't believe the situation they were in. He had dated many girls at school, but none of them had made him feel the way he did in that moment, with Evie. What surprised him most was it was Evie, a runaway his mother had brought home and into their lives. Someone he knew nothing about her past but he knew who she was, who she could have been.

His hand still held hers and his other one pressed to her back holding her up, hers on his upper arm. She gazed up at him, Owen could see a mix of emotions in her eyes; the one that worried him was the one he thought was fear.

Owen cleared his throat, slowly and reluctantly releasing Evie of his hold.

With some distance between them now, neither one of them could find the right words to speak, both just standing there looking at the other.

"Owen, where are you man?" Zane called as he entered the front door.

Evie shook herself awake from her stare and dashed past Owen and upstairs to her room.

Owen watched her leave as Zane came into the kitchen.

"I've been messaging you all morning, why haven't you replied?"

Owen turned his attention to Zane, "My phone's in my room. What did you want?"

"Lacey has invited everyone over for a pool party this afternoon, one last chance to blow off steam before all the exams and assessments. Let's go."

Lacey was a part of their crowd. She was tall and beautiful, and she knew it too. Owen had been out with her a few times at the start of the year, but never felt anything for her close to what he felt with Evie. Even being friends with Lacey since the start of high school hadn't changed any of that.

Owen's eyes drew towards the stairs, thinking about Evie. He knew without a doubt Evie wouldn't come to a pool party, he was struggling to get her to accept his invitation to his own party the next weekend. Lacey's party sounded like a lot of fun, all of their friends would be there and, in a few months, they would be graduating. Owen debated for a brief moment declining, for the chance to stay home and spend time with Evie, but then he realised she probably wanted space from him anyway, especially after the morning events.

"Give me five to get ready," Owen replied, sprinting up the stairs to change into board shorts and get his keys, wallet and phone.

Chapter 27

It is always amazing how when everyone is silent that the smallest noises can be heard. The rhythmic tick of the clock on the wall to the scrawling of pencils on paper, and then sure enough there is always that one person who coughs breaking the utter silence.

The minutes were ticking down. Evie knew the answers to all the questions off the top of her head. She had studied enough, maybe a little too much. Stuff she had forced herself to remember wasn't even relevant to the exam, which made it frustrating.

Finally, the timer on the teacher's desk buzzed, making some of the students jump. Evie looked around the classroom and noticed two students hurriedly rushing to write their last answers before Mr Mason noticed. Evie saw Harley across the room and she looked exhausted. When she looked in front of her, Owen looked relaxed and confident.

Evie handed her completed paper in and headed quickly out the door, keen to get outside to her lunch seat and get some fresh air. She purposely snuck out before Owen was even out of his seat, she didn't want to admit it, but she had been avoiding Owen since Sunday morning. Evie had tried to convince herself that she was doing it out of fear of putting him at risk, but deep down she knew it was the fear that she was falling for him and she couldn't let that happen.

Outside, sitting in the comfort of her table, which was half in the shade and half out, Evie pulled out her bottled water and took a drink. The chicken salad wrap sat in front of her, freshly unwrapped from the plastic wrap, ready for her to eat. Placing her water down, Evie picked up the wrap and took a bite.

"Feeling confident after the exam?"

Evie looked up at Owen walking towards her. She gulped down her mouthful of food as he sat down opposite her at the table.

"Umm, I guess."

Owen nodded as if her response was good enough for him.

"We haven't talked much the last couple of days. Even in the car you've been quiet."

"Nothing to say," Evie replied quietly.

"Have I done something to upset you?" Owen asked concerned.

Evie surprised by his question, as it showed he cared. He cared that in some small way, unbeknownst to him, he had done something that had caused her to withdraw from him. If only he had known the real reason, what would he say then?

"No," Evie answered.

"Okay," Owen studied Evie carefully before going on, "Have you given any more thought to my party?"

Evie looked down at her lunch, avoiding Owen's gaze. She wondered why he was being so insistent to her going to his party. What was the big deal?

"Owen," Evie started, but he cut her off.

"Don't say it wouldn't be a good idea. I think it would be a good chance for you to get out. You're always locking yourself up at home. And we've been getting along lately, you and I, yes?"

Evie eyed him suspiciously. They had started to grow closer, but was it a good thing?

Owen waited patiently for Evie to respond, hoping she would finally agree. He didn't know how else to convince her and he had stopped thinking about why he wanted her there.

"There you guys are," Zane exclaimed walking over to where the two were sitting, and placing himself beside Evie.

Owen's eyes narrowed on Zane slightly, as if in warning, but it went unnoticed.

"Hi Zane," Evie greeted him, with a small smile.

"So, we're going to see you on Saturday, right?" Zane asked Evie, jumping straight to the point, while stealing a piece of chicken sticking out from Evie's wrap and popping it into his mouth with a smirk.

Owen wished silently he could have the same type of confidence with Evie that Zane had.

Evie looked from Zane to Owen.

"Did you tell him to say that?" Evie asked in disbelief.

"I swear to God, I didn't." Owen held his hands up in surrender.

Evie turned back to Zane who was looking between the pair.

"I don't think so, not after what happened at the lake party," Evie tried to sound as convincing as she could.

"This time Owen and I will stay with you at all times," Zane suggested exactly what Owen had previously suggested.

"That won't be much fun for you," Evie countered.

"You were saying yourself to my mum on Sunday that it's important to let loose and enjoy yourself at times. She's forty-three, you're seventeen. If anyone should be enjoying themselves it's you."

Evie wondered how she could persuade the two boys to let her stay at home, in the safety of her room. Her mind drew a blank. She knew it was a hopeless case. Maybe they were right; maybe she did deserve a night of fun. All Evie needed to do was make sure nobody took her photo and she would be fine.

With reluctance, Evie responded with a sigh, "Fine, I'll come."

Zane wrapped an arm around Evie's shoulder, smiling, "There, that wasn't so hard, was it?"

Owen couldn't help but feel jealous at the sight of his best friend in a close embrace with Evie. Wiping the scowl from his brow before either of them noticed, Owen stood up from the table.

"I've got to go catch Mark before Maths," Owen announced, before giving a wave and walking off.

He took one last look over his shoulder and saw Zane no longer had his arm around Evie. The pair were talking happily, Zane said something that made Evie laugh. Owen pushed the pang of jealousy down and headed back into the building.

By Saturday afternoon, Evie had tried to convince herself thousands of times that it was going to be good to go to the party. She couldn't shake the feeling that it was the worst possible idea.

It had been a long and tiring week, filled with exams for all her classes. Once again, Evie wondered why she had tried so hard, yet there was a sense of satisfaction inside her knowing she felt confident that her results would be of a high standard. Not that it would matter. She only had four weeks left at the Taylors. Evie sighed in sadness at the thought but shook the feeling away.

When Owen had told Sandra, that Evie had agreed to go to the party, she got so excited. Saturday morning, Sandra took Evie shopping for a dress to wear to the beach, stating Evie needed something new, much to Evie's protests. In the end, Sandra convinced her that the teal coloured halter dress was exactly what she needed for a beach party.

Standing in front of the full-length mirror in her room, Evie studied her reflection. The dress was beautiful and something she would have worn in her old life. Still she was scared of what may happen and the high possibility of someone taking her photograph at the party, Evie knew she had to take precautions. She tied her hair up in a ponytail and pulled on her cap, which would help in hiding her face. It was a lovely sunny day, so she could make the excuse of shielding herself from the bright sun.

Evie put her phone in the small silver mobile shoulder bag Kelly had lent her for the night and placed it over her head so it hung from her neck and wouldn't get lost. Slipping her feet into the strappy sandals Sandra insisted she needed to complete the outfit, Evie felt as ready as she could be for Owen's party.

Heading downstairs, Sandra was waiting to drive Evie to the beach. Owen had left earlier with Zane to set up for the party.

"You look beautiful," Sandra gushed. "Do you think you need the hat though? It doesn't really go."

"It will protect me," was all Evie said and Sandra just nodded as if she understood.

It was short drive to the beach, no more than ten minutes. Sandra told Evie she would be home all night and to call her if she needed anything, but instructed her to relax and enjoy herself.

Sandra waited patiently while Evie glanced out her window and down to the beach where the party was. Finally, she opened the door and got out. Sandra encouraged her one last time to have fun.

Evie walked from the carpark down to the sand, where she immediately removed her shoes and carried them. The music was pumping already and she could see a large bonfire where people were congregating, dancing and drinking.

Stopping in her tracks, Evie looked back to the car park, thinking she could run back to Sandra's car and escape, but

Sandra had already left. Her heart began to beat wildly in her chest and Evie took a few steadying breaths, moving towards the party.

Chapter 28

"Evie!" Zane shouted out above the music, as he jogged across the sand to her side. "You just made me ten bucks, thank you."

The party seemed to be in full swing already. There had to be at least a hundred teenagers on the beach, between the bonfire, a table of drinks and across the sand. The sun was on its way down towards the horizon, casting shadows across the sand.

"Excuse me?"

"Owen and I had a bet on whether you would show up or not. I bet you would come."

"Owen didn't want me here?" Evie asked in almost a whisper. Suddenly her fear of going to the party was for an entirely different reason.

"No, nothing like that," Zane assured her, "He's going to be so happy that you came. Trust me."

Zane took Evie by the arm and guided her towards the bonfire. Standing near the heat of the flames was Owen, talking to Mark and a girl Evie didn't know, but looked familiar.

"Pay up, Owen," Zane announced as they approached.

Owen looked up at them and Evie could swear his face lit up when he saw her.

"Evie, you came," Owen sounded surprised. Realising he was staring; he turned to his two other friends. "Mark, you've met Evie before. Evie this is Danielle."

"Yeah, I think we have English together," the blonde girl smiled cheerfully at Evie as she waved.

Realisation hit Evie; they shared a class, that's why Danielle looked familiar to her.

"Hi," Evie replied shyly.

"Do you want a drink?" Owen offered and Evie eyed him cautiously. "There's bottled water or soft drinks."

Evie smiled knowingly, "Water, please."

Owen disappeared to get Evie her drink, leaving her with Zane, Mark and Danielle who were talking animatedly about a video that had gone viral on the internet of a dog. It was the most bizarre and normal conversation Evie had heard in a long time.

"You came!"

Evie recognised the squeal of delight immediately as Harley, who ran up and hugged her as she turned around. Harley was wearing a short skirt and low-cut top that left little to the imagination.

"Uh, it was a last-minute decision," Evie lied, throwing Zane a look that told him to keep quiet, to which he just smirked.

"The group is over by the dunes, come say hi," Harley announced, taking Evie by the hand to pull her away from Zane and the others.

Evie dug her heels into the sand, not wanting to go anywhere near Marcus or leave the semi-safety of Zane.

Before she could protest, Owen showed up, handing Evie her bottle of water. It was then he noticed Harley standing next to her, holding Evie's hand.

"Owen, happy birthday," Harley purred, no longer trying to pull Evie away.

Harley smiled flirtatiously at Owen, twirling a finger in her hair that hung down to where her breasts lay half-exposed.

Evie noticed Owen's brow creasing in disinterest.

"Maybe I will come say a quick hello to the others," Evie suggested, pulling Harley away with her in the direction of the dunes.

Owen watched Evie carefully, he didn't want to break his promise to her of leaving her alone, but the last thing he wanted at his own birthday party was to hang out with Harley and her friends. He could tell Evie was doing it in a way to rescue him from Harley's advances, which he was grateful.

Evie glanced over her shoulder to him as the pair walked away and gave him a reassuring smile. He gave her one in return to let her know he would be keeping an eye on her, just from a safe distance.

"Do you think he liked my outfit?" Harley asked Evie excitedly, oblivious to Owen's distaste for her.

"It might have been a little too much," Evie offered gently.

"You're probably right," Harley agreed, tugging at her top to hide her cleavage a bit better.

Evie gave Harley's friends a brief hello. Marcus avoided her eyes, which she was thankful. Evie felt uneasy near him, memories of the lake party coming in flashes to her mind.

Paige jumped to her feet, her phone clutched in her hand.

"Let's take a group shot," she announced, instructing the others to bunch together.

Evie tried to pull away from the group, but Harley had her arm firmly around Evie's waist in a hug, holding her in place. Using the only security, she had in that moment, Evie pulled her cap down over her face and hid from the camera below its rim. If she had to end up in the photo, at least no one would see her. The flash lit up the dune, as the sun dipped closer towards the horizon.

After the photo, Evie suggested Harley and her dance over near the rest of the party, anything to get away from another photo taken of her. Harley gulped down the last of her drink, which Evie assumed was alcohol, and looped arms with Evie ready to go towards the part of the beach most of the teenagers were dancing.

Music pumped from a stereo system that had been set up on the beach. Harley started swaying her hips before they had even stopped walking. Evie started to move awkwardly to the music, not feeling relaxed enough to enjoy herself. She found herself constantly checking the crowd, making sure no one was taking a photo with her in the background.

Two songs in and Harley suddenly stopped, staring past Evie.

"Jesse from my Maths class is here, he is so hot," Harley crooned; Evie could only just hear her over the loud music.

Evie decided to take the opportunity to distract Harley's attention away from Owen. She tried to convince herself she was trying to help Owen out, but she knew she didn't like the feeling she got in the pit of her stomach when Harley always poured herself over Owen.

"Why don't you go say hi to him," Evie suggested carefully.

"Do you think?" Harley asked, unsure.

"What have you got to lose?"

"My dignity," Harley replied seriously, "My chance with Owen."

"Don't you think something would have happened with Owen by now," Evie said gently.

"You know what," Harley stood tall. "You're right. I should make my move."

"There you go," Evie encouraged.

"I'm going to get Owen, finally."

"Yeah, you are... what?" Evie stopped short.

"Something should have happened with Owen by now. I need to stop playing coy and finally do something about it."

"That's not what I..."

Evie tried to stop Harley, but it was too late. Harley shot past Evie and into the crowd in search of Owen.

Turning around, Evie looked around for Owen, surely, he would be close by her; he said he wouldn't leave her. Evie pushed through the crowd in search for Owen, or even if she could find Harley and stop her. How would Owen react to Harley's admission, what if Owen returned her feelings?

The thought made Evie sick to her stomach and she hated to admit it.

Only a few feet from where she had been dancing, was Zane.

"Zane," Evie called to him and grabbed for his arm to get his attention.

"Evie, are you okay? What's wrong?"

Panic crossed Zane's face, worried that Evie was having a panic attack. He tried to think about where he had seen Owen last. Because Evie was hanging out with Harley, Zane had offered to keep a close eye on her, from a short distance.

"Harley's about to profess her undying love to Owen," Evie explained exasperated.

Zane smiled at her and laughter danced behind his eyes.

"That worries you because?"

"Well, because," Evie didn't know how to finish the sentence. She couldn't admit she had feelings for him to Zane.

Zane waited a torturous minute to let Evie stew in her emotions. He couldn't understand why Owen and Evie couldn't admit their feelings for one another. He had noticed it weeks ago. Yet they still danced around one another, scared to admit it to themselves.

"Don't worry," Zane finally spoke, "Owen isn't interested in Harley."

"How do you know?"

"He's my best friend."

Zane guided Evie out of the dancing crowd and around the bonfire. He had left Owen near the drinks stand.

As they rounded the bonfire, Owen came into view. His darkened form came into light from the flickering flames of the bon fire. He wasn't alone though, Owen was in an embrace with Harley. Her arms were snaked around his neck, holding her to him, their lips connected.

Evie froze where she was, her hand slipping from Zane's. Her voice caught in her throat at the sight before them. It hurt in her heart and she felt like a fool. How had she let herself so close to Owen? She couldn't afford to do that. It was too dangerous. Shaking her head as if to wipe the image from her eyes, Evie turned and ran off in the opposite direction.

Owen was standing by the drinks stand, checking there was still enough for everyone. That's when she approached. When Owen turned around, he came face to face with Harley, her eyes wide with passion.

"Owen, I know you don't know me that well but I need you to know, I think you're great and I really like you. I think if you gave me a chance we could really make a go of it," she rambled so quickly, that Owen struggled to make sense of it.

"Harley, I-" Owen started, but Harley silenced him.

Wrapping her arms around his neck, leaning up on her tiptoes, she pulled his face towards her, closing her eyes and kissing him like her life depended on it. Owen placed his hands on her hips and tried to push her away, but she pushed in closer to him. Finally, he managed to push her away, keeping her at arms-length.

"Harley, it's not going to happen, not now, not ever," Owen informed Harley firmly.

"But, I thought-"

"What? If you threw yourself at me, I would be impressed. When have I ever given you any indication that I liked you?"

"Evie said-"

"What did Evie say?" Owen suddenly interested for the first time in what Harley wanted to tell him.

Zane burst in beside the pair.

"Owen, Evie..." Zane panted.

"What? Where is she?" Owen asked, panicked.

"She ran off, I tried to follow her but there were too many people," Zane explained.

Ignoring Harley, Owen strode off to look for Evie. He had promised his mother he would keep her safe. He had promised Evie he would look out for her.

"What happened?" Owen demanded of Zane, who was at his side as they both searched the crowd for her.

"I should ask you," Zane countered.

"What's that supposed to mean?" Owen grunted, stopping to look at Zane.

"Evie wanted to find you, so I was bringing her to you when we came across you making out with Harley."

"She saw us?" Owen rubbed a hand through his hair in frustration.

"Yes, she saw you, she has eyes!"

"We weren't making out. Harley attacked me. I struggled to push her off me."

Silence fell over the two teenagers as their eyes continued darting around the now darkened beach for any sign of Evie.

"Whatever happened, Evie was upset."

Owen's eyes fell back on his best friend.

"She was?"

"You are really stupid, you know that," Zane said in bemusement, shaking his head.

"Later, let's just find Evie first."

They agreed to go separate ways, to search for Evie along the beach. Owen hoped that he would be the one to find her, and soon, so he could explain to her what really happened between him and Harley.

Chapter 29

Evie felt like a complete and utter fool. Not only had she fallen for a boy she couldn't have, but then she went and made a fool of herself running from Zane. She couldn't escape her feelings no matter what she did.

Evie knew she had to get back to reality and stop getting caught up in drama with Owen. There was a bigger threat out there waiting for her. One she had stopped thinking about as much. She wasn't thinking with her head anymore, but with her heart.

Sitting on the dune by herself, she could see the bonfire further down the beach and people moving around. She wondered what Owen and Harley were doing, were they still attached to one another's faces, or were they sitting in the sand laughing and talking together. Evie placed her head in her hands to calm herself and get a grip on what she needed to do.

The trees behind Evie rustled in the slight breeze. She shivered from the coolness as it hit her. The days may have been warm, but the nights were cool. Rubbing her arms for warmth, she decided she should go back to the warmth of the fire and find Zane. He was probably worried about where she was and looking for her.

Standing up, Evie dusted the sand from her behind and heard a twig snapping behind her. Alert and heart racing, she turned to look into the trees. She couldn't make anything out in the dark of the night.

"H-Hello?" she stuttered.

Silence. There was nothing out there. Evie tried to calm her beating heart by telling herself she was overreacting.

"Hey," came a male voice from behind her as a hand touched her shoulder.

Evie screamed, diving sideways from the touch, as if the touch had burnt her. As her body swung around, her heart began to pound so hard it felt like it had already leapt out of her chest.

A dark shadow moved towards her, hands up in surrender.

"Evie, it's okay, it's only me."

Her breathing erratic, Evie did her best to think past it and focus.

"It's Owen."

Just the mention of his name calmed her instantly as she tried to slow her breath by taking a few deeper breaths. She closed her eyes and focussed on her breathing, then felt the warmth of Owen's body against hers as he wrapped his arms around her in a protective embrace.

"It's okay, I'm here. You're safe."

His scent and proximity set Evie at ease, but at the same time made her feel anxious but in a good way.

"I'm sorry," Evie apologised finally.

"It's alright."

"No, I ruined your moment with Harley," Evie whispered, "I was being stupid but I'm okay now."

"I'm glad the moment with Harley was ruined. I wasn't enjoying her company one bit."

Evie pulled back from Owen's hold so she could look into his eyes.

"But you were kissing."

"Correction, she was kissing me," Owen stated, wanting to clear the air right away. "I was trying to get her off me."

"Why?"

"Because I don't like her."

Owen watched Evie intently for a reaction, wondering if he should tell her he liked her. Slowly, Owen leant in towards Evie, drawn to her, wanting to calm her but also let her know he would be there for her. His eyes drifted to her lips, which were slightly apart as she panted her breath.

"Zane!" Evie suddenly exclaimed, surprising Owen and bringing him out of his trance.

"Zane?" Owen's heart fell in his chest.

Evie wanted Zane, Owen thought. He had connected with her from the very beginning while Owen pushed her away.

Evie pushed back away from Owen and started towards the bonfire. Her heart was racing from all the emotions surging through her body. She could feel herself drawn to Owen, wanting to kiss his lips as he held her, his breath caressing her face. Evie knew she couldn't let anything happen between them.

Owen followed Evie towards the party, downhearted by the rejection he felt. Why was it the girl he didn't want would leap into his arms, yet the one he wanted pushed away?

"I'll just call him," Owen suggested, pulling his phone out of his pocket.

Evie turned to him and wandered back. They were closer to the party now but still on the outskirts so it wasn't too noisy to make a call.

Owen held his phone to his ear, "Zane... yeah she's with me... okay, meet you at the food table."

Owen took Evie's hand in his as he stepped past her and pulled her along behind him, guiding her to the food table. Zane was waiting for them.

"Evie," Zane smiled when he saw her, "Are you okay?"

"Yeah, I'm sorry."

"It's all good, as long as your fine."

Zane's eyes fell down to Owen's hand holding Evie's. To him it was just another sign of the two having feelings for one another, although for others it might seem weird; everyone else thought they were cousins.

Evie noticed Zane's gaze and followed it, realising how it looked, she pulled her hand free from Owen's.

"You know what, I think I'm going to go home," Evie announced.

"What? No, you can't do that. It's still early," Zane protested, hitting Owen in the arm to help him talk her out of leaving.

"Please, I came, I've already caused drama. I just want to go," Evie pleaded, looking to Owen.

"Want me to take you?" Owen offered and Zane let out an exasperated sigh that Owen wasn't trying to convince her to stay.

"It's okay; your mum said I could call her. You stay and enjoy your party with your friends," Evie explained.

Owen just nodded. Evie gave Zane a friendly goodbye hug and then eyed Owen carefully before just giving him a wave.

Evie walked away from the party, towards the car park and called Sandra. She told her she would wait in the carpark for her. After the call, she wandered over to a bench seat and sat down in the dark to wait, putting her shoes back on her feet after dusting off the sand that clung to them.

The party noise continued behind her, sounds of music and laughter. Evie closed her eyes and once again wished she could be normal.

When she opened her eyes, Evie looked at the cars parked in the night. One car looked oddly familiar to her and she couldn't pinpoint how. She narrowed her eyes in an attempt to get a better look in the darkness. Evie swore she saw movement inside the car parked across the lot. In the shadows, it looked like someone was sitting in the driver's seat.

Evie's blood ran cold and a wave of anxiety and panic washed over her. She gasped for air as she struggled to breathe. It was him she knew it. What was he doing though, just watching her?

It was then that Evie remembered why the car was familiar to her. The weekend before when she had become lost on her run, there was a car that passed her and then slowed down. The car that had caused her into a panic then, it was the same car now watching her.

Evie stood up, her legs frozen in place but she willed them to move. She wanted to run back to Owen, the safety of the party, but her body wouldn't move. A part of her didn't want to go anywhere near the party. Evie knew he wasn't put off by crowds.

Lights flashed out on the road, coming closer. Sandra! Evie dashed out towards the car and jumped in immediately.

"Eager to leave the party?" Sandra laughed.

"Yes, I need to go, now," Evie stated, watching the other car still out of her window as Sandra pulled away from the parking lot.

"Are you alright honey?" Sandra voiced her concern, "You look very pale. Did something happen?"

"Evie, talk to me," Sandra pleaded, driving the car towards home. "What's going on?"

"My real name is Rhiannon West," Evie said her true name for the first time in over a year and it felt foreign to her. Evie swallowed and took a deep breath before she went on, fresh tears brimming at the corners of her eyes, "Fourteen months ago, a boy from my school, Ryan Scott, killed my family in an attempt to get to me."

Chapter 30

Sandra, taken aback by Evie's sudden confession, she quickly pulled the car off the main road. She pulled up in a carpark at the back of a McDonalds, turned off the engine and looked at Evie.

Evie let out the breath she had been holding. Sandra waited patiently, knowing that Evie was about to open up to her, she didn't want to scare her by rushing her.

Knowing that the blue car had not followed them, Evie relaxed. She told Sandra her story, her hands clasped tightly in her lap, her eyes downward. Evie knew there was no going back once she told Sandra the truth, but it was time.

"It all started about two years ago. I loved going to school and I was an A student. I got along with my teachers and I had a great group of friends. My best friend was Casey, she was crazy and we did everything together," Evie smiled at the memory of her best friend.

"My Maths teacher, Mr Baldwin, pulled me aside one day to tell me about a student in his senior class who was close to failure and if he failed, he wouldn't graduate. I felt sorry for this boy, so I agreed to help tutor him. The student, the one I offered to tutor, was Ryan Scott."

Evie swallowed the lump in her throat, her heart rate started to pick up.

Sandra rested a reassuring hand on Evie's hand, letting her know she could take her time, she wasn't going anywhere.

Taking a deep breath, Evie went on.

"We lined up a few tutoring sessions, meeting in the school library after school. He seemed like a nice boy. He would make jokes, I would laugh, your typical high school stuff. Then things started to change, he became possessive.

"A friend in my year level, Peter, asked me out on a date to the movies and I accepted. The night of the movie, Ryan was there, watching us. I tried to ignore him, but he just kept staring at us when we left the movie, it felt... wrong.

"Peter dropped me home after the movie and he walked me to the door. I swear he was about to kiss me, he was leaning in and then the next thing I knew he was being pulled away from me. Peter was on his back on the ground and Ryan was on top of him, punching him repeatedly. I screamed at Ryan to stop, but he just kept hitting him. My dad came out and pulled Ryan off. Peter was unconscious and bloody. The police came and the police let Ryan go with a warning. Peter spent a week in hospital."

Evie let out a deep sigh. The image of Peter's mangled face still burnt into her mind.

"After that, the obsession Ryan had on me went from bad to worse. If another boy even talked to me at school, Ryan would be there to tell them to back off. Countless times, I would have to pull him off someone he had pressed up against a locker. He would start fights because of me, even if someone just looked at me.

"He would ring my phone at all hours of the day and night. I changed my phone number a couple of times, but he would always manage to find out my new number. Finally, it got too much for me and I went to the police and filed for a restraining order. Ryan wasn't allowed to come within a hundred metres of me or contact me in anyway shape or form. This just frustrated him and made things worse.

"It was Casey's birthday and she was throwing a party. Nearly all of our year level was there. Ryan showed up uninvited. I tried my best to ignore him and keep my distance but Casey hated that I wasn't having a good time at her party. She went over to him and started yelling at him to leave or she would call the police. That's when it happened. Ryan pulled out a knife and stabbed her in the stomach. I watched in horror as my best friend crumpled to the ground. Kids started to scream and run in different directions.

"The police came and arrested Ryan. It was as though he wasn't scared of being arrested. He could have run after killing Casey, but he didn't, he just stood there and watched me cry over my best friend's death. He was charged with the murder of Casey and sent to prison for twenty years. It didn't fix anything though. I suffered from anxiety and panic attacks, nightmares."

Evie gave Sandra a knowing look, her eyes filled with tears from the memory of her best friend murdered right in front of her.

Sandra, horrified by the story so far, refused to let it show. She didn't want Evie getting spooked and stop telling the rest of it.

"My suffering caused my parents to fight. After six months, my family was falling apart, so my parents decided we needed a fresh start. We moved away from the memories and tried to put it behind us, moving to the other side of the country. We started anew.

"After five months at my new school, I was finally starting to settle in. I was getting good grades and thinking about what I wanted to do when I graduated. My nightmares weren't as bad and I was seeing a great therapist that helped me with some tricks on how to manage my panic attacks and anxiety. I had made new friends and my parents were happy again. Even my younger brother, Matthew, who was twelve at the time, was enjoying our new life.

"It all came tumbling down though, with one phone call. The detective who was put on my case rang me one Wednesday night to inform me Ryan had managed to escape from prison and they had reason to believe he was coming after me again."

Evie paused at the thought of Ryan escaping, a shiver running down her spine.

Sandra wanted to reassure Evie that she was safe, but she was concerned if she interrupted Evie she might stop opening up to her.

Five minutes passed before Evie continued.

"I began to live in fear again, always looking over my shoulder, wondering if he was waiting in the crowd for me. I became distant from my new friends first; I didn't want to see any of them ending up like Casey. The local police knew of the situation. Uniformed police patrolled my neighbourhood and did routine surveillance of my school.

"It was three weeks after the detective's phone call that it happened. Ryan found me. He came to our house late one night, my family and I were all home. Dad phoned the police but Ryan broke through the front door. He argued with my parents who were trying to protect me, and my brother. Ryan said he wanted me to go with him. I was too scared to move. He wanted us to be together.

"First, he stabbed my mother in the heart; she had been standing in front of me, shielding me from him. She fell to the ground and I kneeled down beside her dead body, crying. My father told Matthew to hide, so Matthew ran off while my father fought with Ryan to take his knife off him. My father lost the fight, Ryan slitting his throat."

Evie's voice was trembling and she spoke between soft sobs. It was all still so fresh in her mind, as though it had happened only the day before.

"I knew I should have run, but I couldn't. My parents' lifeless bodies lay in front of me. Ryan took the opportunity to grab me, forcing me towards the front door. In that moment I was numb, I didn't care if he took me, but I wanted to stay with my parents.

"That was the moment Matthew chose to fight back. He had a kitchen knife. I wanted to stop him, but Ryan held me against him like a shield probably thinking Matthew would stop, he turned us around and the knife Matthew was holding stabbed me instead of Ryan."

"Ryan was furious with Matthew for hurting me. He retaliated by killing my little brother, stabbing him in the stomach with so much force. I passed out from the blood loss. The police arrived and took Ryan away. Ryan thought I died that night. I was free but I had lost my entire family.

"The system placed me in the care of my only living relative, my father's sister, Aunt Sue. I moved again, started new again. This time I didn't make new friends, I chose to be a loner and I changed my name. I didn't want to risk anyone getting hurt because of me again. I didn't want to get close to anyone in case they took it too far and became obsessed like Ryan had.

"I don't know how, but Ryan found out I was alive. He escaped again but nobody told me this time. I came home from school one day and found Aunt Sue dead in her lounge room; blood surrounded her and the knife still in her side. Ryan wasn't there anymore, or if he was, I didn't see him. I ran. I knew that he would keep finding me no matter what the police did, so I ran and didn't look back. I didn't call the police. I just ran away and I've been running ever since.

"I always give a fake name whenever asked, changing it every time. I dyed my hair dark. I used to be blonde. I steal only what I need, and keep moving. I never stayed in the same place for longer than twenty-four hours. I never spoke to anyone unless required. I never got close... to anyone."

Evie swallowed hard and took a deep breath. Tears streamed down her face, which she tried to wipe away. Sandra reached out and pulled Evie into a tight, comforting hug.

Sandra couldn't believe the heartache and the pain that Evie, or Rhiannon, had been through in her short life. No one should have to go through what she had been through.

The puzzle called Evie was complete. When Sandra had started to search for information about Evie, she only found previous arrests, which she could only assume was Evie, as they all had a different name.

In the end, Evie's story had been more than Sandra could have ever imagined. Everything added up; Evie's panic attacks, constantly wanting to run away, and her fear of putting herself and others in danger.

Sandra held Evie until she calmed down. Her heart ached for Evie after hearing how her entire family was murdered.

"Is that what has you scared right now? Ryan?" Sandra asked cautiously, hoping she was just misreading Evie's paranoia.

There was no way Ryan could find Evie with them. No logical reason he would.

Evie's eyes dashed to Sandra's in fear at the mention of his name aloud.

"I just have this feeling like I'm being watched," Evie confided in Sandra. "I'm probably just over thinking it."

Evie was trying to convince herself, hoping Sandra could talk some reason into her as well to help calm her nerves.

"Evie, I think it's time we go to the police," Sandra replied gently, not wanting to scare her.

Without a second thought, Sandra started the car again and pulled out of the carpark, heading into town towards the local police station.

"We can't," Evie's voice cracked. "Ryan will definitely find me then. He always does when the police get involved. They can't protect me."

"It will be okay, darling."

Evie's heart was racing so hard at this point. Sandra turned the car towards the centre of town, where the police station was. Another five minutes of Evie pleading with Sandra not to do it, they arrived.

Sandra pulled the car to a stop outside the station and turned to Evie to console her.

"It's for the best. They can keep you safe."

"You're wrong!" Evie shouted at Sandra.

Opening the car door and leaping from the car, Evie ran away from the car, the police station and Sandra who was calling out to her.

Breath panting and her feet aching from her shoes not being suitable to run in, Evie pushed on. She backtracked towards the Taylor's house. When she started to feel lost, she quickly used her phone to check her position and get directions.

When she neared the house, she slowed, carefully looking around her. It looked like Sandra hadn't come home yet. She was likely talking to the police. Evie was about to approach the house when the garage door went up. Evie paused, hiding behind a bush in the neighbouring yard.

Brian's car reversed out the driveway and the garage door went back down. Evie noticed she was right, with Sandra's car not being in the garage, meaning Sandra was still not home. From her position, she could see both Brian and Kelly in the front of the car as it drove off down the street.

When the coast was clear, Evie snuck across the front lawn to the front door. After the incident when Evie found herself locked out of the house, Sandra had shown Evie where there was a hidden spare key in a front garden pot. Evie fished out the key and unlocked the front door, dashing inside and locking it again behind her to be secure.

Not wanting to waste any time, Evie rushed up the stairs to her room. She changed into her own clothes, shirt, jeans and hooded jacket. She pulled on her sneakers and took some of the clothes Sandra had bought for her, but only the essentials that were suitable for a life on the road, leaving behind the dresses, skirts and strappy shoes. Evie secured her cap firmly once more on her head.

In the bathroom, Evie restocked her bag with toiletries. As she exited the bathroom, she paused in the hallway and looked over at Owen's closed bedroom door. Biting her lip, Evie debated what she was about to do next, but she knew it was necessary and hoped he would understand.

Once in Owen's bedroom she searched his desk and then his drawers. In the top drawer of the bedside table, she came across his wallet. It was exactly what she had been looking for, hoping he had left it at home. Inside was fifty dollars. It wasn't a lot but it would be a start for her.

Before she left his room, Evie wandered back over to his desk. Taking a blank piece of paper and a pen, Evie began to write. When she finished, she left it in the middle of the desk where he would see it, placing the phone that Sandra had given her on top for good measure.

Hurrying downstairs, Evie took some non-perishable, light-weight items from the pantry and a couple of apples from the fruit bowl. She ran to the front door, took one last look behind her and left.

Chapter 31

"I can't believe you let her leave," Zane complained to Owen for what felt like the millionth time but was more like the tenth.

Owen rolled his eyes at his best friend's annoyance with him. He had let Evie leave the party, but he didn't understand what other choice he had. Evie had made it clear she wasn't interested in him, regardless of what Zane thought he knew.

"Just leave it alone, okay," Owen voiced his annoyance.

Owen moved away from Zane and went to where Mark was standing with Danielle and Jensen. He needed to distract himself from what he was feeling. It was Owen's birthday party and he should be enjoying himself. Still he found it difficult to concentrate as his mind kept wandering, thinking about Evie.

Jensen was telling the group about how he nearly got detention that week for something stupid he did during his Maths class when Owen's phone began to ring. He moved away from his friends and the noise of the party to answer it.

Looking at the screen, Owen noticed it was his mother ringing him. He thought it was odd, as she would have picked Evie up over an hour beforehand.

"Hey mum," Owen answered his phone.

"Owen, I hate to do this to you, but we need you to come home," Sandra spoke in worried tones on the other end of the phone.

"Why? What's happened?"

"It's Rhi- It's Evie." Sandra answered.

Owen's heart stopped briefly at the mention of her name, fear and worry grabbing at his throat.

"Is she okay?"

There was a pause while Owen waited anxiously for his mother to answer him.

"She's run away," Sandra replied gently.

"What? Why?"

"I'll explain it all when you meet us at home," Sandra went on, "Your father and sister are out looking for her, but haven't found her. I'm at the police station working with detectives."

"I'm coming," Owen cut in, hanging the phone up.

Walking quickly back towards the party, people tried to stop him to talk, Owen pushed through, rudely ignoring them. He found Zane talking with Lacey and Xander. He grabbed Zane by the elbow and pulled him away, not wanting to talk to him in front of everyone else.

"What's going on?" Zane surprised by Owen's abruptness.

"Evie's run away," Owen answered, "I've got to go home and help my parents. Can you sort everything out here?"

"Of course, go."

Owen didn't wait for any more reassurance from his best friend; he broke out into a jog across the sand, jumped in his car and drove home, breaking the speed limit here and there in his rush to get home.

He pulled his car up onto the driveway, clipping the kerb with the front tyre. The lights were on inside the house. Owen jumped from his car and ran inside to find out more of what was happening with Evie.

"Mum. Dad," Owen called to his parents as he entered through the front door.

"In here," his father replied from the kitchen.

Walking into the room, Owen saw his father and Kelly sitting at the table.

"What's happening? Where's mum?"

"She's on her way home. Sit down so we can talk."

"No, we need to go find Evie," Owen refused, "How do we even know she's gone?"

"Your mother went to take her to the police station and she ran off from her. We went out to help look for her and didn't find anything. When we came home all her things were gone," Brian explained calmly.

Owen couldn't believe what he was hearing. He sat down in the chair next to Kelly and opposite Brian. He ran his hands through his hair in frustration, trying to make sense of it all.

"Why was Mum taking her to the police station?" Owen finally asked after a moment silence.

"Because Evie needed protection," Sandra replied as she walked into the room and sat down in the last remaining chair.

"Protection?" Kelly queried, speaking for the first time.

Owen could feel his heart stop at his mother's comment. Evie needed protection? What from?

"Evie opened up to me when I picked her up from your party tonight. She told me the whole truth about her past and what she is running from."

"What truth?" Owen pushed.

Sandra took a deep breath to tell Owen and Kelly what they needed to know, leaving out the specific details Evie had told her. Although she had told Brian the situation over the phone, he still listened in.

"Okay, but what I'm about to tell you does not leave this family, do you understand?" Owen and Kelly both nodded in agreement. "Evie's real name is Rhiannon. She's been living on the run for over a year from a boy named Ryan who killed her entire family"

Kelly gasped in shock. Owen watched his mother intently, waiting for her to continue, needing to know more.

"Tonight, after she told me, I tried to convince her to go to the police because she has felt like someone has been watching her. Evie got scared, she doesn't believe the police can help her, she thinks they will be the reason Ryan finds her again."

"Wow," Kelly breathed in astonishment.

"Why wouldn't you tell us something like that?" Owen exclaimed, astounded that his parents and Evie were hiding such a big thing from them. "What if he had found her here? What was to stop him from killing us?"

"Owen, sit down," Brian ordered.

Owen hadn't even realised he was now standing with a clenched fist on the table. Doing as he was told, he lowered himself slowly back into his chair.

"Your mother did what she felt was best and I supported her," Brian stated, reaching over and taking Sandra's hand in his.

"So now Evie, or Rhiannon, whatever her name is, is back out there on the streets, running from Ryan. Why is this guy not locked up in jail?"

Sandra spoke calmly to her children, explaining the best she could about the situation. Kelly seemed scared but also accepted what was going on. Owen seemed agitated and furious. Sandra wondered if it was out of caring for his family or something deeper that he felt for Evie.

When Zane rang Owen to check up on news about Evie, Owen evaded his question, being obtuse and elusive.

Sandra went to her study to try look for any contacts she may have that could assist them. Brian went with Sandra to help her. Kelly went to bed, locking herself in her room.

Owen refused to sleep, even though his parents had instructed him to. He wandered upstairs, pausing at the doorway to Evie's room, the guest room. Looking inside he saw her school bag lying on the floor, the books spilling out from the opening. The dress she had been wearing at his party strewn on the bed, along with other clothes.

Letting out a forlorn sigh, Owen dragged his feet as he went to his own room. He crashed down on his bed, landing on his back, staring at his ceiling. If he wasn't confused about his feelings for Evie before he certainly was now.

Owen realised he didn't know anything about her. He knew Evie's name was a fake and she was a run away, but never did he imagine she was running from something so horrible. Everything started to make sense, every little thing Evie had said or done.

Thirty minutes passed, Owen tried to think of a solution, but he knew if there had been one, Evie would have found it. She was a smart girl.

Rolling onto his side, Owen's phone dug into his side from his shorts' pocket. He pulled it out and looked at it for a minute before realising the simplest idea to find Evie.

Opening his phone, he found Evie's name and called her. While he waited for the call to connect and start to ring, Owen noticed his bedside drawers were open slightly, not how he had left them. Sitting up on the edge of his bed, he was about to investigate when Evie's phone started to ring. Her phone was ringing in his room.

Standing up abruptly, Owen's heart began to race as he looked around for her phone. For a brief moment, he wondered if Evie had been hiding out in his room the entire time. Then he saw it, in the middle of his desk, Evie's phone lit up with his call. Ending the call, Owen walked over to his desk and picked it. Underneath the phone, he saw Evie's letter that she had left for him.

Dear Owen,

I am so sorry. I'm sorry for so many things I wouldn't know where to start. Unfortunately, I don't have the time to apologise for everything.

My biggest regret is lying to you for so long. You looked out for me and helped care for me and I cannot thank you or your family, especially your mum, enough for this. There are no words to express my gratitude.

I can't stay, as much as I wish I could. I want nothing more than to be a normal teenager, go to high school and parties with my friends, but that just isn't a possibility for me.

I tried my best to keep my distance because I didn't want to put you all at risk. So many times, I thought about leaving but I fell in love with you all. You reminded me what it was like to have a family again.

He's found me, I'm sure of it and I don't want any harm to come to you or your family, that's why I have to go again. I don't know where I will go, but I hope that one day I will be able to find my way back to you.

The police can't help me. They tried and they failed. My family and friends died while the police did their 'best'. Their best isn't good enough.

I have to go. I'm sorry.

Love Rhiannon.

PS: I stole your $50, I'm sorry.

Owen's heart pounded in his chest, he reread the letter once more, looking for anything that might help him to find her, help her.

"Mum! Dad!" Owen shouted as he raced from his room to take the letter to show them.

Evie trudged along the side of the highway. It was late at night and there were hardly any cars on the road. She had chosen not to go on any public transport yet. Ryan might have been watching, expecting her to take the easy way out of town.

When a car drove past, Evie would hold out her hand, her thumb up in hopes of hitching a ride. The car would continue on, not even slowing. With each passing car, she would try again. Every so often, the car would blast their horn in warning to tell her to get off the road. Still Evie kept trying and walking at the same time to put distance between her and Ryan.

Evie's legs were tired, but she was glad she had begun running the past week; it meant she could persevere and push on against the pain. She was tired and her body called for sleep, but Evie knew she didn't have time for sleep yet. Not until she was safe, or as safe as she could be.

Another car approached from behind, Evie held her thumb out as she walked on. To her surprise and elation, the car slowed and pulled up to a stop beside her. Turning to face the car with a grateful smile, Evie stilled when she saw the car and the driver inside.

"Ryan," she breathed as panic took hold of her body.

Chapter 32

Two weeks earlier.

Ryan paced back and forth in the dingy motel unit where he was staying. The laptop he had stolen was set up in the corner on the small narrow desk. Lighting a cigarette, he took a puff and blew out in frustration. The bottle of whisky was empty on the side table; he would need to get more when he went out for dinner.

PING! The laptop sprang to life, alerting him to a notification. His heart leapt in excitement. For ten months, it had remained silent. Ten months, two weeks and five days to be exact. It had been the longest time, each hour feeling like a day, each day feeling like a week.

Jumping into action, Ryan rushed over to the desk. Opening the window with the notification he saw it; a new search. He held his breath while he clicked on the various links to find the information he needed. It wasn't a strong lead, but it was a lead all the same. The location was a town not far from where he was.

When he lost her the last time, Ryan created a website, writing his own articles about Rhiannon. When someone viewed his site, he would get a notification and their location. In his plan, Rhiannon would search herself and it would help him to find her. The police continued to hide her from him, keeping them apart. He had followed many leads to dead ends, but the site had remained quiet for the past four months.

Opening a search browser, Ryan typed in the town's name. It was a decent sized town, plenty of places for her to stay if she was there. He searched the town with Rhiannon's name. Nothing. He banged his fist on the desk, the laptop rattling. His head in his hands, he rubbed is face in frustration, trying to clear his head to think clearly. There had to be something. Why would someone in that town be searching her name?

With a new idea, Ryan typed in the town's name once more followed by 'new girl'. The first result was for the local high school, a student run blog for the school. Clicking on the link, there were various photos of teenagers at what looked like a party. Most of the girls were wearing bikinis, drinks in hands or dancing.

Scrolling through the pictures, Ryan stopped on one in particular, his stomach flipped with excitement. It was Rhiannon, except her hair was no longer the golden blonde he loved, she had dyed it dark brown. It didn't suit her, he thought, angry that she had destroyed her beauty.

Reading the comments below the photo of Rhiannon with some girls he did not recognise, Ryan tried to find out more.

"Evie Harrison, Harley Stanton, Paige Michaels and Rebecca Lewis."

"Evie is the new girl."

"Yeah, she's Owen Taylor's cousin."

"I think she's in my History class."

"She's very quiet and keeps to herself."

Ryan frowned at the comments about Rhiannon, or Evie as she was calling herself. Cousin? As far as he knew, she didn't have any family left. He had made sure of that, they wouldn't let Rhiannon and Ryan be together. Then she wouldn't feel guilty about running away with him and leaving their old lives behind as they started their new life together.

It was Rhiannon's father, he caused the drama between them. He was the one who kept her away from Ryan. It was his fault, the mother's too. They would get between them and their love for one another. Ryan had known it would be hard, but he had to remove them from the equation.

Then Rhiannon was sent away to live at her Aunt Sue's. When Ryan finally found her, Rhiannon wasn't at home. Sue wouldn't tell Ryan anything, no matter how much he tortured her. He watched from afar when the police arrived, but never saw Rhiannon. The news outlets all claimed Ryan had taken Rhiannon, that he murdered her. That was a lie. He would never hurt Rhiannon.

Anger fuelled Ryan, searching the 'cousin's' name. He looked very similar to himself, Ryan thought; blonde hair, blue eyes and well built. With narrowed eyes, glaring at the picture of Owen, Ryan tried to locate where he lived, but found nothing. Frustrated, Ryan swiped his arm across the desk sending the laptop flying to the ground with an almighty crash.

Grabbing the keys to the car he had bought illegally, Ryan left the motel, disregarding the mess. He wasn't coming back and he had given a false name anyway.

Slamming the car door shut, Ryan turned the key in the ignition and the car roared to life. He pulled it out of the parking lot and headed in the direction of the town where Rhiannon was.

Driving all day and night, Ryan rolled into town the next afternoon. Not wanting to waste time, Ryan drove straight to the high school. When he arrived, it was the last session of the day. He parked the car opposite the school while he waited and watched.

When the final bell rang for the day, Ryan searched the crowds of students for any sign of Rhiannon. He was about to give up when he saw her. She had her brown hair tied up in a ponytail; Ryan still didn't think that the colour suited her. He watched as she walked with her supposed cousin and another boy with dark hair. The one with dark hair said something that Rhiannon laughed at.

Jealousy coursed through Ryan's body. His fingers gripped the steering wheel so tightly that his knuckles turned white. It took all his will power not to get out of his car and go and take Rhiannon right then, but there were too many people around. It had been so long. He didn't want to risk losing her again. He had to do it just right.

The three teenagers climbed into a large black jeep and drove out of the school parking lot. Ryan followed the car from behind, at a safe distance so to not arouse suspicion. The jeep got further away and another car got between them. Ryan lost sight of the jeep, shouting profanities.

Ryan took up residence in a local rundown motel, everyday returning to the school and watching for Rhiannon. Each day that week, he would lose sight of the jeep, but he was able to figure out the general area she must have been staying.

On the Saturday morning after he arrived in town, Ryan got in his faded old blue car and headed to the corner store near his motel, Sam's. He bought more cigarettes and whisky. As he left the store, he lit a new cigarette, took a swig of the whisky straight from the bottle while he climbed into his car. He drove off in the direction of the school, hoping to retrace the path the jeep had taken each day.

As he drove, he sipped from the bottle. Ryan noticed a girl on the footpath ahead, walking hurriedly. He slowed down to get a better look. As he passed, he saw a brown-haired Rhiannon, panic-stricken. She watched Ryan's car and started to jog in the opposite direction.

Once Ryan was able to turn around, Rhiannon was gone.

The following week, Ryan waited at the school again, resolved to not lose sight of the jeep, Ryan stuck closer to it and followed it all the way back to a two-storey suburban home with a large tree out the front. Ryan stopped further down the street and watched as the three teenagers exited the jeep and went inside the house.

While Ryan waited, he smoked more cigarettes and drank from his new bottle of whisky he had bought that afternoon.

The two boys left in the jeep a few hours later and when the jeep returned, ten minutes later, there was only Owen.

Each day was the same.

The following Saturday afternoon, Ryan drove to the house just in time to see the mother of the family leaving in her car with Rhiannon. Rhiannon wore a cap, which Ryan recognised as her brother's. Ryan followed closely behind, curious to where they were going. A ten-minute drive and Rhiannon got out of the car at the beach. It looked as though there was a party happening on the sand with a bon fire.

Ryan parked the car in the corner of the parking lot. Climbing out, he wandered through the trees and observed from afar. A few hours in and Ryan watched as Rhiannon ran from the bon fire, down the beach and stopped on the dunes.

Ryan snuck quietly through the trees to get closer. She was upset, crying. He moved closer, ready to make his entrance, when another shadow came into view on the beach. Ryan stopped, his foot snapping a twig on the ground. Rhiannon looked into the trees and he stood still like a statue.

"Hello?" she called into the trees, her voice as sweet as he remembered.

Ryan wanted to reach out and hold her, but Owen came up to her. The two stood close to one another, not like family, but like lovers. Jealousy grew in Ryan's gut and he reached into his back pocket of his jeans for his pocketknife. Flicking it open, he watched for his chance. Before he could take it, Rhiannon pulled away from Owen and the two started back towards the party.

Ryan growled in frustration and huffed back to his car where he lit another cigarette and drank more of his whisky. While he contemplated his next move, he saw Rhiannon come up to the parking lot. He hadn't planned on seeing her so soon and alone. He looked around the area for a sign of anyone else. Ryan put his bottle down and put out his cigarette on the dashboard. He reached for the door handle but paused when headlights bobbed out on the road and headed towards the carpark. Rhiannon stood and ran to the car and got in.

Waiting, so she didn't notice him following, he knew where the house was now. Ryan drove off towards the house fifteen minutes later. When he reached the house, he parked a few houses away and waited.

Time passed and the garage door opened. A car left with an older man and a teenaged girl with blonde hair that wasn't Rhiannon. Ryan sat there debating following the car, noticing the other car wasn't in the garage, but he stopped himself when he noticed a shadow from behind the neighbouring bushes move. Rhiannon snuck out and raced into the house.

Curious, Ryan didn't move. Unsure who was inside or what was happening. Not half an hour passed and Rhiannon exited the house again. She had changed her clothes and had her backpack on, but she continued to wear her brother's cap. Rhiannon ran down the street, cutting across lawns and disappearing down a walkway that went between two houses. Ryan couldn't follow with the car, so he sped around the corner in hopes to find her, but there was no trace.

"Fuck!" Ryan cursed, banging his hand against the steering wheel.

Speeding up and down the streets, Ryan searched for Rhiannon, his heart racing. He drank his whisky as he drove.

After an hour of going up and down the same streets, Ryan took a chance, driving out onto the highway, the same one he came into town on. He drove for fifteen minutes, before turning back towards the town. On the way back, he noticed a figure walking on the other side of the highway.

Turning the wheel abruptly, Ryan's car cut across the grass median strip and onto the other side of the highway, heading out of town once more. It wasn't long until he caught up with Rhiannon walking on the side of the highway. Her thumb went out to indicate she wanted to hitch a ride, but she didn't turn around.

Ryan pulled the car up beside her and stopped. Rhiannon turned to face the car, smiling politely, but when she saw Ryan her eyes widened in fear.

"Ryan," she breathed.

Chapter 33

"Rhiannon," Ryan exclaimed, "Get in the car."

Evie's heart thumped quickly in her chest, panic-stricken she was momentarily frozen to the spot.

Ryan let out an exasperated sigh and climbed out of the car, looking at Evie once more over the roof of the car.

"Get in the car, Rhiannon," Ryan commanded.

"No," Evie whispered.

Pushing through her fear, Evie mentally ordered her body to run. Her legs started to move, taking her in the opposite direction, back towards town, away from Ryan.

Ryan banged a fist against the roof of the car, dove inside and squealed the tyres as he turned around, going the wrong direction on the road. He pulled up in front of Evie once more, blocking her way. She moved to get around the car, but Ryan was out of it quick as lightning. He grabbed Evie around the arm and pushed her up against the car, pinning her body with his own.

"Why are you running? It's me, Ryan. We can finally be together Rhiannon. No one can keep us apart."

Evie's heart pounded harder than it ever had, her breathing was fast and her head began to spin. She tried to focus on calming her breathing, refusing to blackout with Ryan. Using the adrenaline coursing through her body, Evie brought her eyes up to meet Ryan's.

"You found me," Evie whispered, trying to figure out how he had found her.

"Of course, I did, I told you I would never stop looking for you. I love you," Ryan replied, obviously misinterpreting what Evie had said.

"H- how?" Evie asked gently, not wanting to upset him.

"I got your message," Ryan smiled at her.

"My message?"

"Yes, when you typed in your name, I got an alert. I came as fast as I could, but I had to wait until the right time to show myself to you. Then I saw that guy who is apparently your cousin?"

Evie closed her eyes briefly, realising she had been her own undoing by searching her name on the internet. If she had just left it alone, she would still be safe; she would still be with Owen.

Opening her eyes again to look at Ryan, Evie knew she would have to play along with Ryan, to keep Owen safe and the rest of the Taylor's.

"He's nobody," Evie lied, forcing herself to lay a calming hand on Ryan's chest.

"Then why were you living in his house?"

Evie could hear the anger and jealousy in Ryan's voice.

"The police made me after I was caught shoplifting. They put me into care with that family. I wouldn't tell them who I really was, so they told the school I was their cousin to be able to enrol me. I had to wait for the right time to escape."

Evie told only a half-truth, lying to keep Ryan focused on what he really wanted. Her.

"I have you now, I will keep you safe. I know a place we can live, away from everyone else. It will take us some time to get there and I need to collect some supplies and my things from the motel. Get in the car."

Even though Ryan bought Evie's story, he still gripped her upper arm tightly as he directed her into the passenger side of his car. He closed the door, locking her in and ran around to the driver's side. Evie felt sick, a mixture of cigarette smoke and whisky fumes filled the air.

Ryan didn't talk during the drive. Evie clasped her hands tightly in her lap, watching the trees then the buildings whizz by as he went over the speed limit. Something felt familiar to Evie about where Ryan was taking her. It wasn't until she saw the corner store; Sam's, that she realised where they were. It was where she had become lost that day on her run and Owen had come to rescue her.

The car slowed as it pulled into the motel a short distance down the road. Ryan dashed around the front of the car to open the door for Evie. He took her hand out and pulled Evie from the car, leading her quickly into one of the motel rooms.

Evie stayed quiet. She didn't call out for help in fear of spooking Ryan into harming someone or even her.

Inside the motel room was a solitary queen-sized bed, a small table with a laptop sitting on top and two dining chairs. The room smelt the same as Ryan's car, with cigarette butts on the side table and empty whisky bottles lay on the floor. Dirty clothes strewn all over the room and a small rubbish bin in the corner over flowing with takeaway packaging. A door off to the other side of the room was ajar, leading to the small bathroom. Wet, used towels lay on the floor, the toilet seat was up and toothpaste stained the sink.

Evie wrinkled her nose at the state of the room. Ryan pushed her down to sit on the side of the bed.

"We should sleep for a few hours, in the morning I will get the supplies for our trip. You're going to love where we are going Rhiannon. There's a cabin with a lake. When the sun sets, you have a beautiful view from the porch. We are going to be so happy together."

"Um, Ryan," Evie tried her best to not sound scared, "Do you think I could use the bathroom first?"

Ryan eyed Evie suspiciously, as though he didn't completely trust her. He nodded once and Evie stood slowly, making her way to the bathroom. She reached for the door handle to close it behind her.

"Leave it open," Ryan instructed.

"But," Evie started to protest then realised she shouldn't push her luck.

Her hand dropped from the handle and she moved to the toilet. Hidden from view of the bed, she had some privacy.

Evie had hoped to use the opportunity to look for an exit, but now she was there, she could see it had only a small window that a Labrador wouldn't even fit out of.

When Evie returned to the room, Ryan welcomed her to lay down on the bed with him. Evie did so uneasily, her heart pounding and she shook with fear.

"Are you cold?" Ryan asked, pulling her to him as he cradled her in his arms from behind, spooning her.

Every ounce of Evie's willpower went into not jumping at his touch. Ryan pulled a blanket over them and nestled his face into Evie's hair. Evie heard him take a deep breath, smelling her hair, she squeezed her eyes closed tight in disgust and tried to gather strength from within.

For over an hour Evie lay awake while Ryan slept behind her, holding her tightly in his arms. If Evie tried to move even slightly, his arms tightened around her, pulling her closer to him. Eventually, Evie's body gave up fighting and she fell asleep. It wasn't a restful sleep, still highly aware of Ryan's presence.

Evie's head filled with her reoccurring nightmare...

Ryan's large frame filled the doorway, intimidating Rhiannon so much she cowered back into the house. With bleached blonde hair blowing in the breeze and his blue eyes piercing through her soul. He looked just as she remembered. He stepped into the house towards her, she tried to scream but no noise would come out.

Rhiannon's mother stepped in front of her to protect her. Her father held Matthew close to him.

"She's mine," Ryan growled in a low voice.

"We've called the police," her father stated forcefully, yet in a calm tone.

"We'll be gone before they get here," Ryan spat in reply.

"You're not taking her," her mother argued, holding Rhiannon behind her, away from harm.

"She belongs with me!" Ryan yelled at her mother, before lunging forward with a long sharp glistening knife.

Her mother screamed in pain as the blade pierced her heart, collapsing to the ground in a limp state. A dark, red pool of blood started to dam around her body.

Tears streamed down Rhiannon's face as she screamed for her dead mother lying in front of her. She fell to her knees beside the lifeless form that was only moments before trying to protect her. It already felt cold when Rhiannon's hand touched her mother's arm. Rhiannon's tears dripped to the ground, mixing with the blood that was now soaking into the knees of her denim jeans.

Her father pushed Matthew to the side, commanding him to run and hide, while he sprang to his feet and fought with the intruder for the blade. Rhiannon watched in horror as they wrestled with one another, her father pushed up against the wall, the dagger edging close to his face.

With an almighty push, her father fought back and attempted to get the knife out of Ryan's hand. Ryan thrust his head forward, banging his forehead against her father's face causing her father to falter, giving Ryan the opportunity to slice the blade through his throat.

Blood poured from the slit, her father grabbed his throat as he stumbled and fell to the ground beside her mother, where Rhiannon continued to cry.

Rhiannon's blue eyes pinned her to her place. Fear gripped Rhiannon so tightly she couldn't bring herself to move, to run and try and escape. Ryan reached forward with his bloodied hand and grabbed hold of Rhiannon's upper arm, pulling her to her feet.

"Now we can finally be together," Ryan sneered at her, "There's no one standing in our way."

It was at that moment her younger brother, Matthew, came running down the hallway with his hand holding a large kitchen knife. Before Rhiannon could warn him to stop, Ryan whipped around, holding Rhiannon in front of him as a shield. It was too late. The knife cut through Rhiannon's shirt and stabbed her right in the stomach. She instantly felt the wetness of her shirt sticking to her as the blood began to seep out and cover her.

"No, I didn't mean to," Matthew cried, his eyes riddled with fear at the realisation of what he had just done.

Pain seared through Rhiannon's body, she wanted to collapse to the ground, but Ryan held her up, tight against him.

"You little shit!" Ryan raged, "Look what you've done!"

Ryan backhanded Matthew across the face, his knife still in his hand. Matthew rubbed his face as Ryan let go of Rhiannon and she crumpled into a heap on the floor beside her dead parents. Ryan stepped towards Matthew and pushed the knife deep into Matthew's gut, holding him by the shoulder, he yanked it up, deep into his gut, blood spluttered out of Matthew's mouth. This time Ryan let go of the knife and pushed Matthew away and he landed on the couch, gasping for breath.

Sirens wailed in the distance. Everything went black and Rhiannon passed out from the pain and loss of blood. She thought she was dead, just like all the members of her family.

Evie woke abruptly from her nightmare, panting. Ryan's arms were no longer around her and his body no longer pressed up against hers. She sat upright in bed quickly at the thought, her head spinning slightly from the movement.

The toilet flushed in the bathroom and Ryan came out of the bathroom, a towel wrapped around his waist. Evie briefly thought about the morning she walked in on Owen in the bathroom. She dashed the image out from her mind. She couldn't allow herself to be caught up in the emotion of not seeing him anymore. She needed to focus on the predicament at hand.

"Morning babe," Ryan uttered as he sauntered towards her, leaning down and planting a kiss on her lips.

Evie froze, unable to react. Her nightmare still fresh in her mind.

"I'm just going to get dressed and head down to the corner store. Want anything?"

"Uh, no," Evie answered carefully, "Thank you."

Evie sat silently, thinking of what she could do to escape, taking everything in. Ryan dressed and smiled over at Evie. He looked around, thinking and then walked over to the side table where a phone sat plugged into the wall. Ryan whipped out his pocketknife and cut the cord easily, making Evie jump slightly.

"I'll be back as soon as I can" Ryan whispered; leaning in and brushing his lips against Evie's again, "Don't go anywhere."

Ryan winked as he walked out of the room, closed the door and locked it.

Evie waited for a few minutes before standing up and running to check the locked door. It wouldn't budge. Moving to the window, the curtains were drawn, Evie pulled them apart to find the windows covered with a timber panel.

"No," Evie wailed as she banged on the window aimlessly.

Looking around the room for anything that might help her, she saw it. She ran across the room and opened the laptop. While it started up, Evie tapped her fingers against the table impatiently; stressing that Ryan could come back at any moment.

Evie bit her bottom lip, trying to think quickly of what she could use the laptop for, as she opened an internet browser. She had an idea and hurried to type in what she needed to, before shutting the window and closing the laptop once more so Ryan wouldn't notice she had been on it.

By the time she laid back down on the bed, it was only a matter of seconds before she heard the rattle of the lock and Ryan entered the room, his arms full of groceries. They were the type of groceries suitable for a road trip; packets of chips, chocolate bars, cans of drink, and biscuits, nothing really of nutritional value.

"How's my girl?" Ryan asked, placing the supplies down on the table with the laptop. Rhiannon's heart pounded fast.

"I'm actually not feeling very well," Evie lied, holding a hand to her stomach.

Ryan looked over at Evie in alarm, "Really?"

He rushed to her side, sitting down on the edge of the bed. He placed his hand on her forehead.

"You don't have a temperature," Ryan mused aloud.

"My stomach keeps cramping and I threw up while you were out."

"We're meant to be leaving now," Ryan moaned.

"I know," Evie acknowledged, forcing herself to place a gentle hand on top of Ryan's. "I guess I could try to get up."

Evie pretended that trying to sit up caused her pain.

"No, stop," Ryan protested, easing her back down to a lying position on the bed. "We will stay one more night. That way you can rest and we'll leave first thing in the morning."

Evie bit her lip to stop herself from smiling in any way.

"You sleep."

Ryan leant over her and pressed his lips to her forehead. Evie nodded solemnly and rolled over on the bed as he tucked the blanket over her. As she closed her eyes, Evie hoped her plan would see her rescued before the morning.

Chapter 34

A knock at the door, made the entire family freeze and look in the same direction as the noise. Owen was the first to recover, jumping from his chair and running to the door to answer it, hopeful that in some way Evie had changed her mind.

Twisting the doorknob, Owen pulled the door open and found a familiar face, but not the one he was hoping.

"Zane," Owen stated, deflated.

"Good morning to you to," Zane replied, pushing inside, past Owen.

"What are you doing here?" Owen asked as he closed the door again.

"I'm here to help you find Evie."

Owen led the way back into the kitchen where his family sat solemnly.

"It's just Zane," Owen announced, leaning against the kitchen counter.

"Zane, darling," Sandra smiled weakly; trying to act like everything was okay. "What brings you here this morning?"

"I came over because I thought you might need help looking for Evie," Zane replied, looking from one family member to the other, taking in their lack of motivation in finding Evie. "Why are you all just sitting there, doing nothing?"

"Zane, it's very kind of you, but there is nothing you can do," Sandra told him. "We've told the police, they will let us know if they see her."

"That's all?" Zane's eyes dashed to meet Owen's, who looked away. "We could be out there, driving around and looking too."

"It's not safe," Brian answered.

"Safe?" Zane asked bewildered. "What's going on?"

Before anyone could answer him, there was another knock at the door. Everyone jumped, ready to answer it this time.

"I'll go," Brian stated as he rose and walked to the front door.

Everyone listened carefully. Brian and another male voice spoke briefly, before the front door closed again. Brian walked back into the kitchen carrying a pizza box.

"Kelly," Owen scolded.

"What?" Kelly responded with surprise, "I didn't order any pizza."

Brian laid the pizza on the kitchen table uninterested in eating.

"Then who did?" Sandra asked, looking around at her family.

No one admitted to ordering it.

"So, I just paid for a pizza no one even wants to eat?" Brian queried, sounding only slightly annoyed.

"I'll have some," Zane offered, reaching over and flipping the lid open, before pulling back in disgust. "Eww, pineapple. Who would order a pizza with only pineapple on it?"

"Who would put pineapple on a pizza?" Kelly protested, scrunching up her nose in disgust.

Owen smirked slightly, and replied in almost a whisper that no one could understand him, "Evie would."

"What was that?" Sandra asked him.

Owen's eyes widened, as he stood up straight and approached the table as if a lightbulb had gone off in his head.

"Evie would eat a pizza with pineapple," Owen explained, "She said it added some sweetness to the pizza."

"Did you get the receipt?" Sandra turned quickly to Brian, understanding where Owen was going with his thought.

Brian handed her the receipt that was slightly greasy and crinkled. Sandra's eyes ran over the slip quickly, looking for a clue that might help her.

"Nothing," Sandra shrugged, putting the paper on the table. "It's just the order for one plain pineapple pizza."

Owen frowned and picked up the receipt to look at it.

"Here," Owen pointed to the top, showing his mother. "The delivery address is our house but look at the name."

"Who's Sam Motel?" Kelly enquired, feeling confused.

Brian looked up from his phone where he had been searching the name.

"There's no Sam Motel in the directory for the area or even the state."

"Is there a motel called Sam?" Zane suggested; to which Brian started a new search and then shook his head.

"The only Sam I can think of is the corner store 'Sam's'," Sandra stated, shaking her head in defeat.

"That's it," Owen exclaimed.

"What's it?" Kelly asked.

"Evie got lost running last weekend. She called me from Sam's and I had to go collect her," Owen explained.

"Why would she order a pizza to tell us she's at Sam's though?" Kelly wondered aloud.

"There's a motel just down the road from Sam's," Brian announced to the group, looking up from his phone.

"Well, let's go," Zane proclaimed, ready to head to the door, but noticed no one was following.

"I think we should call the police," Brian suggested to his wife.

Sandra nodded in agreeance and took her mobile phone, dialling the number. She stood up from the table and walked into the lounge room for privacy while she called them.

"Why aren't any of you moving?" Zane asked bewildered. "Come to think of it, why would Evie run away and then send you clues to where she is? Does she understand the point of running away?"

Owen looked to his father for assistance. His parents had said to keep Evie's secret within the family, but surely Zane could know too. He had helped Owen out so many times with Evie.

"Dad, please," Owen pleaded carefully.

"Only Zane," Brian stated as he stood up and went to check on Sandra.

Kelly chose to go up to her bedroom and take a break.

Owen sat down with Zane at the kitchen table and explained to him everything his parents had told him about Evie, the real Evie. Rhiannon. Zane listened with interest and awe. He found it difficult to believe that poor Evie had been through so much.

"So maybe Evie's in danger. Shouldn't we go get her?"

"Mum and Dad say it's too big of a risk for us, that the police should handle it," Owen explained sullenly.

"What do you say?" Zane probed, giving Owen a daring look.

"I want to help her, but I have to think about my family's safety too. If something happened to Kelly…"

"What if something happens to Evie while we sit here waiting for the police to take action?"

"No one is going anywhere," Brian stated matter-of-factly as he returned to the kitchen with Sandra.

"The police are going to check out the motel," Sandra informed the boys.

The four sat down at the table, unsure what else they could do but wait. Zane reached forward and took a piece of pizza, but picked off the pineapple into the box and eating just the base with the sauce. Owen shook his head in amusement at his friend's actions.

"What?" Zane asked, with a mouth half full of pizza. "It's just a waste otherwise."

Sandra's mobile phone sprung to life and she rushed to answer it.

"Hello?"

Silence, while Sandra listened to the caller, the others waited quietly.

"Okay, thank you for letting me know and for looking into it so quickly."

Sandra hung up from the call and looked at her husband sadly, shaking her head.

"They went to the motel, but it is shut down currently," Sandra explained what the police had told her. She looked to the teenaged boys. "They looked into the motel records and it hasn't been in use for nearly six months. The owners started renovations and then had issues with money and the bank so abandoned it."

"Did they actually look in the motel rooms? Wouldn't it make sense for a murderer on the run to hide out in an abandoned motel?" Owen argued.

"They can't legally enter the premises without the owner's permission and at the moment they don't have much to follow other than a random guess of the name on a pizza receipt. It's not really strong evidence."

"Screw this," Owen exclaimed, standing to his feet and grabbing his car keys from the kitchen counter.

"Where are you going?" Brian demanded.

"To what the police are too lazy to do," Owen stated and started towards the front door.

"Hell yes!" Zane jumped to his feet and started to follow Owen.

"Wait," Brian called out after them.

Owen paused at the open door and looked back at his father, who was now standing.

"I'll come with you," Brian told him, then to Sandra. "You stay here with Kelly. Lock all the doors and keep in contact with the police."

Brian gave his wife a quick kiss on the lips as she whispered to him to be careful.

"It will be fine," Brian reassured her. "But if you haven't heard from us in thirty minutes, call the police."

Sandra nodded resentfully and watched her husband disappear out the front door with her son and his best friend, off to rescue a runaway she had brought home and into their lives.

Getting to her feet, Sandra went about securing the home. Locking all the doors and windows. She made her way upstairs to check to the bedrooms, finding each one empty. Empty?

Sandra swung around and started calling out Kelly's name. She searched Kelly's room, double-checking she wasn't over reacting too soon. Dashing down the stairs quickly, but ensuring she didn't trip, she collected her mobile off the table, ready to call Brian.

Before she could dial his number, she noticed a message on her phone. It was from Kelly.

I've gone to Mel's until everything is safe again. I'll be safe at Mel's.

Sandra breathed a small sigh of relief, but still concerned that Kelly had gone out of the house unnoticed and was attempting to walk the five blocks to Melissa's in a time of uncertainty. Worried, Sandra dialled Melissa's number.

"Hey Mrs Taylor," Melissa answered.

"Hi Melissa," Sandra urged herself to keep her voice calm and sound as normal as possible. "Kelly said she was going to your house, but I haven't heard from her since. Is she there?"

"I'm not home," Melissa replied, sounding confused. "We're visiting my grandmother today. Kelly knew that."

"We must have got our wires crossed," Sandra tried to stay positive. "I'll try her phone."

After saying goodbye to Melissa and hanging up, Sandra went about ringing Kelly herself. The call rang out, with no answer. Sandra attempted to call her a second and third time.

Panic set in and Sandra called the police immediately. Speaking to the same detective she had been dealing with all weekend, she explained her concern. Detective Johnson agreed it was a concern, given the circumstances surrounding the family at that time, and promised to come right over to investigate.

Hanging up, Sandra debating ringing Brian for a few seconds, but decided there was nothing he could do at that time, not until Detective Johnson and come and assessed all the evidence.

For all she knew Kelly could be screening her calls. She could have gone to Melissa's and snuck in using a spare key. They had made sure long ago that both girls knew how to get into one another's houses if no one was home to be ensure they would never be locked outside.

Sandra sat down atthe now lonely table and drummed her nails on the tabletop, waiting impatientlyfor the detective to arrive.

Chapter 35

Owen pulled the car to a stop on the opposite side of the road to the motel. He couldn't fault the police for thinking there was no activity at the motel. Some windows were boarded shut with plywood, skips bins were in the car park and over flowing some of them.

Owen climbed out of his car, standing on the road and shutting the door behind him, just staring at the motel. Brian and Zane climbed out and stood on either side of him.

"What's the plan?" Zane wondered aloud. "We do have a plan, don't we?"

"I guess we just walk around and see if we see anything unusual," Owen shrugged.

"Boys, I really don't think this is safe. If this Ryan kid is as dangerous as Evie told your mother he is, then maybe we should get the police to come with us."

Brian looked up and down the street, taking in everything in their surroundings, making sure they were safe.

"You heard what Mum said, the police can't do anything," Owen stated as he took a step out onto the road and crossed it to the motel.

Zane followed closely behind and then Brian after looking around one last time for any imminent threat.

Brian held up a hand to the glass window of the office to stop any glare from the sun and peered in the window. He saw a desk with piles of paper and some even scattered to the floor. The bin in the corner was full and an unplugged computer on the desk, the monitor tipped on its side. A sign on the slightly ajar door stated the closure of the motel until further notice, with a number to call for enquires.

Zane wandered around the large skip bins in the carpark area, searching for any clues. All the rubbish seemed to be old furniture and room fixtures, likely from the renovations that were never completed. He did note that there was a pile of takeaway food bags and empty drink cups on top of one of the bins, with one of the cups knocking gently in the breeze on the ground as if it had fallen out.

Owen walked along the long building made up of rooms, testing each door to see if it would open, each one locked. Blocking out the sun with his hands, he would look through the windows when possible, having to skip the ones that were boarded up of course. He made it along the entire length of the building before turning around.

Owen looked over at Zane in the middle of the carpark, "Anything?"

"Just a bunch of rubbish," Zane shook his head.

"Come on boys, it's not safe, we've looked, let's get back home before your mother worries," Brian called from the entrance of the driveway, next to where the office was.

"I just don't get it," Owen called over, starting to walk back along the building to meet the other two. "I was so sure that this is what the pizza meant."

"Don't worry, we'll-" Zane started but Owen held up a hand to silence him as he stopped outside one of the rooms that had a boarded-up window.

"What is it?" Brian asked loudly so Owen could hear him.

Owen simply held his index finger to his lips to indicate for them to be quiet.

Owen walked slowly to the door and reached for the door handle to check it once more. He thought he had heard something from inside but couldn't be sure. Before he touched the handle, it jiggled slightly as if there was someone on the inside trying to open it.

Startled, Owen jumped to the side and pressed his back up against the wall. He saw Brian was now standing with Zane in the carpark, between two skip bins, outside the room. The door to the room hidden from the street and the two skip bins provided more than enough room to hide a car if needed, yet there was no car anywhere in the parking lot.

The doorknob jiggled gently again.

"Hello?" Came a soft muffled voice from inside the room, "Is there somebody there?"

Owen's heart began to beat wildly inside his chest. Had he found Evie, locked in an abandoned motel room?

"Evie?" Owen asked quietly.

"Owen!" Came the excited response. "Is that you?"

"Dad, call the police," Owen instructed Brian, who was quick to pull out his mobile and dial the number. "Evie, can you unlock the door?"

"No, Ryan locked me in. He went out not long ago; I don't know how long he'll be gone."

"It's okay," Owen reassured her, trying to pull and push on the door handle in an effort to make it budge.

Zane was by his side now to help him, but it wouldn't move.

"We're going to get you out of there."

"I'm scared, Owen," Evie replied.

Owen could tell even from her muffled voice that she was crying, which willed him even more to get her out of there.

"Zane, go try the office," Owen ordered, "Maybe there is a key lying around."

Zane ran off in the direction of the office to look for a key. Brian rushed to Owen's side.

"The police are on their way," Brian declared.

"Zane's gone to look for a key," Owen nodded in the direction of the office.

Brian hurried off to help Zane, knowing the state the office was in, figuring it would be quicker if they were both looking.

"Are there any windows in there?" Owen asked Evie, trying to sound as calm as possible, in hopes it would pacify her.

"There's nothing, I've looked."

"Don't worry, the police are coming."

"Hurry Owen, if he finds you here..." Evie sobbed from inside. "I don't want you to get hurt."

"No one is getting hurt," Owen stated with more confidence than he felt.

He wondered what he would do if Ryan did show up.

Evie had been lying on the bed wondering if the Taylor's had received her cry for help yet in the form of a pizza. She had ordered online a pineapple pizza and tried to give Owen hints to help them find her or at least contact the police. Evie just hoped that Owen would understand the message. That he would remember their conversation about how she liked pineapple on a pizza. That he would remember only last week, having to rescue Evie from Sam's, which Evie had seen was just down the street from the motel Ryan had locked her in.

After Evie had told Ryan she was unwell and feigned being in pain, she had pretended to sleep as Ryan had instructed her to rest. After about fifteen minutes, she heard the room's door being open and closed then locked. When she dared to open her eyes, Evie saw Ryan had gone. That's when she heard the sound of his car leaving.

It was while Evie waited for her rescue or Ryan to return, which ever came first, she heard an unfamiliar noise from the room next door. Then what sounded like footsteps approached her door and she held her breath, anticipating Ryan to open the door. The doorknob twisted back and forth slightly, as if someone was testing the door to see if it would open and then the footsteps receded, walking away from her room.

Evie stood up suddenly feeling hopeful, listening carefully. Maybe Owen had figured out her clue. She waited, frozen to the spot, to see if she could hear any other indication that Owen was outside, or even the police.

Not long after, Evie heard a muffled conversation coming from the outside. From what she could tell, whoever had attempted to open her door moments beforehand, was walking back towards her room.

"I'm in here," Evie whispered at first, panicked that Ryan was testing her, before quickly realising she needed to take the chance.

"I'm in here," Evie called, a little louder the second time.

Scared she might miss her chance she dove for the door. It was suddenly silent outside, which made her heart beat fast with anxiety and fear. She couldn't figure out if it was a good or bad feeling.

She reached for the door handle and attempted to open the door, even while knowing that Ryan had locked it when he left, she didn't want to not try once more in hope she was wrong.

"Hello?" Evie called again, hoping that whoever she had heard had not yet left. "Is there somebody there?"

The response was almost instantaneous.

"Evie?"

Evie recognised the voice immediately, relief washed over her. A single tear of happiness ran down her cheek.

"Owen! Is that you?"

Evie heard Owen shouting out an order to someone else about calling the police. Brian was there?

"Evie, can you unlock the door?"

"No, Ryan locked me in. He went out not long ago; I don't know how long he'll be gone."

Suddenly Evie's blood ran cold and her fear returned. She had no idea how long Ryan would be gone for or where he had even gone, but she doubted he would leave her alone for long. Tears came more willingly, trickling down her face.

Owen reassured Evie through the door that everything was going to be okay. The door handle flickered in front of her and she heard the thump of Owen pushing his body against the door in an attempt to get it to budge.

"I'm scared, Owen," Evie admitted through her tears.

Owen's muffled voice gave instructions once more to someone else, Evie recognised him say Zane. Zane was there too.

"The police are on their way," Evie heard Brian declare.

More muffled conversation and footsteps retreating.

Owen asked Evie if there were any windows and she told him there were none.

"Don't worry, the police are coming," Owen announced through the door to Evie.

Evie's panic that Ryan would return before then scared her more than anything.

"Hurry Owen, if he finds you here..." Evie cried. "I don't want you to get hurt."

The thought of Owen being hurt in any way because of her made her feel ill for real. She couldn't help herself but cry at the thought of losing Owen or any of his family at the hands of Ryan, all because of her.

Once again, she realised she should never have stayed as long as she had in the one place. If anything happened to the Taylor's she would never forgive herself.

"No one is getting hurt," Owen stated confidently, yet not reassuring Evie in the slightest.

Evie knew Ryan's capability. Police didn't scare him. He was fearless.

Chapter 36

Evie leaned her forehead helplessly against the door.

"Owen, I want you to go," Evie ordered through the motel room door.

"I'm not leaving you here," Owen replied.

"Ryan could return at any moment. I won't risk your life or anyone else's for mine," Evie argued.

She turned on the spot, leaning her back against the door and sliding down to the floor. Pulling her knees up to her chest, she wrapped her arms around her legs, hiding her face in her lap and cried. She should never have involved the Taylors. She should never have sent the pizza.

"Evie, everything is going to be okay, I promise," Owen tried to reassure her from the other side of the door, hearing her crying harder now.

"You can't promise that. You don't know what he's like, what he's capable of," Evie cried.

"No," Owen agreed evenly, "But I know you. I know you're a fighter and I know you won't just give in."

A fresh wave of tears washed over Evie as she broke down once more. Scared for her life, but also scared for Owen's, and the others outside trying to save her. Her parents and her brother tried to save her they all died trying. Ryan took everything from her that night. She refused to let him do that to her again.

Evie wiped the tears from her face with her hands and took deep breaths to try control her crying. She closed her eyes for a brief moment to compose herself.

"Police are two minutes away," she heard Brian announce from the other side of the door.

"Did you hear that, Evie?" Owen asked, "The police are almost here. It won't be long now."

"There were no room keys. He must have ditched them in one of the bins, maybe," Zane explained as he approached Owen. "Is she okay?"

Owen shook his head in response, his hands leaning on either side of the door.

"Evie," Owen called to her gently.

He waited, studying the door. Silence.

"Evie, I'm staying right here with you, okay?"

Silence still from inside the room, before an interruption on the outside.

Sirens sounded in the distance. Owen looked over his shoulder to the driveway of the motel as police cars swarmed the area, two of them driving into the car park. Police officers scrambled from their vehicles and ran to them at Evie's door.

"Step back please," one officer ordered as they approached.

Owen stepped back slightly, to the side to make way for the officers.

One reached for the door handle and attempted to open it, with no luck.

"Did you think we didn't try that already?" Zane asked bewildered with their actions.

The officer just eyed Zane, before motioning to the other officers over by the cars. One moved to the rear of their vehicle, opened the back and pulled out a large metal battering ram.

"Miss," the first officer called through the door, "If you can hear me, I need you to move away from the door. We're going to break the door in. You need to find a safe place to protect yourself."

Two officers carried the battering ram over to the door. Then with four of them holding it, they swung it once, twice before pushing it into the door with force.

The door burst open towards the inside of the room, splinters shattered across the floor and bed.

The officers holding the batting ram moved back away from the door. The first officer moved to enter the room, but Owen pushed past him and into the room.

"Hey," the officer called.

"Evie?" Owen ignored the officer and moved further into the room, searching for Evie. He looked in the attached messy bathroom and found nothing.

"Evie!"

Owen turned in a circle, the officer reaching for him to pull him out of the room. Owen shrugged him off, but he grabbed at Owen's arm again and pulled him in the direction of the door. Brian and Zane stood outside the doorway, blocked by another officer.

That's when Owen saw her. Evie huddled up in the far corner of the room, beside the bed. He stilled, the officer stopped tugging his arm when realising what Owen saw.

Evie curled in a small ball, her head dipped down. Even with arms wrapped tightly around her legs, Owen could see Evie shaking in fear.

Pulling his arm from the grip of the officer, Owen took a few steps to close the distance between him and Evie. He knelt down beside Evie and put his hands on either one of her arms.

"Evie," Owen whispered gently.

Slowly, Evie raised her head and looked up at him tentatively.

"It's okay," Owen reassured her, "You're safe."

Evie shook her head slowly, "I'll never be safe."

"Come on," Owen held out a hand, "Let's get out of here."

Evie studied Owen's hand, before looking up at him once more then took his hand for him to help her to her feet. He put an arm around her waist and held her close to him as the officer led them out of the motel room.

They walked past the officers at the door, who kept Brian and Zane at bay. Owen continued to hold onto Evie as they made their way over to the closest police car. An officer held the back door open and Owen guided Evie to climb into the car. Before Owen could climb in too, a female officer approached and climbed in beside Evie.

Owen frowned at being separated from Evie, but he didn't want to alarm her all the same.

"It's okay," Owen spoke calmly, "I'll meet you at the station. I'm going to be following right behind you."

Another two officers climbed into the front of the car, it started, the female officer closing the door to the back and the car pulled out of the motel parking lot.

The remaining officers set up a crime scene while they waited for detectives and CSI to arrive. The police interviewed Owen, Brian and Zane individually before leading them away, instructed to go home.

"Finally," Owen muttered as they climbed into his car. "I promised Evie we would be right behind her and meet her at the station."

"I messaged your mother earlier to let her know we had found Evie," Brian stated from the back seat.

"Is she going to meet us at the station?"

Brian looked down at his phone and shook his head, "I haven't heard back from her."

Once they arrived at the station, Owen stormed in ahead of the other two, eager to see Evie, to let her see that he was there. As they entered, they saw Evie escorted by a detective and a woman they did not recognise.

"Evie," Owen exclaimed at the sight of her looking forlorn.

Evie didn't respond, simply ducking her head down and avoiding eye contact. She wrapped her arms around herself as if for protection and comfort.

"Excuse me, sir," the detective stood slightly in front of Evie as if to protect her.

Two officers stood up on either side from their desks, readying themselves to stop any altercations that may arise. The detective held up one hand to indicate for them to stand down and they sat back at their desks, watching carefully still.

"Owen," Brian chastised his son, before turning to the detective. "I'm sorry. We are the Taylors. My name is Brian and my wife is Sandra, who works for Social Services. We are Evie's temporary guardians."

"Mr Taylor," the detective greeted Brian formally with a handshake, "I'm Detective Michaels and this is Mrs Wickens."

He motioned to the woman beside him, who was holding a file of notes and looking very business-like, smiling at the Taylors kindly.

"Miss West has opted to go into protective custody and Mrs Wickens will now be watching over her case," Detective Michaels explained.

Owen's brow furrowed at what the detective was saying and tried to look at Evie who continued to avoid eye contact with any of them, especially Owen.

"What?" Owen baulked, "Evie is coming home with us."

"Miss West has chosen not to continue her stay with your family and we will see that she is provided with the utmost highest level of protection," Mrs Wickens tried to reassure him.

"Evie, what are you doing?"

Owen tried to get her attention by moving closer to her, Evie simply side stepped further away from him.

"Where's Detective Johnson?" Brian inquired, "He's the one that's been in contact with my wife. Does he know what's going on? Has anyone spoken to Sandra about this?"

Detective Michaels and Mrs Wickens exchanged a look which didn't go unnoticed by Brian, Owen or Zane.

"Detective Johnson is currently occupied. I think its best you go home Mr Taylor and speak with your wife," Detective Michaels suggested forcefully.

"You're not telling us something," Brian concluded, stepping closer to the detective. "What's happened?"

The detective let out a breath he had been holding and dropped his shoulders ever so slightly in defeat.

"Detective Johnson is with your wife," Detective Michaels finally answered.

"What?"

"Why?"

"It seems your daughter, Kelly," Detective Michaels paused slightly, unsure of how to proceed and wanting to do so cautiously. "She's missing."

The blood drained from Brian's face as the words sank in. Owen's eyes darted from trying to get Evie to look at him to the detective.

"What did you say?" Owen breathed, not believing what he said.

"No, no, no, no, no, no, no, no," Evie cried out, turning all eyes on her.

Evie could feel her heart racing, she found it hard to breath and there was a ringing in her ears. Anxiety and panic coursed through her body at the detective's words.

Her hands covered her ears, not wanting to hear what the detective had said, willing the words to disappear. Her eyes shut tight Evie sunk to a crouched position, cowering on the floor, her knees up to her chin.

"Rhiannon," Mrs Wickens voice echoed with her real name, but Evie couldn't focus on that fact.

He had her. Without a doubt, Evie knew that Ryan had Kelly. It was all her fault.

Chapter 37

"He has her," Evie mumbled aloud.

She wasn't saying it to anyone in particular, more just to herself. Confirming what she already knew, deep down.

Rocking back and forth on her heels, Evie tried to focus on her breathing, attempting to calm herself down.

It was useless. No matter what she did, someone would get hurt because of her. When she had arrived at the station with the police officers, she immediately declared that if she was going to cooperate then she needed to be able to remove herself from the Taylors. She wanted them safe and she wanted them to have police safety also. Detective Michaels had been all too accommodating and Evie now understood why; he already knew that Kelly was missing.

Muffled voices of anger and confusion filled the air and Evie opened her eyes and looked up. Brian was on his phone trying to call Sandra, Owen and Zane were shouting at the detective. The two officers and a few others had jumped in to hold them back, afraid they might get physical. Detective Michaels was trying his best to soothe the situation, which got more heated when Brian didn't get an answer from Sandra.

Mrs Wickens crouched down beside Evie, one arm around Evie's shoulders and the other hand gently rubbing Evie's arm in a consoling way. The feeling wasn't comforting, but more irritated her. She pushed Mrs Wickens away and stood up suddenly, holding onto the desk beside her to keep her balance as her head spun.

Owen stopped arguing with the detective when he noticed Evie was now standing and ashen faced, swaying slightly. Mrs Wickens was hovering over Evie, but Evie simply pushed her aside. She took two unsteady steps towards them, nearly falling over her own feet. It was obvious to Owen that she was on the brink of an anxiety attack; he had seen her suffer from them enough to know the signs.

In one swift movement, Owen was in front of her, his arms cradling her carefully so she wouldn't fall over.

"Are you okay?" Owen whispered to her, concerned.

"He has her," Evie murmured, finally looking up into his friendly blue eyes.

"Who?" Owen looked down at Evie trying to read her eyes his own etched with concern.

"We don't have time to argue about this. My daughter is missing!" Brian argued with the detective then turned to face Owen, "We need to get back home, now."

Owen nodded once in acknowledgment.

"Jimi, Carl," Detective Michaels barked at two officers standing nearby. "Escort the Taylors home. Stay with them until Detective Johnson or I state otherwise."

The officers stood behind the Taylors, waiting for them to leave the station.

Brian turned to face Evie, "I'm sorry, I'm glad you're safe, I really am, but I need to go home to Sandra."

Evie watched on blankly, wondering why no one was listening to her.

Owen remained by Evie's side, watching her, hoping she would change her mind and go home with them.

"Owen, now," Brian ordered from the doorway where he stood with Zane in tow.

Owens eyes drifted to his father and back to Evie, before he let his hands fall from her sides, making sure she was able to stand on her own. Then he followed his father out of the station, a brief glance back to see Evie standing on her own and Mrs Wickens fussing over her.

"I don't feel right leaving Evie there," Owen complained once they were in the car driving home, escorted by two officers.

"She's safe where she is," Brian replied, trying once more to call his wife but to no avail.

"If she is so safe with the police, why was she always running and hiding?" Owen argued.

Zane sat silently in the back seat, not saying a word.

When Owen pulled the car into the family driveway, Detective Johnson's car and two patrol cars parked out front on the street. Two officers that sat in one car gave a knowing nod to the just arrived car. Two other officers stood to either side of the house.

Brian entered the kitchen, shaking hands with Detective Johnson, who stood to greet him. Owen and Zane followed in after, Owen throwing his car keys haphazardly onto the kitchen bench and turning to face the detective with arms crossed.

Sandra rushed to Brian and threw her arms around him, letting the tears she had been holding back all day start to flow now that her husband was home to support her. After a minute, she calmed and pulled back from Brian and smiled weakly at the boys standing in the doorway.

"Where's Evie?" Sandra asked looking back up at Brian.

"She's at the police station," Brian explained.

"She's chosen to go into witness protection," Owen spoke, irritation evident in his voice.

"When we find Kelly, we'll talk about Evie," Brian stated to his son and then turned to Detective Johnson. "What can you tell us about my missing daughter?"

"There is no evidence of Kelly being taken," Detective Johnson spoke.

"What does that mean?" Owen demanded, stepping forward.

"Owen calm down," Brian ordered his son. "Zane, why don't you two..."

Brian nudged his head towards the living room.

"Come on, man," Zane encouraged his best friend, leading Owen out of the room against his will.

Detective Michaels talked in hushed tones with another officer, while Mrs Wickens tried to encourage Evie to follow her out of the station. Evie resisted and stormed towards the detective who looked up at her when she approached.

"Is everything alright, Miss West?"

"No. Nothing is right," Evie spat at him in frustration that no one seemed to be listening to her. "Ryan has Kelly and none of you are out there trying to find him!"

Detective Michaels turned to face Evie straight on, giving the other officer a nod who stepped away to go on with his work. Mrs Wickens came up from behind Evie, placing a hand on her shoulder, but Evie just shrugged it off.

"Did Ryan mention to you that he was going to kidnap Kelly?"

"No, but-" Evie started, but Detective Michaels interrupted her gently yet firmly.

"At this stage there is no evidence that shows Ryan has taken her, no struggle of any sort. For all we know she is at a friend's house and not informed her parents. We are all taking precautions with Ryan still out there. There are police officers on watch at the Taylors and unmarked police watching the motel where you were."

"Ryan isn't stupid, he won't go to either of those places again," Evie argued, "He's escaped prison twice and stayed hidden. He found me when I was hiding."

Detective Michaels breathed a sigh of defeat and decided to allow Evie to have her say. Out of anyone, she might be the only person who knew how to track down Ryan, whether he had the Taylor girl or not.

"So, what do you suggest we do?"

Evie took in a deep steadying breath to calm her nerves and feel brave.

At the end of the day, Evie knew if it came down to her life or someone else's because of Ryan, she would give hers. Kelly didn't deserve this. The Taylors didn't deserve it. It was Evie's fault for involving them. She never should have gone home with Sandra that first night.

Images of Rhiannon's family flashed through her head. Her mother lay in a pool of her own blood, her father close by. The pain of the kitchen knife slicing into her belly by her own brother right before Ryan killed him in retaliation for hurting her.

Evie squeezed her eyes shut in an attempt to remove the memories. Her heart pounded so hard, she thought it would leap from her chest. Focussing on what she was attempting to do, save Kelly's life, Evie focussed on calming her breathing.

"Give him what he really wants," Evie whispered, before speaking more confidently, "Give him me."

Chapter 38

Evie pulled her cap down on her head as she exited the police station, quickly descending the stairs while looking both ways and hurrying down the street towards the train station.

Once on the train, Evie sat down nervously in a spare seat and watched out the window at the platform scanning every face she saw. Her palms were sweaty and she rubbed them against the thighs of her jeans to dry them.

The train jolted forward as it started to move and begin its journey. Evie breathed a small sigh of relief but also of despair that maybe she was wrong, maybe her plan wouldn't work. What if she couldn't help to find Kelly, what if Ryan didn't have her at all?

As Evie watched aimlessly out the window, her fingers knotted in her lap, she felt someone sit in the vacant seat next to her making her jump slightly at the intrusion. She turned to look at her new companion and her breath caught in her throat when she saw his blue eyes smiling at her.

"Hello beautiful," Ryan crooned at her gently.

Leaning in, Ryan went to brush his lips against Evie's, but she managed to move her face in time so his lips met only with her cheek.

"I'm sorry," Ryan apologised, sitting back up straight, Evie's eyes darting to his in surprise. "I don't know how the police found you. I went out briefly to get something and when I got back the pigs were everywhere."

Evie's brow furrowed in confusion then realisation dawned on her. She knew she needed to play the role if she was going to get an opportunity to save Kelly.

"Where were you?" Evie asked, "I thought you already had all the supplies we needed. I was sick and you left me."

Ryan's head bowed as he shook it in despair. Evie took the opportunity to take a quick glance over the back of her chair to see if anyone was watching them. Nobody seemed interested, which she was grateful for and scared her.

"I made a mistake, but forget about that."

"What mistake?" Evie pushed gently, unsure she wanted to know the answer.

Had he taken Kelly and murdered her? Was she safe? What if Detective Michaels had been right and Kelly had just gone to a friend's house and hadn't contacted Sandra. Questions milled around in Evie's mind, but she took another steadying breath and tried her best to focus on Ryan and getting some answers from him, or it would have all been for nothing. She would have given herself to him once more and for nothing.

"Never mind about that," Ryan answered, taking Evie's hands in his and holding them to his chest. "We're together again and that's all that matters and I won't let anyone come between us again."

His words made Evie uneasy once more. Who had he thought got between them this time?

"We'll get off at the next station," Ryan continued on, oblivious to Evie's fears she was sure he could see all over her face. "I'll get us a new car and we'll get out of this town before the police start looking for us again."

"What about your other car?"

"I left it with a pretty little present in the trunk, easy for the pigs to find," Ryan skited, proud of himself. "It will keep them distracted while we make our escape."

Ryan leaned in and at the same time pulled Evie towards him, so their foreheads were touching. Evie swallowed the lump forming in her throat, praying her sweaty palms wouldn't give her away. He still smelled of cigarettes and whisky, making Evie wonder if he had stopped drinking at all in the time they had been apart. Ryan's cold blue eyes looked deep into her as he spoke.

"In less than a day, we will be in our own little paradise at the lake house. Together forever," Ryan whispered.

Evie's heart pounded in her chest, she was sure he could hear it. Dizziness and made her sway in her seat slightly, but with Ryan holding her she hardly moved. Evie tried her hardest to push her panic attack away, she needed to stay focussed, and it was up to her to save Kelly.

It didn't take long for the train to reach the next station, stopping with a hiss of the brakes. Ryan held Evie's hand tightly, no chance of her running from him, guiding her out of the carriage. He led the way along the platform and down the stairs to the carpark.

Evie allowed Ryan to direct her through the cars, she didn't fight him, she knew she had to let this happen. Ryan walked past the parked cars, looking in windows and testing door handles to see if they would open. When they had reached the further most point of the carpark, Ryan rounded a small hatchback car and looked around the parking lot to see if anyone was around and to check if they were out of surveillance range. He let go of Evie's hands and took off his jacket. Evie watched on in silence, wrapping her arms around her chest for comfort and control.

Ryan held his jacket up against the small windowpane at the back of the passenger side and used a rock Evie hadn't seen him pick up and hit it against the glass which shattered on impact. Clearing the edges of the window so he wouldn't cut himself, Ryan then pushed his arm through the small hole, reaching for the car door on the inside, unlocking it before removing his arm. Lifting the handle, the door opened easily and he held the door open for Evie.

Still not wanting to arouse suspicion, she climbed in the passenger seat, but not before looking around to see if anyone was watching; she couldn't see anybody. Her action didn't go unnoticed by Ryan, who also glanced around the car park again himself. He assumed she was simply checking that no one was watching them steal the car. Once Evie was in the car, Ryan closed the door and rushed over to the driver's side. Evie lent across the front seat and unlocked the door for him and he climbed in.

Ryan pulled a pocketknife from his pocket and flicked it open, making Evie flinch slightly in fear.

"It's okay, baby," Ryan reassured her, "I won't hurt you."

He lent forward and pulled wires out from under the dash, using the knife to thread the covering and cutting the wire. Evie watched out the front windscreen for any movement or persons watching their actions. There was nothing and no one.

The car flickered to life and Evie's attention turned to Ryan once more, who smiled proudly at her before easing the car gently out of the car space and driving out of the parking lot.

Out on the street, Ryan reached across to Evie, taking her hand and pressing it to his lips as he steered with his other hand. His driving was slightly erratic which scared Evie, who once more wondered how much he had been drinking.

Five minutes passed and they were still driving through the outskirts of town when Ryan picked up the speed, feeling confident he had pulled off the perfect plan. It wasn't long before they made their way onto the highway where Ryan pushed his foot down on the accelerator and forced the small car to power past other cars, some which honked at them as they passed and veered in and out of traffic.

Ryan smiled in confidence at Evie when he saw her clutching the door of the car with on hand and bracing herself against the dashboard with the other.

"Relax, Rhiannon," Ryan attempted to comfort Evie, reaching over he squeezed her thigh gently.

"Can you please slow down and watch the road!" Evie pleaded, ignoring his touch and staring in fear out the front of the car.

"I've got this, baby," Ryan gloated and leaned over to kiss Evie's cheek, the car swerving suddenly as he did.

"Ryan!" Evie screamed, pushing him away.

Ryan laughed an evil laugh, Evie thought, and her heart raced faster than it ever had before. The fear this time kept her fully alert and she knew there was no chance of passing out, which she half wished for in that moment so she wouldn't have to witness his erratic and scary driving.

"Remember that Fast and the Furious movie we saw?" Ryan asked Evie.

Evie's eyes darted to him suddenly in disbelief, he was talking about the movie she went and saw with Peter on their date. The same date he ended by attacking Peter on her doorstep when he tried to kiss her. Evie wondered if Ryan was delusional enough to believe it was actual a date he had with her.

"I'm just like Vin Diesel," Ryan boasted, "Only hotter."

He winked at Evie and she turned to look out the windscreen just in time to see Ryan approaching a slow-moving truck at high speeds.

"Ryan!" Evie screeched and braced herself for a head on impact.

Ryan simply turned the steering wheel with a sudden jerk and put the car in the other lane, only there was already a car in that lane. Slamming on the brakes and twisting the wheel again to avoid a collision the car skidded sideways.

Evie knew she was screaming but it was as though there was no noise and everything was happening in slow motion. As the car skidded sideways, Ryan lost control and the car began to flip. Evie's hat fell from her head flew in front of her face, her hair falling free. She lost her grip on the door and felt her body bounce and jolt around in the seat. Shards of glass surrounded her like falling snowflakes. She closed her eyes briefly, fearing it would spray in her eyes.

The car flipped a total of three times before landing on its roof in the middle of the road. Car tyres screeched in the background and Evie feared other cars would plough into them from behind.

Panting from shock, Evie tried to slow her breathing and gasp for air as she dangled from the seat, held in place by the seatbelt she had secured herself with when leaving the train station. Her body ached all over and her forehead felt damp. Touching her finger to her skin, she drew them back stained in bright red blood.

Still panting, she craned her aching neck to look at Ryan who was groaning in pain. He was lying in an awkward folded up position on the roof of the vehicle. He hadn't been wearing his seatbelt. It looked like he had flung around his seat like a rag doll in a washing machine.

Feet pounded the road as other drivers abandoned their own vehicles to run towards the upturned car, glass crunching underfoot as they approached.

Chapter 39

The front door opened, surprising everyone inside the house. Sandra ran to the front door, followed closely by Brian, hoping it was Kelly coming home. Owen and Zane stalked out of the lounge room and stopped in the archway. Detective Johnson, who had stayed towards the back, stepped through the family members, when he saw it was Detective Michaels.

"Michaels? What are you doing here?" Johnson asked confused. "You're meant to be with Miss West back at the station sorting out her protective custody."

Michaels rubbed the back of his neck knowing he was going to get in a lot of trouble for what he was about to tell him. He looked from one family member to the next, their eyes all on him in interest. It didn't make what he had come to inform Johnson about any easier.

"Can we talk outside?" Michaels indicated towards the front door and Johnson followed him outside, closing the front door behind them.

The Taylors and Zane watched on through the window as Michaels spoke to Johnson, his hands moving about as he spoke. Johnson's eyes widen and he looked red with anger.

"You what?" Johnson growled, loud enough the family inside could hear.

Michaels looked like he was attempting to explain something hurriedly and Johnson rubbed a hand over in face to as if to ease a large headache that was forming. A pointed finger in Michaels face, Johnson was obviously upset with him as he reprimanded him.

Opening the front door, Johnson returned inside, faced with an anxious family, wanting to know what was going on. Michaels stood off behind him, looking ashamed and frustrated with himself.

"There's been a development," Johnson spoke cautiously, trying to find the right words to break to news to the family.

"Is it Kelly? Is she okay?" Sandra choked back a sob as she spoke.

"We still have no word on the where about of your daughter," Johnson answered gently.

"Then what is it?" Brian asked, wrapping a comforting arm around his wife.

"It seems that Detective Michaels allowed Miss West who volunteered to use her as bait to draw Mr Scott out of hiding. Miss West was convinced that Mr Scott is the reason for your daughter's disappearance," Johnson explained.

"That's what she meant," Owen cut in, all eyes turning to him. "Evie said something like 'he has her' right before we left her at the station. She was having an anxiety attack and wasn't making much sense, but we left to come home."

"So where is Evie, I mean Rhiannon, now?" Sandra pushed for answers.

Johnson looked back at Michaels who bowed his head ashamed and then back at the family who were waiting eagerly for a response.

"We don't know," Johnson replied and there were gasps throughout the room. "The plain clothed officers detailed with following Miss West lost sight of her on the train. Surveillance footage shows Miss West and Mr Scott exiting the carriage together at the last minute at the first stop, holding hands. It didn't seem like Miss West was resisting either."

Colour drained from Owen's face and his blood ran cold. After everything they went through to rescue her, she willingly runs away with him. It didn't make sense.

"Why would you let her risk her life like that?" Owen demanded to know, looking straight at Michaels.

Stepping forward, Owen was ready to punch Michaels in the face from frustration and anger. Zane quickly stepped in front of him and managed to push his best friend away before he did anything that would land him in handcuffs.

"I get you are upset, but we have people out looking for them and we're going through any surveillance footage we can find," Johnson tried his best to ease the family's fears.

Before anyone else could talk, the front door opened again and an officer stuck their head inside, looking between both Michaels and Johnson.

"Detectives," he spoke, "We have something we need you to look at out here."

Everyone in the room exchanged looks. Johnson asked the Taylors to stay in the house, but they ignored him and followed him outside.

The officer led the way, followed first by both detectives and the Taylor family right behind them. From the back, they could just make out what the officer was saying to the detectives as they rushed along the footpath and across the road.

"It wasn't there in the patrol we did an hour ago. We stopped to check it out as it matched the description given of the suspect's vehicle he was last seen driving. There's no sign of the suspect and the keys were left in the ignition but turned off."

The group approached the small park that was a short distance from the Taylor home. The same park Owen had sat on the swings with Evie on two separate occasions.

Parked on the kerb was a faded blue car. The park was deserted and the officer who had stayed with it was busy wrapping police tape around the scene so no one could get near the car.

"Have you searched the car?" Johnson asked, pulling a set of gloves out of his pocket and pulling them onto his hands.

Johnson ducked under the police tape while Michaels stopped and kept the rest of the group behind the line.

"No, sir," the officer replied. "I came and got you right away."

Johnson opened the driver's side door and sat in the seat, flicking through the centre console and in the glove compartment. The car smelt of stale cigarette smoke and spilt whisky; an empty bottle lay on the floor of the passenger side. Climbing back out of the car, Johnson moved around to the back of the car.

"Can we get this opened, please," Johnson ordered.

One of the officers hurried over with gloved hands, pulled the car keys out of the ignition and carried them to the back of the car. Sticking the key into the hole, he unlocked the trunk and stepped back to let the detective open the lid.

Johnson pulled the lid of the trunk up and peered inside, almost instantly calling out over the lid.

"We've got her! Get an ambulance out here right away!"

Sandra's hands flew over her mouth to cover her wails of crying as Brian hugged her tightly in his arms.

"Is it Evie?" Owen demanded to know, the other officer preventing him from getting too closer to see.

"It's Kelly," Johnson declared, carefully leaning in and gently carrying her out of the trunk to lie her down on the soft grass. "She's unconscious, but she's breathing."

Owen breathed a sigh of relief at the sight of his limp sister's body lying before him. Time stretched on and it seemed like forever, when in fact it was only a matter of minutes until the sound of sirens in the distance grew closer.

It all became a blur once the paramedics arrived. They did their initial checks of Kelly before moving her onto a stretcher and rolling the bed into the back of the van. Sandra climbed in the back with them, staying with Kelly, holding her hand.

The ambulance pulled away and it wasn't until Zane patted Owen on the shoulder, that he broke his stare at the blue car in front of him.

Owen torn with his feelings. When the detective had announced it was Kelly in the trunk, Owen was relieved his sister had been found and was safe again, but at the same time, he felt despair and fear that it wasn't Evie.

"Let's get to the hospital," Zane suggested, pulling his friend away from the scene the police were going over with the now arrived crime people.

Zane drove Owen's car with Owen in the passenger seat and Brian in the back. He dropped them off at the hospital entrance then took the car to find a parking spot.

Brian ran into the emergency department with Owen hot on his heels. By the time they had located Sandra, she was outside a room, waiting on a chair. When she saw Brian and Owen coming towards her, she embraced them both in tight hugs.

"The doctor is in there with her now," Sandra explained, indicating towards the closed door behind her. "The paramedics said her vitals were steady. Initial thoughts are she has been knocked out in some way."

After a long wait, the doctor and a nurse come out of the room. The doctor spoke with Kelly's family, explaining she had a concussion and swelling on her brain. They wanted to keep her in until she showed signs of improvement and no brain damage, though she was still unconscious.

The family waited in the small room, listening to the monitors beep. Zane nudged Owen and indicated toward the door. Owen nodded, but leant down and gave his mother a kiss on her cheek before leaving the room.

"Thought you could do with a break," Zane uttered as they walked down the hospital hallway. "Let's get some drinks for everyone and you can clear your head a bit."

"Thanks, man," Owen muttered, "And thank you for being here."

"Where else would I be?" Zane shrugged with a laugh, which made Owen give a weak smile.

Two nurses and a doctor pushed past them as they ran down the hallway towards the emergency entrance.

"We've got two patients coming in, single car roll over on the highway. One female; estimated age to be eighteen, and one male; estimated age to be early twenties. No identification on either of them."

The double doors at the end pushed open with paramedics pushing two trolley beds along the hallway towards where the boys were walking. Nurses and doctors came from various directions to join them and take over the emergency care.

"Watch out," ordered a nurse and the boys jumped to the side of the hallway.

On the first bed that wheeled past them was the male. Covered in blood, he looked a mess. Zane looked away slightly horrified.

The second trolley wheeled past with the female. Her face covered with an oxygen mask and blood stained her long dark hair but Owen recognised her right away.

"Evie!" Owen called out and started to follow the doctors and nurses who were wheeling Evie down the hallway. They pushed through another set of double doors labelled 'staff only', but Owen ignored the sign and followed through.

"Hey, you can't be in here," yelled a nurse who shoved him back out.

"That's Evie," Owen declared, trying to look past the nurse who wasn't allowing him to pass. "I know her. I need to see if she's okay."

"You need to stay out here and let the doctors do their job. If either of you try to come in here, I'll call security," the nurse gave a warning look to both Owen and Zane before disappearing back through the door.

"Are you sure it was Evie?" Zane questioned his friend gently.

"One hundred percent," Owen murmured debating going through the doors again. He didn't care if security kicked him out; he needed to check that Evie was okay.

"Let's go tell your parents," Zane suggested, "They can let the police know where she is."

"The guy must have been Ryan," Owen mused aloud.

"All the more reason to get the police over here, come on."

Owen allowed him to pull him back down the hallway towards his sister's room, casting an eye back on the doors where Evie had disappeared.

Chapter 40

Evie's eyes felt heavy. Every time she tried to open her eyes, she couldn't. Her body ached all over but she couldn't move. Breathing was difficult and felt like someone was smothering her.

Feeling trapped, Evie struggled to straighten her thoughts. The last thing she remembered was dangling upside down in the upturned car that Ryan had rolled. Ryan! He was a crumpled mess on the roof, moaning in pain but not moving.

That's when she remembered the whole reason she was with Ryan, Kelly. Was she okay? Had the police found her? Was she alive? The thought made her blood run cold.

Evie felt lost in a haze of darkness, which stretched on forever.

Days passed until late one evening when Evie's eyes began to flutter open like a butterfly drying its wings in the sun for the first time after emerging from it cocoon.

Taking in her surroundings, Evie realised she was in a hospital bed in a private room, with a machine beeping beside her and a cannula in her arm attached to a drip. She moved her legs slightly trying to get feeling back into them, when she was able to do so she breathed a sigh of relief knowing that it was a good sign. Her head ached and when she strained to sit up, pain shot down her neck.

Moving her feet once more, her left leg knocked something on the bed. Adjusting herself slightly to look down along the bed she noticed a male leaning against the bed, facing away from her, a head of blonde hair. She froze, her heart rate picking up. Ryan was there with her. Nobody would have known where she was and that's what scared her most.

The door to the room opened quietly and a nurse walked in, pausing briefly when she saw Evie was awake.

"Well, look who decided to wake," Nurse Sarah whispered, aware that Evie had a sleeping visitor lying on her bed.

"Please help me," Evie struggled out, keeping her volume low, to not wake Ryan.

"That's usually what we do in the hospital," Sarah smiled as she checked the monitor and made some notes on Evie's chart.

"You need to call the police," Evie spoke in a hushed tone. "He's dangerous," she indicated with a small nod of her head towards Ryan's sleeping body.

Sarah frowned slightly, "He seemed like a lovely young man while I was talking to him today. He's been here every day waiting for you to wake up."

Evie shivered. Ryan would not let her out of his sight again if he could help it. Everything she had tried to prevent had happened and it was all her fault.

"Please call the police," Evie's voice strained once more, a single tear escaping the corner of her eye, which didn't go unnoticed by Sarah.

"Oh sweetheart, everything will be okay," Sarah reached out and patted Evie's arm. "I'll go get the doctor."

"No, wait-," Evie tried to stop Sarah from walking out, but she closed the door to the room before she could.

Ryan began to stir; Evie's voice had been a little louder and had obviously woken him. Gripped with fear, Evie froze wondering if it was too late to pretend to be asleep still. She knew he had heard her, so there was no point. Waiting, bated breath, Evie watched as Ryan moved more and his head slowly rose from the bed and turned to face her.

Owen! It wasn't Ryan at all, but Owen. He was here, with Evie. Owen had been with her for days while she slept. How did he find her?

"You're awake," Owen smiled at Evie and sat upright. "How do you feel?"

"Kelly, I didn't help-," Evie began, not concerned for herself but for the wellbeing of Kelly.

"She's fine," Owen told Evie, cutting her off, "They found her trapped in the trunk of Ryan's car around the corner from the house, next to the park. She spent some time in hospital, but she's home now resting."

Evie breathed a sigh of relief knowing Kelly was safe with her family again. Then something Ryan had said to her made sense, he had said he had left his car with a pretty, little present in the trunk, easy for the police to find. He was talking about Kelly.

The doctor came in at that moment followed by Nurse Sarah. Owen stood up and pushed the chair he had been sitting in off to the side so it was out of the way.

"I'm just going to step outside and call mum to let her know you're awake," Owen announced, smiling at Evie before leaving the room.

Once the door closed behind him, the doctor turned to face Evie, "Nurse Sarah mentioned you wanted the police called because you didn't feel safe around the young man."

Evie shook her head slowly, "I mixed him up with someone else."

"As long as you're sure," he offered.

"I'm safe with Owen," Evie confirmed with a nod.

The doctor smiled and began to check Evie over. He told Evie how she was very lucky to have survived the car accident. She had come out with some fractured ribs, a collapsed lung, bruising and a gash to her head.

It was a good half an hour before the doctor and nurse left the room. Owen came back in followed closely behind by his family, Sandra led the convoy, rushing to Evie's side and scooping her in a hug gently to avoid hurting her too much.

"You silly girl," Sandra chastised her, "Don't you ever do anything so silly again, do you hear me?"

Evie smiled weakly in response, looking past Sandra and noticing Kelly standing by the door.

"Kelly, I'm so sorry," Evie apologised, "I never wanted any of this to happen."

"I'm fine," Kelly replied quietly, "I will be, thanks to you."

"Me? But I didn't do anything."

"The detectives determined the timeline of events," Brian spoke for the first time, "It seems that once you left the police station, Ryan dumped his car and Kelly in pursuit of you instead."

"Is he," Evie started, swallowing a lump in her throat, "Where is Ryan?"

Evie looked from one face to another and they all looked between themselves before Sandra sat down on the edge of the bed taking Evie's hand in hers.

"He's here in the hospital," Sandra spoke gently, breaking the news to Evie as carefully as she could. Evie's heart stopped. "Ryan's in ICU in a critical condition. They don't know if he will survive or not yet. It's fifty/fifty."

Evie's heart pounded. She didn't know what she expected to hear, she knew she would never feel safe with him out there. Evie wondered if it made her a bad person, to wish that he were dead. He had taken so much from her, her family, friends and her freedom.

The Taylors left soon after, Nurse Sarah asking them to leave to allow Evie a chance to rest. Sarah would refer to Evie as Rhiannon and it made her feel uneasy once more. What if Ryan was okay and somehow found her in the hospital?

Two days later, with frequent visits from the Taylor family, Owen more so and even Zane dropped in to say hi, Evie was given the all clear by the doctor to leave the hospital. From what information she could get, Ryan was still in ICU and clinging to life.

On her last day in hospital, Evie received a visit from Detective Michaels, accompanied by Mrs Wickens. Detective

Johnson had been previously and taken Evie's statement, but the last time she had seen Michaels and Mrs Wickens was the day she convinced them to use her as bait for Ryan.

"Miss West," Mrs Wickens spoke formally, "It has been decided by a judge that you have no choice but to go into witness protection until the situation with Mr Scott is maintained; whether that be by his death or his containment in a high security prison. You are to come with us now and we will take you to your new location and give you a new identity that you will live by."

Evie's jaw dropped open in surprise; Sandra had told her she would be collecting her in an hour.

"I thought that I would be going home with the Taylors," Evie croaked, unsure of what she actually wanted to do. It seemed logical to go with Mrs Wickens. The Taylors would be at risk if she stayed with them again.

"Mrs Taylor will be informed of the court ruling once you are in protective custody," Detective Michaels informed her.

Evie had already changed into some clothes Sandra had brought in for her the day before. Otherwise she had no other personal items; they had been destroyed in the accident. Even her cap, her brother's cap, was gone forever. Yet another thing Ryan had taken from her.

"We need to leave immediately," Mrs Wickens announced.

Evie simply nodded and followed Mrs Wickens out of the hospital, escorted by Detective Michaels. Outside the hospital, she climbed into the back seat of a dark SUV that Detective Michaels was driving and with Mrs Wickens in the passenger seat. Behind them was a police car with two officers inside.

Mrs Wickens gave Evie a file to read through about her new life. Evie flipped through the pages trying not to get overwhelmed with it all. Her new name was Gabrielle Porter and she would be living with a woman who was an undercover agent who would pose as her mother, Mandy. They would live in a small town where Evie would attend school and be able to finish her senior year. Their story was a single mother raising her teenage daughter after losing her husband in a house fire when Gabrielle was two. They recently moved to town so Mandy could be a freelance writer and finish her novel while working at the local café.

In the file was a photo of Mandy, she looked nothing like Evie, except for dark hair. Evie assumed she would need to tell people she took after her father, but as luck would have it all photos of him had burnt in the fire.

Owen reached for the door handle to Evie's hospital room to open it. He had offered to accompany Sandra in collecting Evie from the hospital. Sandra knew he was being over protective; it had become so obvious he had feelings for Evie. He pushed the door open and stilled when he looked inside.

"Where is she?" Owen asked his mother.

Sandra poked her head inside the room to see it empty. Turning to the nurses' station, Sandra spoke to one of the nurses who worked on a computer behind the desk.

"Excuse me, but we're here to pick up Evie from room twelve and she's not there."

The nurse looked up at Sandra and furrowed her brow.

"Your name?"

"I'm Sandra Taylor and this is my son Owen. I'm down as her emergency contact," Sandra explained.

The nurse tapped on her keyboard and looked at the computer screen.

"It says here she was discharged over an hour ago," the nurse revealed, "By a Jeremy Michaels."

"Who the fuck is that?" Owen burst into the conversation.

"Owen, language, calm down," Sandra chastised her son, "It's one of the detectives from the police station. I'll give him a call."

Sandra pulled her phone out of her handbag and began to dial, holding it to her ear. Owen stood off to the side of the walkway and watched his mother as she paced back and forth while having a heated conversation.

"Why weren't we informed before now?"

Hanging up she wandered over to Owen, placing a sympathetic hand on his upper arm.

"What's going on?" Owen asked, concern etched in his voice and a little frustration.

"Evie has been taken into protective custody by order of a judge," Sandra explained to him, "There's no way around it. She's gone."

Fire burned in Owen's eyes, but he looked away from his mother trying to fight his feelings.

"Whatever," Owen grunted, "Let's go home."

Owen marched off down the hospital hallway, ignoring his mother's pleas to talk to her. Sandra knew he was hurting but was too proud to let it show.

Chapter 41

Gabrielle was the new girl at school arriving a little over a month earlier. She kept to herself and when not at school usually locked herself away at home with her mother. Some of her peers had tried to engage her in their conversations, she had even had a party invite when she first arrived, but Gabrielle would politely refuse and end the conversation.

Collecting her things from her locker to complete her homework, Gabrielle closed the door and headed towards the school exit. It was a short walk home and she enjoyed every minute of it, knowing she would soon be locking herself indoors until the next school day. She hated her life but at least she was alive and this time she would do anything so no one else came in harm's way.

Arriving home, Gabrielle was surprised to see an unfamiliar white sedan parked out the front of her house. Stopping in her tracks, her heart began to race. Could it be her past had found her and tracked her down already? She knew that the witness protection agency was full of shit when they said she would be safe in their program.

Gabrielle started to back track and ran towards the centre of town, she needed to get to the café where her mother worked.

Diving through the door, the little bell attached at the top rang out loudly causing patrons and staff alike to look up in her direction. At one of the back booths was a group of students Gabrielle recognised from some of her classes. She avoided their curious stares and hurried to the counter. Beth, the older woman that worked with Mandy approached Gabrielle.

"Gabrielle, are you okay?" Beth asked.

"Where's my mum?" Gabrielle choked out between pants for air. Her lung was still recovering from the accident and running probably wasn't her best idea.

"She went home early today," Beth explained, "Said something had come up in the family."

Concern and sympathy crossed over Beth's face, worried that Gabrielle was only learning now that something was wrong with a family member.

"How about I call her and let her know you're here," Beth suggested, reaching for the phone and dialling before Gabrielle could sort out her thoughts and object.

After a brief conversation, Beth hung up the phone and Gabrielle waited for what Beth was going to tell her. All she needed to hear was one of two words. One word would tell her to run. The other would tell all was safe.

"Your mother is a strange lady sometimes," Beth muses.

"What did she say?" Gabrielle gripped the counter as she waited, her knuckles turning white.

"She said everything was fine and to pick up some canned asparagus on your way home."

Gabrielle released her hold on the counter and began to steady her breathing.

"Um, thank you Beth," Gabrielle murmured, "I guess I better get home."

Gabrielle walked back towards her house, confused. Asparagus, their safe word, it meant everything was okay. If Mandy had told her to bring home a can of tomatoes, Gabrielle would have known that she was no longer safe and needed to run.

Stopping next to the white sedan parked out the front of her house, Gabrielle looked at it before glancing up at her house. Everything seemed fine, but Gabrielle had learnt many times that appearances could be deceiving.

Walking up the pebble path, Gabrielle opened the front door slowly and cautiously entered the house. Voices floated through the air from the lounge room, Gabrielle wondered who could possibly be visiting.

Slowly, Gabrielle wandered into the lounge room to see Mandy sitting on one of the couches facing Detective Michaels and Detective Johnson on the other.

Gabrielle's breathing picked up along with her heartbeat and she felt slightly faint at the prospect that they were in her living room. For them to visit meant there had been a development with Ryan Scott and Gabrielle didn't know what she was hoping to hear.

Both men stood as Gabrielle walked around the couch to sit down next to Mandy.

"Sorry if we scared you," Johnson apologised.

Gabrielle simply shook her head and clasped her hands in her lap, picking nervously at her nails.

"You're probably wondering why we are here," Johnson went on, Michaels sitting quietly beside him giving nothing away.

"I'm assuming it has something to do with Ryan," Gabrielle murmured quietly, finding her voice.

Both detectives looked at one another, as if to decide who will break the news to the frightened teenaged girl.

Detective Michaels spoke, "As you know, Ryan sustained critical injuries in the crash, due to him not wearing his seat belt. He had internal bleeding and he had severed his spinal cord meaning he would never walk again if he survived."

Gabrielle swallowed, trying to moisten her dry mouth. He would never walk again, that certainly would prevent him from chasing her. Maybe she was free after all, is that what they were telling her?

"He's been on life support for the past two weeks; the machine was the only thing keeping him alive. Last night a judge made the decision to turn off his life support. His family wanted nothing to do with him, he was dead to them the moment he committed the murders on your family."

Gabrielle bowed her head, remembering that night all too well like it had only happened yesterday. She knew nothing would ever rid her of those images of her family bleeding all over the floor.

"Miss West," Detective Michaels use of her real name made her eyes shoot up to his, "Ryan died last night. You no longer have to worry about him coming after you."

Gabrielle stared at him stunned, unsure of what to feel or say in that moment. For over two years her life had been ruled by Ryan's actions.

"Rhiannon, do you understand what the detective is saying to you?" Mandy asked, looking to the detectives for permission to take over the conversation, looking back at the frozen figure beside her.

"Rhiannon," Mandy went on, "You no longer have to hide. You don't have to pretend to be anyone but yourself. You don't have to go by any other name but your own. News bulletins will read that Rhiannon West is alive and well."

"That movie was great," Zane commented stretching out on the lounge.

Owen simply shrugged, not fussed about the movie.

"Man, you have to get out of this slump," Zane commanded, "It's been two months. If she wanted to contact you, she would have by now. She's in protective custody. She won't break that, even for you."

Owen threw a cushion at his friend, hitting him square in the chest.

"Shut up," he demanded, trying to act as though he wasn't even thinking about Evie. "You don't know what you're talking about."

"So, you're not thinking about Evie then?"

A knock came from the front door, Owen jumped up to answer it.

"That'll be the pizza," he commented.

"You didn't answer my question," Zane called after him from the lounge room.

Opening the door, Owen stood stunned when he saw who stood on the doorstep, not the pizza delivery he was expecting.

"Hi," Evie gave a small timid wave, suddenly unsure of herself.

Owen couldn't move, worried his eyes were deceiving him. He had dreamt so many times about running into Evie over the past two months that he was scared that at any minute he would wake up. Had he fallen asleep during the movie with Zane?

Evie stood awkwardly, wondering if she should have called first.

"Man, you don't have to flirt with the delivery guy to get the pizza, do you?" Zane mocked as he came out from the lounge room. His jaw dropped when he saw Evie standing in the doorway.

"Evie!" Zane exclaimed in excitement and rushed forward to hug her, "Rhiannon. Sorry, I don't really know what to call you. You probably have a different name now anyway."

Evie giggled, Zane's antics putting her more at ease. She eyed Owen who still stood there just staring at her. Zane followed her gaze and nudged his friend out of his trance.

"What are you doing here?" Owen muttered, immediately cursing himself for making it sound like he wasn't happy to see her. When actually, he was over the moon she was there, but still it frightened him. How long would she stay? What if she was just passing through to say goodbye for good.

"Uh-," Evie wasn't sure how to answer that. "Are your parents at home?"

"They should be home any minute," Owen answered, "They just went out to pick Kelly up."

"Invite her in," Zane growled at Owen leaning close to his ear, although Evie could hear him and she smiled shyly.

"Oh yeah, sorry," Owen stepped back, "Come in."

Evie walked inside, taking in her surroundings. The home was the same as she remembered. Nothing had changed in the time she had been away. Owen led her into the kitchen to the table where the three of them sat down.

"Would you like something to drink?" Owen offered.

Evie shook her head, "I'm fine thanks."

At that moment, the door to the garage opened and Kelly walked through first.

"Is the pizza here yet?" she called out as she walked towards the kitchen, "I'm starv-"

Kelly's voice trailed off when she saw Evie sitting at the table with Owen and Zane.

"Kelly stop acting like you've never eaten before," Sandra scolded her daughter as she entered behind her.

When Sandra saw Evie, she raced over to her with a squeal and open arms. Evie stood up from her seat smiling and embraced Sandra.

Sandra held Evie back at arms-length and studied her.

"Are you okay?" Sandra questioned her.

Evie nodded, smiling at Sandra's mothering.

Brian stepped between the pair and gave Evie a brief hug. Kelly moved over and gave hugged Evie.

"Do the police know you're here?" Sandra questioned.

"In a way," Evie replied, taking a deep breath she knew she needed to get it out and tell them, "I'm not longer under protective custody."

A chorus of 'what' and 'why' filled the room.

"They turned Ryan's life support off two weeks ago," Evie explained. "He's dead."

"Why didn't the police tell me? Why didn't you come here sooner?" Sandra asked.

"Mum!" Owen warned his mother, "Let her speak."

Evie smiled at Owen appreciatively.

"I came back briefly just after it happened," Evie went on, "I needed to see for myself that he was actually gone. After, I had to go home and sort out things with lawyers. I'm the only surviving member of my family, I inherited all of my parents' and Aunt Sue's assets. I also wanted to visit my family. Say a proper goodbye. I never got that opportunity before."

Evie's head hung down in sadness, but she quickly recovered and looked up at everyone watching her.

"I just wanted to come by and say thank you, for everything you all did for me. I also wanted to apologise for everything I put you through."

Evie's eyes fell on Kelly.

"I'm fine," Kelly assured her.

"Well, no more apologising for things you can't control," Sandra announced. "Where are you staying? How long are you here for?"

"I'm staying at a motel currently, just until I can find a place to rent more permanently," Evie revealed, "I want to finish high school. I didn't want to start at another new school and I couldn't bear to return to my old schools with everything that's happened."

Sandra shot a look to her husband that only he recognised and nodded his head once.

"Stay here," Sandra offered.

Owen nearly choked on the water he was drinking at his mother's sudden suggestion. He didn't hate the idea of Evie living with them but wondered how he would be able to control his feelings for her in such close proximity. The last thing on Evie's mind would have been a relationship with anyone, surely.

"What? No, I couldn't, I'll be fine in a place of my own. Honest."

"I won't take no for an answer," Sandra declared. "You can have your room back. We still have all the clothes and school supplies we bought for you. I'll just come into the school and explain what's happening and we can simply change your name on the roll to Rhiannon West."

"Actually, I wanted to ask you," Evie suddenly looked very nervous, unsure of what Sandra's reaction would be. "I was sort of thinking I could be Evie Harrison again. Not just at school, but I want to legally change my name, if that's okay?"

"Of course, that's okay," Sandra answered happily, wiping a tear that ran down her cheek, "But why do you want to do that?"

"I don't have a family anymore," Evie explained, "It was only as Evie, living in this home with all of you that I felt like I had a family again."

Sandra smiled at Evie's explanation

"Also, I was warned by my protection agent that everyone will know Rhiannon is alive and the news will be all about her. I don't want to be spread all over the news. I just want a normal life finally."

Sandra hugged Evie once more and smiled.

A knock on the door broke through the room and Evie's instinct made her jump as she looked at the door. She took a deep breath, knowing she was safe and always would be from now on.

"That will be the pizza," Owen commented, but it was Zane who stood up this time, noticing Owen couldn't take his eyes off Evie.

"I'll get it," Zane announced.

He returned quickly with four pizza boxes and laid them out on the table, grabbing a piece right away from the box nearest to him.

Sandra smiled at Zane's actions and turned to Evie, "Hungry?"

"Starving," Evie winked at Kelly who smiled back at her.

The family sat down around the table, started to pull pizza slices out and began to eat.

Owen, who was sitting beside Evie leaned over towards her and whispered so only she would hear, "Sorry, there's no pineapple ones."

Evie glanced up at him and smiled. The warmth Owen felt seeing her smile so genuinely made him smile in return. Evie looked free.

Epilogue

Evie was placing her books back into her locker after class, finding the things she needed to go study in the library, when Harley came bounding up beside her.

"Are you coming to Simon's on Saturday night?" Harley asked for the third time that week.

Evie knew that Harley was excited about the party more so because it was being hosted by Harley's new boyfriend. It seemed that in the two months Evie had been away, Harley had moved on from her obsession with Owen and started dating Simon.

It had been two weeks since Evie had returned to school. At first Evie was reserved towards hanging out with Harley and her friends, she had heard some of the rumours that were going around about her disappearance from school. Some were the standard, her mum had returned early, taking Evie back home. Other rumours ranged from teen pregnancy to being in jail for drugs to armed robbery.

Harley had been surprised and excited to see Evie when she walked into their first shared class of Biology on her first day back at school. She had waved Evie over eagerly asking her a thousand questions. Evie simply told Harley she had needed to go home to sort out some family things and was back to finish off the senior year.

Evie made sure to explain to Harley that Owen wasn't actually her cousin, but a family friend. Evie didn't know why she had to clarify that part of the story, but she felt it was important. It didn't take long for Evie's excuses to spread through the school like wildfire. It probably helped that Owen told his friends the same thing and being one of the most popular people in school, everyone wanted to know everything about him.

"Yes Harley, I'm coming," Evie smiled at her, closing her locker door.

"You're not going to pull out last minute, are you?" Harley looked at her concerned. It was obvious she was remembering how Evie had been previously in regards to parties.

"I'll be there," Evie assured her.

"Great," Harley squealed, "Got to run. See you in class."

Before Evie could speak another word, Harley had rushed off down the hall.

"Did I just hear right? Evie Harrison is actually accepting a party invite without having to be coerced?" Zane's voice teased from behind Evie.

Turning around, Evie found Zane leaning with one arm against the locker beside Evie's.

"Yes, you heard correctly," Evie stuck her tongue out at him.

"Is this a new Evie or something?" Zane asked her.

"More like the old me," Evie winked at him.

Evie turned on her heel and started to walk away from him.

"Where are you going?" Zane called after her. "It's lunch time."

Evie walked backwards as she called back to him, "Library, I need to catch up on my studies. That part of me has never changed."

Saturday morning, Owen staggered sleepily out of his bedroom towards the bathroom. As he reached for the door handle, the door opened on its own.

"Oh, sorry," Evie apologised looking up at him, "It's all yours, I just finished."

Owen's eyes opened, suddenly no longer tired.

"No, you're alright, sorry I should have knocked," Owen stuttered, he was still getting used to Evie being in the house again.

"Lucky your dad fixed the lock," Evie smiled shyly at him, her cheeks blushing slightly.

Owen laughed, remembering the time Evie had walked in on him in the bathroom.

She stepped past Owen towards her bedroom, "I guess I'll see you tonight at the party."

Owen's brow furrowed slightly, "You're not coming with Zane and me?"

Evie shook her head gently, "No, I'm heading over to Harley's to get ready together and going from there."

"Of course, right," Owen muttered, "See you at the party."

Evie haltered in the hallway for a few more seconds before giving him a tiny wave.

Owen watched her walk away, closing her bedroom door. He knew when his mother offered Evie the spare room to live in again that things would become complicated. Over the two weeks Evie had been living with them again, Owen had tried to give Evie her space.

While Evie had been in witness protection, Owen wanted nothing more than to have her back at home again, but now that she was there Owen was more aware of his feelings for Evie. He couldn't deny them to himself anymore. The issue was Owen didn't know how Evie felt about him. He doubted she felt anything.

Evie danced on the makeshift dance floor with Harley, Rebecca and Paige. This party was different for her compared to the Lake Party and Owen's birthday. For the first time since becoming Evie Harrison, she felt completely free to be a teenager and have fun. Evie hadn't felt that way since Casey's death. Pushing the thought to the back of her mind, Evie continued on dancing with her new friends.

Owen and Zane arrived to the party with their friends greeting them as they walked into the house, the party already in full swing. Owen's eyes searched the party desperately, trying to locate Evie.

"Chill, man," Zane spoke only loud enough for Owen to hear, "She's safe, she's with Harley."

"That's not the most reassuring thing," Owen mumbled.

Zane laughed, patting his friend on the back and dragging him further into the party. He did his best to distract Owen from thoughts of Evie, though he knew how his friend felt, even if he couldn't admit it to himself or others.

The pair moved through the house to the backyard, Owen catching a glimpse of Evie dancing happily with Harley and her friends. His eyes narrowed when he saw Marcus nearby, but had no time to do anything about it with Zane pulling him outside.

"I need water," Evie called over the music to Harley, fanning herself with her hand in an attempt to get cool.

Leaving the girls behind, Evie pushed her way through the masses to the kitchen, pouring herself a glass of water from the tap. She sculled the liquid instantly, before refilling the glass and going outside to get some air.

Outside in the night air, Evie instantly felt cooler. Taking a deep breath, she moved around some of the small crowds to find her own space off to the side. Someone pushed past her, knocking her forward and causing her to spill her full glass of water down the back of someone.

"What the..." growled Owen as he felt the cool liquid saturating the back of his shirt.

He turned around quickly to curse at the person who had spilt their drink on him only to find Evie standing before him. Owen immediately relaxed at the sight of her and raised an eyebrow at her in question.

"Did you just throw your drink on me?" Owen asked curiously, a hint of a smile on his lips.

Evie stood in fright, expecting Owen to go off at her.

"I'm so sorry," Evie started to babble an apology, "Someone bumped me, it's just water, I swear."

"Evie, calm down," Owen laughed, "It's okay. I'm not angry."

Evie visibly relaxed at his words.

"You looked like you were going to kill her," Jensen blurted out.

"Shut up, Jensen," Zane scowled at him before Owen could respond, his eyes not leaving Evie's. "Let's go guys. Give these two a chance to talk."

"They live together, they can talk whenever," Tyler rebutted.

"Get a clue," Mark whispered.

The group of boys peeled away, leaving Evie and Owen standing alone together.

"I really am sorry," Evie repeated.

"You looked like you were having fun in there," Owen stated, ignoring her apologies.

"Yeah," Evie smiled in agreeance, "It feels good to finally not be looking over my shoulder constantly, to be me again."

"So, this is the real you?"

"Well, minus the name change," Evie replied with a small smile, "But the normal teenage stuff; school, parties, friends..."

"Boyfriends?" Owen asked, before he could stop himself.

Evie's eyes shot to Owen's in surprise. She wondered what he meant by that? When she last stayed with them, her feelings certainly grew for Owen, more than a friend or family. Though Evie had no idea of his feelings towards her, for all she knew he hated the fact she was back. Did he even forgive her for all the danger she put him and his family in?

"I just meant," Owen stumbled on his words, trying to find an excuse for what he said.

"I don't know," Evie saved him, shrugging her shoulders, she wandered over to the edge of the yard and Owen followed her, the pair sitting down on a bench seat near a couple of rose bushes. "I went on a few dates with boys before everything with Ryan happened. After that I never gave it much thought, I was always too busy running away."

Evie looked out across the lawn back towards the house party, avoiding Owen's gaze.

"What about now?" Owen broke the silence that had extended between them.

"Now?" Evie repeated looking at him in confusion. What was Owen asking her?

"Uh, well," Owen had never felt so unsure of himself when it came to girls before, but Evie was different. "What if Zane asked you out again? Would you go out with him?"

Immediately, Owen chastised himself internally for asking Evie the question. He didn't want her thinking of Zane in that way. Owen wanted her to think of him in that way.

"Zane?" Evie asked. Was Owen trying to tell her he thought she should date Zane? "He's a good friend."

"Yeah, he is." Owen murmured; his eyes trained on Evie.

Evie felt unsure of herself and the situation they were now in together. She didn't know what to do or say as she wringed her fingers in her lap nervously to distract herself from her feelings.

"Evie," Owen spoke softly.

"Evie!" Harley's voice rang out across the lawn, over the music at the same time Owen spoke.

Evie's eyes darted to Harley, before she stood up from where they were sitting and gave Owen an apologetic smile.

"I better go," Evie stated, "I'll see you at home."

Owen simply nodded. Deep down he wanted to grab Evie, pull her back to him and kiss her. He wanted to kiss her, but he didn't want to cause a scene. Not at the party where half their school was attending.

Evie skipped across the lawn to Harley and headed back inside to the party.

Owen sat silently on his own until Zane came over and joined him.

"How'd you go?" Zane asked his friend.

Owen eyed Zane and shook his head.

"Man, you two need to just admit that you like each other."

"You don't know that," Owen argued.

"I've known you cared about Evie longer than you have known yourself," Zane declared. "And Evie, it was kind of obvious she felt the same when she got all bent out of shape at your party when Harley tried it on with you."

Owen thought about what his friend said and looked at Zane in a questioning way. Zane simply nodded.

Owen knew what he had to do. Before he could talk himself out of it, he stood up and strode into the house to find Evie.

Evie was dancing once more with Harley. Paige and Rebecca had gone off with their boyfriends to make out. Simon approached Harley from behind and started moving in time with her, his arms wrapping around her waist. Evie smiled at Harley, happy for her that she had found someone.

Suddenly, a hand grabbed Evie's wrist and started pulling her away from Harley and out the front door. Evie went to scream and pull her arm free, but noticed it was Owen. Unsure what he was doing, Evie followed him as he led her outside.

The front yard was empty, the party mostly being contained to inside the house. There was a random straggler leaving or a passed-out body in a bush. Plastic cups and bottles littered the lawn.

Owen guided Evie to the darkness of the shadows to the left, away from the view of the front door.

"Owen, what's going on? Is everything okay?" Evie asked Owen, her voice full of concern.

Owen's eyes searched Evie's, he didn't say anything. Letting go of Evie's wrist, he gently stroked Evie's face with his hands, cradling her face in his palms.

Evie felt the butterflies in her stomach, her heart raced and her mind became fuzzy. She knew it wasn't one of her panic attacks, but normal teenaged hormones. The excitement of what might happen next, what she hoped was about to happen.

Slowly, Owen leaned in towards Evie, his lips gently brushing hers. He was checking to see if she was okay with what he was doing, giving her the opportunity to push him away and yell at him if that's what she wanted to do.

Evie didn't do any of those things. Instead, she gently held onto his elbows, keeping him near her.

Owen's hands moved away from her face and he wrapped his arms around her waist and deepened the kiss.

Evie wrapped her own arms around his neck, pulling him closer to her, all the pain of the previous two years washing away.

Time seemed to stand still. It was only the two of them in the world. Nothing else in that moment mattered.

Pulling apart, Owen rested his forehead on Evie's as he looked at her and sighed.

"Please don't ever run away again," he pleaded with her.

"I'm staying right here," she breathed, "Where I belong."